BAIT AND SWITCH

SUBTLE DECEPTIONS
BOOK 2

ELLE KEATON

ONE

Gabriel

Monday before noon, late November.

"SERIOUSLY? You have got to be kidding me."

With a grunt, followed by an extra-long and extra-deep sigh, Gabe nudged the body in front of him with the toe of his hiking boot. Maybe he was wrong, maybe Peter was taking a power nap. He stared down and willed Peter to move, to sit up with a "Gotcha!" and a snap of his fingers. Maybe he'd even give himself away by laughing at Gabe's reaction.

But he did none of those things. His ex stayed on his back, his arms all akimbo, angled awkwardly by his sides. His left hand was tucked underneath his back, the right almost touching his hip. There was no blood, no other signs of violence, just an obviously broken neck.

It was near freezing today and the filthy, bird poop-covered deck of the *Shangri-La*, the only boat at the marina in worse shape than *The Golden Ticket*, was no place to take a breather.

With his neck at an impossible angle—and in that getup—he was definitely not taking a catnap.

Wavelets rolled up and slapped against the side of the sailboat, emphasizing Gabe's morbid thoughts. He didn't laugh, but Peter had officially been caught dead in a hideous outfit.

He was deflecting. Even Gabe, notorious for avoiding the serious, could recognize a good deflection when it hit him in the face. In his defense, it was a hideous tracksuit, one Gabe had never seen Peter in—when he was alive anyway.

"Fuck."

He and Peter may have been past tense, but he'd never wished him bodily harm. A parking ticket? An audit notice from the IRS? Maybe, but never this.

Never dead.

"A baby blue tracksuit, like some sort of common Jersey gangster?" He paused and crossed his arms over his chest. "Have you been binge-watching *The Sopranos* again? Tony is not the role model you think he is," Gabe said to the dead man. There was no response from the corpse, for which he was eternally grateful.

But, just in case he was wrong about the *my-ex-is-dead* part of the day, Gabe crouched next to Peter's remains and tentatively reached out his hand, pressing his index and middle fingers against Peter's neck. Nothing. He wasn't even warm to the touch. How long had he been at the marina and on the *Shangri-La?*

How long had he been lying there dead?

Out of the corner of one eye, Gabe spotted the errant tennis ball that had ultimately been responsible for the unpleasant discovery. Slowly, it began to move, the slight wind sending it rolling off the sailboat's deck and onto the pier, where it bounced once and then dropped into the bay with a gentle bloop. Ranger Man's dog, Bowie, trotted to the edge of the dock and peered over the side, his tail slowly wagging back and forth. Even Gabe, who'd never owned a dog in his life, knew Bowie was considering a quick swim to retrieve his toy.

"Don't you even fucking think about it," Gabe said to the dog. "I do not have the bandwidth for this—*this-ness*." He waved a hand in the corpse's direction. "You jumping into the bay is the cherry on top that I don't need. You and I both know your owner would pin the blame for your wet ass on me."

Bowie side-eyed him, huffed, and plopped down on the dock to rest his head on his paws. Totally waiting for Gabe to turn his back again.

Gabe rose to his feet to stare out over the slate gray waters of Riddle Bay. Maybe a perfectly reasonable explanation for *this* would erupt from the surface of the water like the Creature from the Black Lagoon, with a comic bubble declaring SOLUTION floating in the air above it. Maybe the monster would return Bowie's ball too. Where was Swamp Thing when he needed him? He could exchange the ball for the body; it seemed like a reasonable trade.

Peter's death was going to be trouble. No offense to his dead ex-boyfriend, but Gabe did not need the drama a corpse was going to bring him. He could feel a tension headache starting to form behind his eyes.

Surely it wasn't grief. Surely he had no tears for him.

Since a week ago Sunday, when Casey Lundin had informed Gabe that someone had been by the marina asking about him, Gabe had been waiting for the other shoe to drop. From Lundin's description, he had known the person who'd done the asking could only be Gabe's ex, Peter Vale. A long seven-plus days of worrying had followed, but Peter himself had never returned—until today.

The shoe had dropped. Painfully.

Had Peter come to warn him that the Colavitos were planning to measure him up for special-edition cement loafers? That seemed fanciful. Peter was more likely to throw Gabe to the wolves than to save him from them.

No, what he was feeling wasn't grief so much as disgust and anger. Who would do this?

Gabe had spent the last week pondering Peter-related questions and not coming up with any answers: *Were Larry Colavito and his nephews planning to ambush him in the dark of night? Why had Peter ventured to Heartstone Island? How the fuck had he found Gabe anyway? And when was he coming back?*

The answer to that last question was lying in front of him. There was no coming back from this.

He sighed—again—and stepped back. The *Shangri-La* moved slightly underneath him, bobbing up and down in the cold waters of Riddle Bay. Today he could see the rocky bottom and a school of tiny fish flashing through the water. Calling the Twana County Sheriff's Office was the next order of business, but he resisted. He was already anticipating the questions they would ask that he did not have answers to.

Why had Elton chosen today to have a dental emergency?

Gabe had avoided interacting with Ranger Man all week until that morning. Considering they both lived on sailboats moored at the same dock, that was a feat in itself. Although for Gabe, the *Ticket* was less home sweet home and more of a rustic camping situation. But first thing that morning, before he'd even ventured to the grocery store across the street for a hot coffee, there'd been a knock on the hull. He'd immediately known it was Lundin; there was a certain exasperation to Lundin's hammering. That and the fact that they were the only two who lived at the marina.

"What?" Gabe had called out through the galley window.

All he'd been able to see through the glass was Lundin's denim-covered legs. They were nice-looking legs.

"I'm taking Elton in for an emergency dental thing, a new cap or something. Can you keep an eye on Bowie? I don't want to leave him in the truck for an extended period, it's too cold out today."

Gabe tried not to be offended that Elton hadn't asked Gabe to drive him. He was an adult, his feelings weren't hurt because Elton had called Ranger Man and not him. But he did have a new cell phone, Elton *could* have called him.

"Won't be more than three or four hours with the drive," Lundin continued, "maybe less. Elton seems to think the actual procedure won't take that long."

"Sure. Bowie and I are tight. He can hang out with me, I don't have anything going on," Gabe had agreed casually.

He didn't have a life anymore. Not unless he counted worrying about the Colavitos, the Anderson brothers, and why Peter hadn't returned yet. He'd headed topside to let the dog aboard.

The sight of Casey Lundin waiting on the pier, his arms crossed over his broad, flannel-encased chest, made Gabe's stupid heart skip a beat and brought to mind the Brawny paper towel guy.

He'd covered his reaction with a cough. As he had ever since they'd met, Gabe refused to entertain all the physical ways Casey ticked his boxes because Ranger Man's personality did nothing for him. He was a popsicle with an unpleasant coating of fuzz. Cold and gritty. Unyielding.

"At least one of you can be trusted not to do anything too stupid. Go on, Bowie, I'll be back as soon as possible."

Case in point.

Lundin's rescue dog had jumped onto the *Ticket* like he belonged there, his favorite orange tennis ball clutched in his jaws. With a curt "Thank you," Lundin had stalked off without a backward glance. Presumably headed to Elton's to pick him up.

"Okay, doggo, I guess it's just you and me. Nice to have some company."

For the most part, Gabe had stayed aboard *The Golden Ticket* over the past week. It seemed best to avoid the public eye and Lundin, especially with the excitement from the week prior. The last thing he needed was more unwanted attention. He'd been lucky to have been treated as a mere bystander after the shooting at the hospital.

It's called hiding, Chance.

Okay, he had been hiding. Which clearly had been a pointless exercise since Peter had somehow found him. How the fuck?

Gabe had falsely believed the dock was defendable, a refuge. Safe from a land invasion due to the locked entry to the marina, protected from water attack because the weather was too cold for anyone but arctic fishermen and harbor seals. Invasion by air was too ridiculous to consider, even for Larry Colavito. And while there was always the possibility of a James Bond frogman-style attack from under the waves, that also seemed like a lot of effort to go to for a washed-up grifter.

Thus, Gabe had kept to himself. Read a couple of thrillers. Organized his few possessions. Ate premade meals from the store across the road. Slept.

Nothing weird had happened and Peter had never shown up again.

Just minutes after Lundin and Elton had departed, Gabe got a call from the marine supply place in Westfort on his new-to-him burner phone, saying his order had arrived. He and Bowie had driven into town, adding a quick stop for some groceries that weren't corn chips and a blessed triple Americano.

And returned to a corpse.

A fucking corpse.

Ew, not fucking.

Hands jammed into his coat pockets, he stared down at what was left of the man he'd briefly been involved with. Peter's head was at an unnatural angle, his body oddly stiff. Gabe didn't know much about rigor mortis, but he hazarded a guess that rigor was why the body appeared uncomfortable as it lay on the decking. Maybe that's why his arms seemed weird too.

"Seriously? Why me?"

What if the corpse hadn't appeared just this morning? Maybe it had been dropped off at some other time during the week. Immediately, Gabe knew that idea was ridiculous. He would have heard someone walking on the pier. If nothing else, Bowie would have heard intruders and sounded the alarm.

Plus—bending down again, Gabe brushed the back of his hand against the blue nylon polyester fabric of Peter's jacket—it wasn't wet, not even damp. Rain had been coming down steadily for days until early that morning, when the deluge had abruptly stopped, like someone in the clouds closed the faucet. Gabe hadn't gotten to bed until late since he'd been up rereading a tattered and worn Travis McGee novel borrowed from Elton, but the absence of the thrum of the rain had woken him.

"Goddammit."

"Who are you talking to?" a deep voice asked from behind him.

Gabe spun around, heart pounding. He'd been so focused on The Corpse he hadn't heard Ranger Man open the gate or start walking on the dock. He revised his opinion that he would've heard trespassers. But Bowie would've. Probably.

"Ah, yeah ... Uh, no one. Not really. Just you know, this guy." Gabe moved back from Peter's body, the boat rocking unevenly as he climbed off the *Shangri-La*. As tall as he was, Ranger Man was sure to be able to see the dead man from where he stood. Gabe had only wanted to make sure there was nothing he could do for Peter.

"The fuck is that?" Lundin demanded, stomping over to the side of the dock and peering at the deck of the *Shangri-La*.

"Ah, *that*, that?" Gabe glanced at Lundin.

"Yes, that. Wait." Lundin's eyes narrowed as he edged closer to the sailboat, risking a dunking. "That's the guy who was here last week. Is he—"

"Shh!" Gabe said automatically, as if saying the four-letter word too loudly would alert the local flying monkeys. "Yes, he seems to be. And no, I didn't do it. I found him that way."

"Isn't that what they all say?" Lundin took a big step backward, away from Gabe and the derelict boat, as though death were contagious. He supposed that often it was.

"I didn't kill Peter," Gabe said to the world in general. "Bowie and I went into Westfort to pick up the new stove after you left, and we got back not too long ago. I only ... er, *noticed* ... him because Bowie's tennis ball landed funny and bounced onto the deck. And there he was. Is. Just *there*. I know it's difficult for you, but don't be such an asshole. You know I didn't kill him."

"Do I, though?" Lundin shot him another, narrower, more suspicious glance.

"Seriously?" Gabe threw his head back to stare up at the clouds mirrored by the relatively calm waters of the bay. As he watched, they slowly parted to reveal a tantalizing hint of blue.

I will not scream. I will not scream. I will not scream.

"Casey, you left your wallet in the truck."

In tandem, they both turned to look down the dock. Elton Cox was walking toward them. Gabe felt slightly vindicated that neither Lundin nor Bowie had noticed the old man opening and shutting the gate. Hah, they must've driven to the dentist in

Elton's truck. It wasn't just Gabe's Honda the old man didn't trust. The Ford was built like a tank, maybe he just felt safer in it.

"You two look serious," Elton said, drawing closer. "Something going on?" He looked from Gabe to Lundin.

"No," they chorused.

"You're supposed to be at home waiting for the rest of the funny gas to wear off," Lundin added.

"Well, it wore off on the drive back, didn't it?" Elton sounded a tad grumpy. "I don't feel like being stuck at home, and like I said, you left your wallet in my truck."

Approaching them, Elton held Lundin's wallet out to him. Gabriel noted that it was made of canvas and Velcro and was well broken in. It suited Lundin.

"Did you pick that up at a vintage place? Or have the nineties come calling and I wasn't around to meet them?" Gabe asked.

"What?" Lundin frowned. "No. What are you even talking about?"

He accepted the billfold from Elton and tucked it into the back pocket of his jeans. The jeans, Gabe absently noted for the second time that day, fit him very well.

What was wrong with him? There was a body only a few feet away.

Elton stopped next to Lundin. "What's going on?" he repeated, looking once more at Gabe and then Lundin.

Gabe had no choice. He moved aside and pointed toward the *Shangri-La* and the body of Peter Vale.

"That's a dead man."

Elton seemed remarkably calm. Maybe it was residual funny gas from the procedure; his jaw did seem a bit puffy.

"Yep. No doubt about that," Gabe said glumly.

Gabe was not happy about Peter's demise, but Lundin

seemed even less so. Honestly, though, the central core of Lundin's unhappiness was hard for Gabe to gauge. Was it the body? The inconvenience of it all? Gabe? All of the above?

"How did he get there?" Elton asked.

Ranger Man also looked expectantly at Gabe, as if he might have a reasonable answer.

"Your guess is as good as mine." Gabe did his best to telegraph his irritation with Casey. "After you left, I drove into Westfort and didn't get back until about an hour ago." The stove had been fairly easy to install, just like Elton had promised, and then he'd decided to reward Bowie for his patience by tossing his ball for a few minutes. "I doubt he was here when Bowie and I took off. The rest, as the saying goes, is history. I suppose he could've been here and I didn't notice, but I don't think so."

"Have you called the sheriff already?" asked Elton.

"No, of course he hasn't called the Sheriff's Office." Lundin scoffed. "I bet if I hadn't shown up when I did, Karne would have dumped the body into the bay."

Gabe did not look at Lundin. He refused to allow himself to glance the ranger's way. He hadn't *truly* considered getting rid of the body. He knew as well as Lundin or Elton that if Gabe had dropped the body into the bay, the tide would probably just have brought Peter back in eight or so hours. Especially with his luck. And even though they hadn't been friends by the end, Peter did not deserve that.

"Well, one of us is going to have to call them." Elton crossed his arms and raised his bushy eyebrows.

Instinctively, Gabe stuck his hands in his coat pockets, but he didn't find the cold plastic of his cellphone. "My phone is in the galley. And I don't know the nonemergency number." He glanced over to where what had been Peter lay. "This doesn't seem like an emergency to me. Does it to you two?"

With a shake of his head and an expression that clearly

projected *Do I have to do everything around here?*, Lundin dug his phone out of his pocket and tapped the screen.

While the call connected, Elton moved to the edge of the dock to peer at the deck and Peter's body. "Huh." He shook his head. "Weird."

"What?" Before Elton could answer, they heard the burr of the connection on Lundin's line and then the tinny sound of someone saying, "Althea Mortine, Twana County Sheriff's Office, how may I direct your call?"

"Althea, Casey Lundin here. We have a situation at the marina." He glared at Gabe, as if it were his fault a dead body had appeared on the *Shangri-La*.

It probably was. He hated to think so, but he was the only person on Heartstone with a connection to Peter. Peter had even stopped by to see him at the marina. But Gabe had been elsewhere, learning new facts about himself that he'd been avoiding thinking about over the past week. He'd spent so much time not thinking about his life, it was a shock he hadn't declared himself brain-dead.

"There's a dead person on one of the boats down here," Lundin said.

The announcement was followed by indistinguishable chatter.

"One second." Lundin put his hand over the mic and eyed Gabriel. "Do we know the victim's name?"

"Peter Vale," Gabe provided, albeit reluctantly.

It wasn't as if TCSO investigators wouldn't be able to figure out his name on their own. All they had to do was check Peter's ID. Assuming he had any on him and it was the right one. Distantly, Gabe knew he should be more upset, but Peter showing up dead was just the last thing in several long weeks of What the Fuck Now.

"Right," said Lundin to the person on the phone. "We're not

going anywhere. Yep, me, Elton, and Gabriel Karne." More chatter. "Yeah, he's the new owner of *The Golden Ticket.* Thanks, bye." He tucked his phone away again. "They're on their way."

Great. Another damn Monday making itself known in the most unpleasant way possible.

TWO

Casey

Monday noon-ish

BEFORE THE TWANA County deputies arrived, Casey hustled to the end of the dock and tucked Bowie away on *The Barbara* and made sure there was a chew toy to keep him entertained. He grabbed his parka too. The air temperature seemed to be dropping instead of rising and who knew how long they'd be standing around.

Gently accepting the toy, Bowie also shot Casey a Look. The squeaky part of the toy would be excised before the afternoon was up. Possibly before Casey made it back down to the scene.

The murder scene.

Had Peter Vale been killed at the marina or somewhere else and dumped on the *Shangri-La?* There was no blood that Casey had been able to see, although the man's neck was obviously broken.

Bowie huffed and plopped down on his bed, the toy gripped between his jaws.

"Yeah, I'm buying you off. Behave yourself."

A dead body was bad enough, they didn't need Bowie tripping up the responding deputies. Or doing his best to herd them around the dock, although it might add a little amusement to this dreary and deadly Monday.

Fingers crossed that at least one of the deputies would be Bree Eagan. Of all the TCSO deputies, she was the one he trusted the most to do her job. The rest had been under Rizzi's thumb for too long or were just too wet behind the ears. They'd either guzzled the punch and never looked back or generally walked around looking like they'd been caught in headlights.

One last "Be good" and Casey departed.

Out on the pier again, he jogged back over to where Elton and Charming Fucker were waiting. It wasn't raining yet. But looking up at the swirling clouds, Casey predicted that would change soon. Maybe there'd even be snow. In the distance, the sound of sirens reached his ears.

"I told them it wasn't an emergency," he griped when he reached the spot where the other two men waited. "Sirens means we're going to have everyone on the island with a scanner stopping by to see what's going on."

It was mid-November. Nothing of interest was going on until the Heartstone Celebration of Togetherness that took place the last weekend of the month. It was the community's way of celebrating the Indigenous peoples who had populated Heartstone long before Europeans arrived. The first few years, it had been met with resistance, but any more it was something folks looked forward to, and it brought the community together. But since it was still a while away, police activity now would not be ignored.

"If one of the responders is Rizzi or Emmett Spurring, sirens are inevitable. You know how they like to hear the sounds of their own bells and whistles," Elton said.

Casey glanced over at Karne, who looked like he wanted to disappear into the pilings or run for the hills but was forcing his feet to stay put. He felt a smidge of pity for him. A smidge.

"So, what are we telling them about this Vale guy?" Casey asked.

"What do you mean, what are we telling them?" Karne demanded.

"You know this guy, or you did?" Elton asked, looking at Charming. Apparently, he hadn't filled Elton in while Casey had been taking care of Bowie.

A multitude of emotions flashed quickly across his face, the final one of which Casey recognized as resignation.

"Yeah, we were"—he paused and waggled his head, possibly considering word choice—"together for a while. I can't hide that we knew each other," Karne said slowly. "But it was over. We still had some loose ends to tie up, but I haven't seen him in person for several weeks."

Something—guilt, fear, maybe both—sparked in Karne's eyes but disappeared before Casey knew what it was for certain. Regardless, there was more that he wasn't telling them.

"You didn't kill him?" Elton asked Gabe directly. Lundin's gut said that Gabriel was being honest when he'd said he hadn't, but a person couldn't always trust their instinct alone, or the word of a grifter.

"No, I didn't." Karne sounded offended that Elton had asked the same question that Casey had earlier. "I've never killed anyone. Jesus Christ."

"Who did the breaking up?" Elton asked.

"Meh, it was mutual. We stayed living at the same address because we were both too lazy to move, and it worked all right. Up until it didn't. I didn't tell him where I was headed when I left town, so his appearance here was a surprise. A big surprise. How did he know where to find me?"

"But he showed up, didn't he? Because this is definitely the same person who stopped by last week," Lundin pointed out.

"Yeah, but he never came back. I'd think you would know."

Restlessly, Karne moved closer to the *Shangri-La* again, staring at his ex. His body language screamed upset and disturbed. With a full-body shudder, Karne jammed his hands into his pockets.

Elton moved to stand by Karne's side, eyeing the corpse again.

Casey didn't want to think that Karne could be a killer—after all, Elton and Bowie both liked him. But then, so did he.

Dammit.

A thought struck him, making him want to smack himself in the forehead. Pulling his phone from his pocket again, Casey tapped the screen to access the single security camera, which unfortunately faced the gate and parking lot. Quickly, he scrolled through the most recent feed. The camera only activated when there was motion, and no one but himself and Karne had left or entered through the locked gate that morning. He scanned back through the week, and it stayed the same; in fact, Karne had only left a few times, returning with bags Casey recognized from the store.

Tucking his phone back into his coat pocket, Casey crossed his arms over his chest and considered what Karne was telling them and what he wasn't. Casey added up the other bits and pieces he'd figured out about the man since his arrival on Heartstone. "You and the dead guy were both con men?" It wasn't really a question.

Karne turned to him and Casey was on the receiving end of another Look. He probably should have combusted right where he was standing. Good thing Casey was as practiced at giving looks as he was at taking them.

"When you put it like that, *fine*." Karne growled the words and stepped closer to Casey again. "Peter and I were in the same line of business, but I am done with that. However"—he twisted his torso to scowl at the heap that was the *Shangri-La* and its cargo—"it is possible others involved in our last business endeavor might have had some complaints."

Casey lifted one eyebrow. "Could these *business partners* have done this? Do you know if Vale had other enemies?"

"Of course, he had other enemies," Karne snapped. "And no, I don't know who they are. We did not have that kind of relationship. And yes, our final group project could have resulted in this."

Casey was tempted to ask what kind of relationship he and Vale had had because it sure as hell didn't sound like much of a personal one. But with lights flashing and sirens screaming, two TCSO cruisers screeched to a halt on the road in front of the marina. They partially blocked the street, as well as blocking in the three vehicles already parked in the lot. Islanders were going to have a lot of questions.

"I think we keep it simple when we talk to them," Elton said thoughtfully. "We know that Gabe didn't do this."

Did they, though?

Casey met Karne's glance and knew Karne was thinking that Casey probably wouldn't argue if the deputies decided to take him in for questioning. That thinking was on Casey. Karne bugged the crap out of him, but he would never condone harassment of an innocent person. Maybe it was time to tell him more about what happened with his brother.

"They'll question me since I knew him," Karne said, interrupting Casey's train of thought. "And they'll probably want me to go to the station. But I swear, I haven't seen Peter in weeks, and that time was through a car window as I was driving away. The last time we talked was over a month ago. Maybe longer. Like I said, it was over. We were headed in different directions." Karne huffed a quasi-laugh. "He didn't even know my mother died. That's how fucking close we were at the end."

Something about that statement didn't sit right with Casey. Not that he thought Karne was lying, he didn't. But from the little he knew about Gabriel Karne, he just couldn't see him in a relationship that basically consisted of two strangers. Karne liked to talk, to be with people. He reveled in what Casey's work partner Greta would call *connection*. Even Casey, who prided himself on being an introvert and liked none of those things, could see that.

Elton harrumphed. "How did he get here, then?"

The old man was on the same wavelength as Casey. If Vale and Karne weren't close, what had brought Vale to Heartstone?

"I have no idea," Karne said. "None at all."

"Right, then," Casey nodded. "We'll try and keep it simple for whoever shows up. Easy enough since I don't know anything and neither does Elton. But once they're gone, we need to have a sit-down. They'll want Karne to go into the station with them, but there's security feed of the dock, and no one came in through the gate this morning except the three of us."

"What?" Karne spun to stare at him. "Why didn't you say something about the security feed?"

"I just did."

"Fuck you. It would have been nice to know there's proof I didn't kill Peter, because I didn't."

Casey started to point out that Karne still could have been responsible for Vale's death, that Vale could have come in by boat. But Casey couldn't make himself believe that Karne was a killer. He doubted Karne had access to anything bigger than a rowboat and the idea that he could kill someone, drop the body into a boat, row it to the dock, and somehow heft deadweight onto the dock and then onto the *Shangri-La* was ridiculous. Unless Peter had arrived via water of his own accord.

Casey glanced at Karne, distrusting the direction his thoughts had taken.

The entrance at the end of the pier rattled. The sheriff himself, Eli Rizzi, and a deputy waited impatiently on the other side of the chain-link gate. Casey abandoned his musings and strode over to open the lock and let the sheriff and deputy onto the dock.

THREE

Casey

Monday afternoon

DEPUTY BREE EAGAN had excellent instincts; if Sheriff Rizzi allowed it, she was going to become a great investigator. Casey had often wondered if Eagan would leave the island for a better chance at advancement. He doubted Rizzi would give her the room to grow. The good ol' boy just wasn't that kind of leader.

Casey shivered even with his parka zipped to his chin, chilled from standing outside and in one place for too long. The wet and chilly weather he'd felt coming had rolled in along with the sheriff. A gentle sleeting rain had begun to fall, and a foggy mist had settled over the bay. In a way, the weather was a complement to the scene. Death was depressing and violent death even more so.

On one side of the dock, Chief Rizzi was interviewing Karne, while Deputy Eagan was taking down Casey's statement near *The Barbara*. Casey didn't envy Karne. From where Casey stood twenty feet away, he could see his expression was a mix of frustration, anger, and sadness. Rizzi was not going to get far with the TCSO's star suspect.

The county coroner, a local guy named Brett Davidson, was also on the scene. He'd arrived not long after TCSO. There wasn't a bustling team of people like on TV shows, just Rizzi, Eagan, Davidson, and the ambulance drivers who would remove the body to the hospital.

Of average height and a bit on the heavy side, Davidson was in his fifties. The coroner was an appointed official whose qualifications were that he'd "been interested in the position," owned a funeral home, and he and his wife had taken a certification class from the state. Casey supposed Davidson was marginally better than what they'd had before. For decades before his appointment, the coroner had also been a county prosecutor.

Davidson would confirm the manner and probably cause of death and then the body would be transported by ambulance to the hospital. It was up to TCSO to gather evidence and catch whoever was responsible for the killing. As far as Casey was aware, this was only the second homicide this year, with Dwayne Perkins being the first.

"So, just to make sure I have the facts correct, you arrived, and Mr. Karne was standing on the pier near the ..." Eagan looked down at her notes. "The *Shangri-La*. You didn't see anyone else, and the gate was locked."

"The gate is always locked."

"Who else has a key?"

"At the moment, Elton, Karne, and myself. I changed the lock a while back, but none of the other owners have come to collect theirs."

"Huh, okay." She glanced up, waiting for Casey to say more.

"I'd been trying to get a hold of the marina board to get

permission to change the lock, but it's a process, so I took matters into my own hands. It's not as if I'm difficult to track down."

"And when you arrived, Mr. Karne was—"

"Talking to my dog."

"I doubt your dog will be able to answer my questions," Eagan said dryly.

Casey replayed his return in his mind's eye.

"I'd dropped Elton off back at his house and picked up my car. Karne was watching Bowie for me, and I came back here to pick him up. Bowie, not Karne," he clarified.

"How did your dog seem? Jumpy? Out of sorts?"

"Irritated that his ball had dropped into the bay."

Eagan's cheek hitched up, exposing a dimple that appeared and disappeared again when she pressed her lips together.

"And the victim, Peter Vale, was unresponsive when you arrived?"

"Definitely unresponsive," Casey agreed.

"Do you have any thoughts on who might have done something like this? Or how Mr. Vale might have gotten onto the dock?"

Casey had done his fair share of speculating while waiting to be questioned. The *who* had to do with Karne, but the how? Casey had theories but no hard facts.

"Whoever it was must have come by boat," he offered.

Casey had already emailed a copy of his security camera's video to the Sheriff's Office from his phone. And he'd played the feed for the officers after they'd arrived. After he'd left to pick up Elton, all there was to see was Karne and Bowie leaving and then returning about an hour or so later. No one had come through the gate. No one but Charming Fucker and Casey had parked in the lot.

"The camera is set on the gate and parking lot, not the dock.

Might have to add one that has an eye on the boats." *Might.* He scoffed at himself. He'd be adding another camera as soon as he could get online to order one.

"Thank you. If we need anything else, we know where to find you." Eagan tucked the waterproof notebook and pen back into her uniform coat pocket. "We'll be in touch, but if you think of anything else, please reach out."

The ambulance drivers had wheeled the body down the pier and were now loading the shell of what had once been Peter Vale onto the bus. The thump of the doors shutting had a disturbing finality to it. Casey had only met Vale once while he'd been alive, and their exchange had been less than five minutes. Less than three minutes, really. And yet, Casey felt the tug of responsibility toward him. He watched as the coroner, who'd followed the drivers, gave some instructions and then got into his car and drove off.

"*The fuck* I will come down to the station right now. Am I under arrest?"

Casey and Deputy Eagan turned toward where the sheriff and Karne were standing. Rizzi looked rough. Not that the man ever modeled sartorial elegance, but he currently had a coffee stain down the front of his uniform and hadn't bothered to tuck his shirt in all the way. It was a decoy, Casey knew. The man was sharp and liked to fool people into thinking he was a hick.

Karne's statement, incredibly, hadn't been said with heat. It had been just that, a statement and a question. Eagan blew out a puff of air, shook her head, and moved toward the two men.

"If you need to talk to me further, give me a time and I'll come down to the station. In my own vehicle. I'm not going anywhere, especially not on *The Golden Ticket*. There's literally nothing to indicate I had anything to do with this tragic event except that I knew him back in the city. I'm freezing and so is everyone else. And I'm hungry. Coffee is also a thing I need."

Rizzi looked like he was considering arguing, but as Karne had pointed out, he wasn't going anywhere. And they had no reason to arrest him—not yet.

"Coffee sounds like a plan," Elton agreed. "I could use some too." He rubbed his hands together and shoved them back into the pockets of his oversized parka. "How about it, Eli? Gabriel will be available when you want to talk to him further. Heck, I bet he'd be willing to come down later after a nice hot cuppa."

It was easy to forget that Elton knew everyone on Heartstone. Eli Rizzi had moved to the island years ago as a wet-behind-the-ears deputy and worked his way up to the position of sheriff, but Elton had his own influence that was difficult for the sheriff to ignore. The old man had a way about him that made it seem like he was asking a thing when in truth he was telling Rizzi how things would go down. Casey hid his smirk.

The sheriff frowned and appeared to be considering the suggestion. He focused his attention on Karne again. "Expect a call from Chief Deputy Spurring before long."

Karne nodded. "Noted."

"Stay away from the boat. Don't touch it, don't even breathe on it." The sailboat in question had been cordoned off with crime scene tape. Rizzi gave Karne another hard stare. "If we find out anything that you didn't tell us, even if it's that you're a Raiders fan when you said you rooted for the Hawks, we'll be talking to you even sooner." It was as if Rizzi couldn't resist giving an order.

Who was Casey kidding? Of course the man couldn't. Beside Karne, Deputy Eagan shifted her weight from foot to foot. He figured she found Charming Fucker irritating, but just as likely it was Rizzi.

Karne's head moved up and down robotically, and his lips were pressed firmly together. Knowing what he did about him, Casey figured it was to keep words like *fuck* and *you* from spilling out. As much as Casey also disliked and did not trust the sheriff, Charming telling him to fuck off would not relieve any of the current tension.

Without acknowledging Karne, Rizzi gave Eagan a jerk of his head and turned away, striding down the pier toward the gate. The crime scene tape flapped in the wind and would probably be mostly torn off by morning. Eagan didn't roll her eyes at her superior, but Casey suspected she wanted to.

"We'll see you soon," she said, and turned to follow Rizzi.

By unspoken mutual agreement, Elton, Gabe, and Casey moved to the middle of the dock and watched the TCSO vehicles depart.

"My place?" asked Elton. "I was serious about a warm-up."

"I could use a drink," Karne said with a tired sigh. "Remind me why I don't want one."

Elton shot him an indecipherable look. "I imagine a strong cup of coffee is a better choice."

"Peter encouraged me to stop drinking. The issue was that once I did, I realized I had no interest in being with him. He was such a high and mighty asshole about it." Karne rolled his shoulders and shoved his hands deeper into his pockets. "He was right about the drinking, but he didn't need to rub it in."

"Did he?" Casey asked, curious about Gabe's relationship with the dead man.

"What? Rub it in that quitting the bottle was a good thing? Oh yeah, he did. Peter liked to be Right About Things. Don't get me wrong, he could be very charismatic when he wanted to be, and it did come in handy."

"When you two were running a game?"

Casey appreciated Elton's word usage. Game, con. Same coin.

"Yeah," Gabe replied, "but it came in handy in general, too.

You really can get more bees with honey. How about that coffee?"

"I got a new jar of instant the other day," Elton said.

"You did not," Gabe replied, shooting the older man a deadly glance while also pulling a vomit face. "That stuff will put you in an early grave."

Elton snickered, enjoying the effect of his joke.

While Gabe and Elton slowly walked toward the gate, Casey turned and jogged back to *his boat* to let Bowie out. He was rewarded with a yip. The dismembered toy had been spread across the saloon.

"Yeah, I know. It was too long."

Wiggling past him, Bowie raced out of the cabin to leap from the deck to the pier and ran to catch up with Elton and Karne.

"What am I, chopped liver?" Casey called after him. Bowie did not slow down. Apparently, he was not even chopped liver. Bowie caught up with the other two men at the dock's entrance, graciously accepting pets while they waited for Casey to catch up with them.

It was the off season, he reasoned, so there was no point in checking in at park headquarters. If anyone did need him, they knew how to contact him. Plus, Greta was back from vacation and had offered to staff the office for the week.

"I'll ride with Elton," Gabriel said, "and get a ride back with you if that's okay."

Casey suspected that Gabriel was avoiding unwanted questions about Peter Vale. But as he let Bowie into the Wagoneer and slid behind the wheel, he realized that Elton wouldn't hesitate to ask hard questions, and Karne already knew that about the man.

So that wasn't it.

FOUR

Gabriel

Still Monday

SHIT.

Peter was dead. *Gone forever* dead, not just on a pleasant vacation in Jamaica and dead to Gabe. Gabe didn't know what to think. He didn't *want* to think about it. He'd hardly begun to process his mother's death and now Peter was gone.

Too much death.

"Why do you think Peter stopped by the marina last week?" Elton asked, keeping his attention on the road.

Gabe would have offered to drive, but for one, Elton wasn't giving up the truck's keys unless he was drugged by a professional and Heartstone didn't have much traffic this time of year. And two, even though it was only a few minutes' drive, Gabe didn't want to be behind the wheel. He was too shaky.

"Honestly? No idea. I have no clue how Peter found me. Like I said, we haven't spoken for weeks." He sucked in a breath like he was eight years old and about to tell his mother he'd done something she'd specifically told him not to. "We got into hot water recently, and I decided it was time to lie low. Sans Peter. That's the real reason I came out here. And I was curious what my mother had left me."

If being chased by an armed man and a guard dog counted as a deciding factor, then that was it. Gabe had been planning to leave town anyway, but it had happened a tad more dramatically than he'd intended.

"I figured it was something like that, son. Are you thinking that the trouble has followed you?" Elton should have sounded more concerned. If he'd had all the facts, maybe he would have been. Gabe was keeping as many of those facts to himself as long as he could.

"Honestly, I don't see how it could have." Gabe sagged back into the comfort of the Ford's passenger seat. "I ditched my cell phone and my car—the Honda was Heidi's— and I haven't used any credit cards, just my stash of go money. I didn't even know Heartstone Island existed. If I didn't know where I was going, how would they?"

"Hmm." Elton tapped the steering wheel with his thumb as they eased into the spot in front of his house. "You know, Casey ran a check on you. Maybe the search triggered something?"

Yes, Gabe did know Ranger Man had checked his background, but he'd put it out of his mind because he still had to pay that fucking trespassing citation and thinking about the ticket pissed him off. Opening the truck's door with his elbow, he slid to the muddy ground, landing with a squelch. Was it possible that the Colavitos had found him via Lundin? He shook his head; it seemed outrageous, and yet Peter was dead.

"Maybe? But how would it? It's not like I'm on an FBI watch list—at least, I don't think so." Gabe said, waiting for Elton to slowly extricate himself from the Ford. "So these people, whose names I am not speaking aloud if I don't have to, possibly found me because of Lundin's background check? That seems far-fetched, very Jason Bourne, and really, I'm a tiny fish in a very big sea. *Was* a tiny fish because I'm not diving back in. I suppose it's possible they could have had somebody watching for any mention of me, but what a waste of resources."

The idea was outrageous. Yes, the Colavitos wanted him dead, but Gabe felt like it was more of a *You're dead if you return to Seattle and we see your face* rather than a *We will hunt you down and take care of it ASAP* kind of dead.

"You know you're going to have to explain your relationship with the victim to Eli Rizzi."

Gabe opened his mouth to agree that yes, he figured that, but also maybe he could cut a few corners, when Lundin's Wagoneer pulled in and parked beside Elton's truck.

"LET ME GET THE COFFEE STARTED." Elton started for the kitchen.

"Nah, you just got back from the dentist, take a load off. I'll start up the coffee, I need something to do anyway," Gabe announced.

Elton didn't argue. He was definitely feeling the effects of the dental work. Taking off his jacket and hanging it up, he headed for his recliner instead.

Gabe stepped into the kitchen. A bonus to making the coffee was that the hospitality might stall the inevitable questions he knew were coming his way. What else could he tell them? Nothing. Knowing more about the Colavitos than they already did wouldn't do Elton or Casey any good. Gabe couldn't even dig up a pithy comment from his dead mother.

But even Heidi would agree that it was time to be a bit more honest—murder was serious. Something soft brushed against his leg. He looked down to see that Bowie had followed him into the kitchen and was snuffling along the tiled floor like a doggy vacuum cleaner. Gabe should have realized that retreat was useless; Lundin had joined them and was now leaning back against the doorframe.

He fought a scowl and reached into the cabinet for the whole beans. He didn't normally have the urge to strangle someone while also wanting to jump their bones. Gabriel frowned at his thoughts and then gave a mental shrug. Most likely this was a Ranger Man-specific reaction.

"Well," said Ranger Man, crossing his damn arms over his stupid chest again. The flannel had been shrugged off, and his long-sleeved t-shirt strained under the responsibility of keeping him covered. Asshole.

"That's deep." Gabe dumped a handful of beans into Elton's grinder.

There was a long, annoyed silence. Gabe enjoyed it.

"This is not the time to fuck around, Karne."

Gabe held down the power button, forestalling his reply for a few seconds longer. Unfortunately, Lundin was still there when he lifted his hand off the grinder, eyebrows raised in expectation. Dammit.

"It's always time to fuck around. Maybe that's your issue, you've never been given permission to just fuck it." Neither had Gabriel, but he didn't let that stop him. "What do you want to hear from me, Ranger Man? That I'm a con man? That Peter and I grifted people? That the con is what I learned growing up on my mother's knee?"

It's con artist, *Chance.*

One thing about Heidi, she did have pride in her work.

Leaning back against the counter, he faced Lundin. "I don't know what to tell you that you would be willing to accept. Believe. Whatever."

"Tell us about these people who you think killed Peter. We can't fight shadows."

Well, fuck. When he said it like that.

Gabe didn't *think* the Colavitos killed Peter, he knew they did. At least as much as he could without having witnessed the murder. He just didn't know how they'd done it. Someone must have followed him to Heartstone, however impossible that was. Which hinted that the family was, in fact, not willing to drop their vendetta as long as Gabe stayed out of Seattle. He pictured the second go-bag stuffed in the closet in Elton's spare room. He still had money, he could take it and disappear.

Except that disappearing didn't feel comfortable the way it once had. Almost as if he'd disappeared himself so many times that the real Gabriel Karne was starting to vanish. Fading a bit every time until he was eventually going to evaporate to nothing if he kept it up.

He rubbed his belly, trying to rid himself of the hollow feeling in his stomach.

"Casey, give Gabe a chance to sit down with his coffee before you interrogate him," Elton called out.

"Yeah, what he said." Turning back around, Gabe poured grounds into the waiting filter, sucking the earthy scent of roasted beans into his lungs. There was almost nothing better.

Lundin didn't immediately respond to Elton, so Gabe glanced over his shoulder and—dammit, maybe there was something better than fresh ground coffee beans. Ranger Man continued to glower, his arms still crossed. And Gabe still wanted to jump his bones. He wished he could blame his reaction on being accused of murder, some kind of weird dopamine thing. Something to distract himself from reality. But why this guy? Why some angsty, semi-feral guy ten years younger than him who possibly hated his guts?

You never did like things easy, Chance. Peter was easy.

Thankfully, Gabe was well-versed in keeping his mouth shut when absolutely necessary. He didn't speak another word until the coffee was done brewing and had been poured into the two mugs he'd gotten down.

"You can pour your own," he told Ranger Man. He carried the filled mugs into the living room. Handing one of the cups to Elton, Gabe made himself comfortable on the couch with the other.

With a steaming mug of java in his hand, Lundin stalked back into the living room and occupied one of the chairs at Elton's table. They both stared expectantly at him. It was slightly unnerving. Gabe swallowed a sip of the still molten coffee and contemplated where to start. He let his attention wander outside the window behind Lundin to where the cars were parked, trying to best frame what he was going to tell them. It was like preparing to tear a bandage off a partially healed wound. Might as well do it fast.

"Peter and I gamed the wrong crowd. Lazy research. We thought the Andersons were stupid frat bros wanting to make fast cash—and they were—but it turned out that their uncle is Larry Colavito, the head of Seattle's homegrown version of the Mafia. They must've gone crying to him when their investments didn't go as planned. Larry has deep feelings about his family being made to look stupid."

"And?"

"And? And what? We destroyed any evidence. Deleted the files. Moved the money. That was"—Gabe rolled his eyes up to the ceiling—"five or six, maybe eight weeks, ago. And was also the last time that Peter and I talked."

"Did you give the money back?"

"What?" Gabe drew his eyebrows together. It was as if Lundin didn't know him at all. "You're familiar with the phrase 'a fool and his money are soon parted'? Well, they are fools, and we kept their money. They can mark down the cost as learning a lesson."

"And it looks like your ex got a final lesson, doesn't it?"

When he put it that way.

Gabe's share of the cash was tucked safely away in Elton's closet. Considering he'd abandoned his new SUV and last home address, Gabe didn't have any qualms about keeping the money. But he did need to consider Elton's safety.

"What exactly happened that brought you here to Heart-stone?" Elton asked. "There must have been something that scared you."

If the question had come from Ranger Man, Gabe probably would have flipped him off. But this was Elton, the first genuine person in Gabe's life. Ranger Man was probably bona fide too. But since he pissed Gabe off, he didn't get an automatic pass, and besides, he was too sexy for Gabe's own good.

"I'd already packed up to leave, knew it was time. Probably past time. I'd been feeling twitchy for a week or so, like someone was watching me, following me. I headed over to Beacon Hill and left my car in an alley, picked up Heidi's. Just had the feeling that Peter and I had overstayed our welcome. But before leaving town, I drove past an address we'd been using and ended up being chased by a dog and shot at. The rest, as they say, is history. I got rid of my cell phone, ditched the credit cards. The plan was to lie low for as long as possible."

Lundin snorted. "How long did that last for you? A few hours?"

"Fuck off," Gabriel retorted, but there was no heat to the two words. Lundin had a point; he hadn't done a very good job of avoiding the limelight. If Ranger Man had just let one night at Fort Hood slide, Gabe might have been successful. Maybe if he hadn't done that background check.

Silent for a moment, they all sipped at their cooling coffees.

Gabe didn't know what Elton and Lundin were thinking, but he was trying to figure out how to spin his relationship with Peter and Gabe's recent relocation to Heartstone Island when he talked to the cops.

Before he came up with much of anything, his phone vibrated. Dragging it out of his jeans pocket, he glanced down at the screen. It wasn't a number he recognized. He read it out loud.

"That's the Sheriff's Office," Elton said. "Rizzi said Spurring would call."

Gabe glanced at Elton and then across at Casey. And when had his brain decided to start using Lundin's first name anyway? Ranger Man suited him just fine.

"The sheriff?" Gabe repeated with a roll of his eyes. "How much are you willing to bet they want me down at the station right now?"

Elton shook his shaggy head. "Not taking that bet. The odds aren't looking good, kid, might as well cooperate. Casey and I have your back."

"Well, fuck," Gabe said glumly, while also amused that Elton was calling him kid. Whether Ranger Man had his back or not was an entirely different discussion.

"I'd say that about sums it up." Elton pushed himself to his feet. "Might as well find out what they want to talk to you about."

FIVE

Gabriel

The Monday that just won't stop Mondaying

THE TWANA COUNTY Sheriff's Office made its home in a low-slung brick building located just across the slender isthmus that connected Heartstone to the peninsula. Years ago, the structure had probably been painted some shade of white, but the color hadn't aged well. Nowadays, it was an off-putting mossy-greenish hue that made Gabriel think of milk that had gone bad. Or a decomposing body. The deputy he'd talked to earlier met them in the lobby.

"Thank you for coming in on such short notice, Mr. Karne," Deputy Eagan greeted him, her expression carefully blank. "We've got an interview room set up down the hall. Do you need water or anything to drink?"

"Uh, no. But thanks for offering."

"I'll wait out here."

Elton had insisted on coming with him. His reasoning had

been along the lines of: "If nothing else, they won't try anything fancy if I'm there."

Gabe appreciated the support even if it made him feel like a naïve kid. And he was all for nothing fancy happening. Regardless that his bed was currently on an almost derelict sailboat, it was his bed, and he liked sleeping in it.

"Are they known for trying underhanded stuff?" he'd asked. "And, more importantly, are you sure? You had that dental work done today, don't you want to take it easy?" Gabe had had to admit that the old man looked reenergized, and his jaw didn't seem to be any puffier than it had been earlier.

"It wasn't brain surgery," Elton had said dismissively, his bushy eyebrows drawn together. "I'm perfectly fine."

And he was stubborn, but there was no reason to point out what everyone already knew. Ranger Man had declined to join them, saying something about taking Bowie for a walk. Gabe was envious, he didn't want to go to the station either. After Elton promised he'd call and fill him in, Lundin had driven off, presumably heading someplace that Bowie approved of.

"Fine, stay, have it your way."

With an impatient wave of his hand, Elton settled into an uncomfortable plastic chair across from the currently empty front desk and pulled a paperback-size book of sudoku puzzles out of his pocket. Gabe noted that a placard with the name Althea Mortine engraved on it sat near a blotter and keyboard on the desk.

The interview room was what Gabe had expected, cramped and dingy. Four chairs and a small square table sat smack in the middle of the space. The room smelled of disinfectant and despair, if despair was the vague scent of dirty socks. Gabe did his best not to breathe too deeply.

"Please take a seat," Deputy Eagan said. "Chief Deputy Spurring will be joining us in a few minutes."

"What? Not the sheriff?"

Gabe hadn't been part of a murder investigation until he'd arrived on Heartstone, but he damn well knew Sheriff Rizzi had homed in on him since his arrival. He was the one who'd interviewed him at the marina, after all. Why wouldn't he have more questions? Gabe was the one who knew Peter personally. Didn't crime statistics prove that most people were murdered by someone they knew, a boyfriend, husband, or other family? Reluctantly, he pulled one of the chairs out and sat down on it, trying to mentally prepare himself for whatever questions they had.

Without replying, Deputy Eagan took the seat next to Gabe, scooting the chair out a bit and sitting so she faced him. Gabe had been expecting her to sit across the table from him like he'd seen on TV shows. This felt much more personal and that was likely the point.

"This interview will be recorded," she informed him.

Gabe nodded that he understood, and Eagan leaned forward to press a button set into the table.

"First, please state your name and acknowledge verbally that you understand this conversation is being recorded."

"My name is Gabriel Karne, and I understand this is being recorded." Maybe he should have brought a lawyer. Except he didn't know any, and he had nothing to do with Peter's death. Murder, he corrected himself.

"Thank you. Please start at the beginning of your day today and take me through it."

Nodding, Gabe went over the day again, starting with Casey Lundin stopping by to tell him he was taking Elton to the dentist and asking if Gabe would watch Bowie.

"Almost right after he left, I got a call from the marine supply place about an order, so I drove into Westfort to pick it up. I'm sure you've checked to see when I arrived. The old guy at the counter and I chatted for a bit, he'll remember me."

"You didn't see anyone suspicious hanging around the marina before you left? No one you didn't recognize?"

"I mean, I'm new to the island, I don't know many folks, but I didn't see anyone before I left or when I returned."

Eagan was taking notes in a small notebook with a spiral binding at the top. She flipped to a new page and started to speak, but before she could ask her next question, the door was flung open and Chief Deputy Spurring filled the doorway. Gabe wondered if he'd been listening in and timed his entrance. Grimacing, Spurring glanced at Eagan and then Gabe.

What was Gabe thinking? Of course he had been listening in.

On the way to the station, Elton had filled Gabe in on Spurring. At least what he could in the time they'd had.

"I've known Emmett since he was a boy, and he wasn't much more likable back then. He's a Heartstone lifer like me, but, unlike me, he threw his lot in with Eli Rizzi. Now that Deter Nolan is gone, you'd be hard-pressed to find a more pro-Rizzi deputy."

"That's just wonderful, not," Gabe had muttered.

"Be careful around him. He's second-in-command and holds a lot of power in the county."

"Even better."

"We figure they want you take the fall for this, so maybe don't antagonize him. It will be much easier for us to try and find out who really did this if you're not behind bars. I'm serious, Gabriel."

There'd been no time to argue with Elton that there was no "us" in the finding-out equation.

Now Spurring hitched his uniform slacks up before taking the remaining chair across from Gabriel. He didn't bother to introduce himself, but Deputy Eagan took a second to verbally note that Chief Deputy Spurring had joined the conversation.

"How did you know the victim?" Spurring demanded bluntly, sitting forward so his face was inches from Gabe as he spoke. He had bad breath.

"Peter and I had been partners, but that was over."

"Partners exactly how?"

A muscle in Gabe's jaw flexed and he forced himself not to flinch at Spurring's proximity. "We were business partners, and in the beginning, we were bed partners." He could not bring himself to utter the word lovers. They'd never been lovers, and the word annoyed him anyway.

"Bed partners," Spurring repeated with a sneer.

"Do you have an issue with that?" Gabe was curious if the man would rise to his bait.

From the tic at the corner of Spurring's eye, he did in fact have a problem with same-sex relationships. Gabe wondered what the cop would think if Gabe told him that he was bi. He briefly imagined the top of Spurring's head popping off and smoke billowing out of it. It was very satisfying.

"We've done a background search on you," Spurring said, changing the subject and dragging Gabe back to real life.

"I figured you would. Isn't that one of the things cops do when they're investigating a murder?"

Beside him, Deputy Eagan shifted in her seat.

"There are gaps in your employment history and home addresses. Can you explain them?"

"Do my past jobs or addresses have anything to do with Peter's murder? If they do, please enlighten me."

Chance ...

Right. Do not antagonize the zoo animals.

"Please, just answer the question, Mr. Karne," Deputy Eagan said.

"I'm largely self-employed and, as far as changes of address ..." Gabe shrugged. "Maybe I didn't always notify the state, but that's not a crime." He had no idea if it was or wasn't. Maybe it was when it came to paying taxes.

"How did you and the victim first meet?" Spurring sneered the question.

Oh boy. Gabe's resolve not to antagonize him was crumbling. It would be so easy. He could tell the man suffered from a bad case of fragile masculinity; it wouldn't take much for him to shed his thin veneer of pleasantness.

"We met at an LGBTQIA+ business networking event. As one does."

Gabe had attended to see if he could make some "business connections," but instead he and Peter had met and hooked up that night. It was only later that they'd realized they had similar "business" interests.

And one thing had led to another, as these things sometimes do.

The questions continued in the same vein and same condescending tone. Spurring seemed determined to trip Gabe up in a lie about his and Peter's relationship, but there was nothing for Gabe to lie about.

The small room was growing warmer by the minute, and the stench of body odor also increased the longer the three of them sat there. Was it a special scent they piped in from somewhere? He was trying to take shallow breaths, but he was starting to feel nauseous.

Eventually, he had enough of the questions. He realized that Eagan had stopped taking notes half an hour earlier and Spurring was repeating himself, his face gradually turning deeper shades of red until Gabe worried the man was going to have a stroke then and there.

"We know that you had a relationship with the victim."

"Are we back to that again? We already established that Peter and I had—operative word is in the past tense—a relationship. I don't know why he was on Heartstone, and I don't know what he wanted to talk to me about because he never came back."

"Why did you end your relationship?"

"Um." Gabe pretended to think. "That's not your business. But if you want to know the truth, Peter didn't do it for me anymore, if you get my drift. No zing. The magic was gone. Our time in the sack was performative at best. Does that answer your question?"

Gabe saw Eagan's cheek dimple quickly before she schooled her expression. The shade of red that Spurring's face had turned was not listed even on the big box of crayons.

"I'm not under arrest?" He directed the question at Eagan, who shook her head. "Then, as far as I understand these things, I'm free to go. I came down here voluntarily and now I'm leaving on my own." He rose to his feet. "If you need to ask me new, different questions about my sex life, you know where to find me."

"We're watching you, Karne. When you make a mistake, know that we'll catch it. You had something to do with Vale's death and I'm—we're going to prove it."

Gabe rolled his eyes. There was always that one guy who had to have the last word.

"READY TO HEAD BACK to your place?" Gabe asked Elton when he emerged from the back of the station.

Elton slowly stood up. "Yep, let's blow this popsicle joint. It was nice speaking with you, Althea." The older woman who had taken the seat behind the front desk smiled and nodded.

Gabe waited until they were back in the Ford and he had his seat belt clipped.

"Althea, huh?"

Elton didn't bother responding; instead, he put the truck into reverse and backed out of the parking spot.

"I'm hungry and all I can have is soup."

Gabe smirked. Elton could deflect all he wanted but Gabe was pretty damn sure romance was afoot between Elton and Althea.

"Soup sounds delicious."

Nodding as if it hadn't been him who'd made the suggestion in the first place, Elton pressed on the gas and they rumbled down the road.

SIX

Casey

Tuesday

CASEY'S PHONE VIBRATED, dragging him out of a pleasant enough slumber. With bleary eyes and sluggish fingers, he grabbed for the damn thing and squinted at the screen. Damn, it was just after six in the morning. He should be up already. He peered at the number, knowing it was familiar, but he had been deep asleep.

Blinking several times, he tried to force his brain into working order. *Bingo*. The number belonged to Rowan Leary, his acquaintance-friend who flew helicopters for the Park Service. The phone vibrated again, and Casey pressed Accept.

"Leary, what's going on?"

Casey was already sitting up. No doubt this call meant he would have to be up and out ASAP. Rowan wouldn't be calling if there wasn't an emergency.

"Sorry to call so early, Casey, but we've got a missing person.

Someone from the brush crew." The brush crews drove themselves up The Valley, riding together in vans and pickups. "Sounds like they didn't realize he'd been missed until this morning when his girlfriend called around. Both drivers thought he was in the other car."

"Keep talking, I'm putting you on speaker while I get ready."

This was not the time of year to go missing. It was cold and wet, and the days were short, making everything about a search that much more difficult. Casey grabbed a thick pair of socks from his dresser and started to put them on. It would be cold as fuck in the forest today. The last thing anyone wanted was a rescue worker needing to be rescued themselves.

"I'm assuming you're calling Greta? I'll stop and pick her up too. What can you tell me about the missing person?"

With Bowie by his side, Casey exited *The Barbara* and walked quickly down the pier. He'd learned early on in his residency at the marina not to move too fast when it was frosty out. His ass had felt the impact for days.

"Carlos Garcia, mid-twenties. This was his first season up The Valley, but he's done other work for us in years past. From what we can piece together, he just didn't show up at the pickup point. The last carpool was around four p.m."

"That's a long damn time to be out in the cold." Temperatures were getting steadily colder as the official change from fall to winter drew closer.

"Yeah," Rowan agreed. "Wires got crossed, not good. I've talked to both drivers directly, and neither remembers seeing Carlos. His girlfriend has tried his phone and it goes to voicemail."

Either because he was out of service range or battery. Also not good.

Opening the gate, Casey let Bowie squeeze through first and

then relocked it after he'd done the same. Not that it would keep someone from dumping a dead body there, he thought grimly.

Covering the mic, Casey yelled, "Bowie, get back here! We don't have time for the cat. Sorry about that," he said to Rowan.

With a doggy roll of his eyes, Bowie trotted over to the car and waited for Casey to catch up. Once Bowie was safely in the back, Casey buckled himself in and started the engine, continuing to listen to what Rowan had to say about the missing person.

"Not much else to tell you. I already alerted Tor and his team. We just need experienced searchers before it's too late for this guy."

Brush work was fast money this time of year, but the conditions could be dangerous. Weather conditions were always iffy and there was little to no oversight. The work was exhausting, there was always the risk of serious injury, and they were paid by the pound, which meant the quicker folks made more money but encouraged carelessness. Casey found it ironic that most folks had no idea where the holiday wreaths they hung on their walls and doors, or the pretty salal leaves that were often added to bouquets, came from. Or the effort that went into harvesting just the boughs themselves—it was back-breaking work.

"I figure we're an hour out, hopefully less."

Travel time was, obviously, unavoidable, but even two more hours out in the cold for Carlos Garcia was too long; fingers crossed, they would find him quickly, alive and relatively uninjured.

"That's all I've got for you," Rowan said.

"Great, see you when we get there." Casey set his phone back in the cup holder and focused on the road in front of him.

He was proud of his tracking abilities. After a lifetime spent as much in the forest as possible, he was pretty damn good at finding people. But Greta was even better. His partner had incredible instincts when it came to locating lost hikers, campers, and other creatures. Once she'd located a cat that had escaped its owners and spent a few days in the woods. The only other being Casey personally knew who was better at tracking was Bowie, and he had the advantage of an incredible sense of smell.

"WHAT DO you know about this guy?" Greta asked from the passenger seat, her go-cup gripped tightly in her hands.

Bowie was staying with Greta's partner, Abby, for the day. He wasn't an official tracking dog and he'd probably get in the way. Casey made a mental note once again to research training schedules when things calmed down. When they'd pulled out of Greta's driveway, Bowie was happily playing fetch with Abby, not caring that he was being left behind.

"Nothing that I haven't told you already. Male, mid-twenties, has worked for Rowan's group before so should know not to wander off. The crew is heading up The Valley at first light." This time of year, the sun didn't rise until just before eight a.m. "Fingers crossed, he's waiting for them up at the site. But since he didn't answer calls to his cell phone, I'm not holding my breath."

"Don't these crews generally stick together?"

Casey shot her a Look; the question had to be rhetorical.

"It's part of their training, you know that."

"Training," she scoffed. "We both know what that means."

Greta had a point. Training was often five minutes of pep talk before they headed into the woods with sharp tools.

"We'll talk to the team—obviously. Maybe one of them can tell us more about him. I, for one, would love to learn that he has backwoods survival experience."

Being an experienced outdoors person didn't ensure

survival or even that the worker would be found, but it might help. Casey navigated around a deep pit in the road but managed to hit another in the process.

"Did they bring a pothole installer up here?" Greta griped. "Blessed be the inventor of the thermal go-cup with a tight lid."

"Maybe they did. Maybe potholes keep the riffraff out? But I'm pretty sure there's been some equivalent of the go-cup since the Romans. Probably before that."

"And now I have an image of Sasquatch hanging out in the forest with his hollowed-out stone mug."

"You're welcome."

They passed by the sign advertising Snowcap Estates. Somehow it looked even more tattered and bedraggled than it had only ten days ago. There weren't any signs of construction, just the orange survey tape fluttering in the wind.

"Mmph," said Greta. "I'd sure like to know whose pockets were lined in order to push that through."

"And why has it been sitting for as long as it has? Not that I want a brand spanking new development up here, but they were so hot to do it. Came in right away, cut all the trees down, and now, nothing. I hate it and the people responsible for it."

"Ironic, considering the LLC that got their hands on the land chose Trillium as their business name, yet they've probably destroyed a huge swathe of the plant's habitat. Fuckers."

Casey had to agree. Trillium was exceedingly slow-growing and hated to be disturbed. It was illegal to pick or harvest the native species growing on state land, but sadly, Snowcap Estates was privately owned.

"Definitely fuckers."

Another quarter of a mile and the ingress leading to Gordon MacDonald's property appeared out of the mist. The driveway looked a bit sad and lonely in the gray drizzle, and a strand of yellow tape had blown all the way to the road, where it caught on some Oregon grape. Casey wondered if Calvin Perkins had been found yet. As far as Casey knew, he hadn't been seen since before his brother Dwayne was discovered on Gordon's land with a bullet hole in his head.

"No news about Perkins?" Greta asked, seeming to read Casey's thoughts. She was often very good at knowing what he was thinking.

"Nope." He grunted as the truck's tires thudded in and out of another massive dip in the road. "Have you heard anything?"

"No time to tap into the rumor mill yet, we only got back Friday." Greta stared out the passenger window. "The Snowcap Estates folks know this road is impossible, right? They'll have to have a year-round work crew on call. Or convince the county to pave the whole thing."

"Maybe that's what's taking them so long," Casey said.

"Maybe." But she didn't sound convinced.

Slowing to a crawl, Casey muscled the truck around a hairpin turn that eventually connected to the service road they were aiming for. Then, with skill and a little bit of luck, they would find the work crew and Rowan somewhere along the next stretch of road.

"Where the hell is Perkins?" Greta said, returning to the subject of the missing brother. "I'd expect him to be rampaging around trying to get revenge for Dwayne. I cannot believe all this happened while Abby and I were on vacation."

"Yeah. Definitely eventful while you were out of town. Do you think Calvin could've killed his own brother?"

"I mean, in a meth-fueled rage maybe? Together they were idiots, but they were inseparable. I think that most likely they finally fucked with the wrong person."

That's what Casey thought as well, but the question of Calvin Perkins's whereabouts nagged at him. It had been well over a week now. Had he been killed as well? Injured? The

Calvin Perkins Casey had known most of his life was not the kind of person to sit around and wait for justice to prevail—or wait to dole out his version of justice, at least.

"So." Greta drew out the single word casually, in a way that had Casey's mental antennae twitching wildly. "What's the skinny on this new dockmate of yours? You're not the only bachelor at the marina any longer."

Casey groaned inwardly and clutched the truck's steering wheel. He'd skimmed over the details of Gabriel Karne's arrival, but somehow she'd homed in on exactly what he was trying to avoid. Or rather, *who*. And she'd waited until Casey was trapped behind the wheel of the truck before bringing him up. Diabolical.

"I doubt he'll be a neighbor for long." He hoped that sounded offhand and dismissive. "I don't think he's long-term liveaboard material."

The truth was, for someone who didn't check the standard *hot-blooded-male-must-have-sex* boxes, Casey had spent an awful lot of time thinking about Charming since his arrival on Heartstone. He'd given himself several sternly worded lectures, but his brain had ignored every one of them, instead bombarding Casey with out-of-the-ordinary thoughts and yes, also images. Charming Fucker was the very last person on earth Casey expected, or wanted, to pique his interest.

"Why wouldn't he be? And don't be shy, share all the details."

Dammit, he'd either sounded too dismissive or not offhand enough when he'd mentioned Charming Fucker. Greta had always been the Sherlock Holmes of figuring out what Casey didn't want to talk about, and he didn't want to talk about Gabriel Karne. The man infuriated him, and that was that. He wasn't at all intriguing with a sensitive side to him that Casey sensed he'd kept hidden most of his life. Nope. And now Casey was mad at himself for thinking like this at all, much less about Gabriel Karne.

"Well?" she prompted.

Casey had to bite his tongue to keep from responding with *That's deep.* Karne had used those exact words yesterday, and they still weren't funny. Or charming. They were damn irritating.

"Let's see." Casey skipped past the part where he'd discovered Karne trespassing at the park and given him a ticket. "From what I know, his mother recently passed, and she left him *The Golden Ticket.*"

"Huh. Because everyone needs a creaky old sailboat in their life."

Casey repressed a snort. Karne and *The Golden Ticket* deserved each other.

"Do you think he was responsible for the body found at the marina yesterday? I doubt it since you haven't said anything."

Of course, Greta had already heard about Peter Vale. Casey was shocked she hadn't called him yesterday to get the scoop. She'd probably intended to do it at the office today, but he'd bet being trapped in a vehicle was even better from her perspective.

"No. He says not, and I tend to believe him. But he did know the guy."

Quickly, Casey filled Greta in on the discovery and their theory about how Vale had gotten there.

"That's nuts! Who would break into the marina and leave a body? Was he killed there, do you think?"

"My security feed doesn't show anyone coming or going, so whoever it was must have come by water while Karne was in Westfort. It's possible he could have arrived alive, but I'd say from the condition of the body that the victim was already dead when he was dumped."

"That forensics course you took to satisfy continuing ed credits is paying off."

"Very funny. Are you Watson, then?" He shook his head in mock disgust. "But I would say there had to be two other people involved. How else would a person carry a body, a literal dead-weight, and lift it from one boat to another? Unless they were very strong."

"But no one saw anything because it's winter and there's hardly any traffic this time of year, foot or otherwise."

Whoever had killed Peter Vale had to be familiar with the obscure Riddle Bay Marina and Heartstone Island. Had they been keeping an eye out, so they knew when Casey and Karne were both gone? Or had it been an opportunity presenting itself at the perfect moment?

If it were chance, they'd been damn lucky. If the dump was purposeful, some sort of message, it put a different light on everything. Was it a message to Karne? And if that was the case, why not leave Vale on the *Ticket*? Why choose the *Shangri-La*? Were they locals? The marina seemed to indicate so.

Casey was driving himself to distraction.

"Those are good questions. Hopefully, Rizzi and company are looking into them." Greta sounded thoughtful. In his peripheral vision, Casey saw her head move as she turned to look at him.

"But that's not what I meant when I asked you about your new neighbor. What's he like? Is he hot? And don't do that jaw-clench thing at me, I can think a guy is hot even if I don't want to get it on with him."

"For Christ's sake, Greta." Casey did not want to talk about Gabriel Karne with Greta. She had this way of weaseling information out of him when he least wanted to part with it.

"So, he is hot? Because I'm just saying, you not confirming or denying is suspicious."

Dammit, Greta.

Casey could lie and say Karne wasn't hot, but Greta was already on alert—how, he had no idea. Even if Casey planned on putting it off as long as possible, they would eventually meet, and Greta would give him The Look and promise a later conversation. Because Gabriel Karne was hot.

"I suppose he's attractive. But his personality leaves something to be desired."

"What? He didn't just fall at your feet when you glared at him?" She snickered at her own stupid joke.

"Ha, ha, ha."

"Casey, I think it's about time you met someone who interested you. I only wish I'd been around to witness it. Were you broody and stern? I bet you were, that's your go-to reaction when someone gets under your skin."

Luckily, Casey spotted the turnout where the brush crew was working and pulled the truck over.

SEVEN

Casey

Tuesday in The Valley

TEN OR SO WORKERS WERE HUDDLED UNDER the protection of a massive six-armed cedar tree that was working hard to beat out the Douglas firs that surrounded it. The group watched Casey park behind a beat-up silver extended cab truck and a red van that Casey was surprised could still make the trip.

"That thing's held together with duct tape and bailing wire," Greta commented as she unbuckled her seat belt.

Casey mentally thanked Rowan for giving them the exact GPS address of Carlos's last known location since there were miles of fire roads and trails leading off in all directions. Today, the search would focus on the trails that headed down The Valley, based on the assumption that the missing Carlos would try to get to civilization if he was able. Hopefully, with skill and luck, they would find him today. Alive.

Of course, when folks were lost, it could be hard to know

which direction was up and which was down, especially if they were disoriented or injured. As he set the parking brake, another van pulled up, an Olympic Rescue logo on its side. Casey recognized the driver, Tor Torkelson, another experienced search and rescuer. There were three other people with Tor that he didn't know.

Everyone got out of their vehicles and gathered at the front of the van. Tor introduced his team and Casey shared what Rowan had told him over the phone call.

"Would be nice to have a little more information," Casey said at the end.

"We'll work with what we've got." Tor slapped his gloved hands together. "Let's talk to these folks first and then do our best to find Carlos. Fingers crossed it doesn't take long."

The six of them walked over to where the group waited for them. Some looked concerned, but most were obviously impatient and ready to get on with their day.

"Thanks for waiting," Greta said. "Please fill us in on Carlos Garcia so you can get to work. Did anything seem off yesterday? Was he nervous or twitchy? Maybe ill?"

"He was okay yesterday." The speaker had long dark hair, most of it tucked up into a knit cap, but stray strands were doing their best to escape. Everyone wore practical clothing, heavy gloves, and hiking boots. "We took a break at the usual time. I think Carlos was there."

He glanced around for confirmation, but no one seemed willing to provide it. There were a few shrugs and *maybe*s.

"I didn't talk to him," added another. "Not after we all got started."

"Did any of you see him wander off or go in a different direction?" Greta asked. They all shook their heads.

Most of the brush harvesters were migrant workers and all were paid in cash for what they cut. Possibly, they were nervous about sharing information or felt like they were ratting on a friend. Or they could even be worried about having to talk to authorities themselves. Casey sighed; he didn't give a crap what their status was. He didn't want anyone dying on the unforgiving terrain.

The harvest leases were generally divided into grids so the shrubs and evergreens weren't overharvested during the season. Crews were instructed precisely where to go, and each team was supposed to have an experienced lead, but Casey wasn't impressed with Cap Guy.

"So," Casey said, drawing out the word. "Carlos could have gone missing at almost any time over the day?"

Looking around at each other, the workers nodded, some hesitantly, some more vigorously.

Dammit. Not having a time frame for when he disappeared made things more complicated. Carlos could have been missing for almost twenty-four hours instead of just the twelve they'd calculated. The likelihood of his being okay was plummeting with every word spoken and minute lost. They all had training and first aid supplies, but if they found him, would it be enough until they could get him to safety? Was he close by, or had he wandered miles away?

"Yeah, I guess he could've." The only woman on the crew pointed at the earbud dangling from one ear. "I'm usually listening to something. It's not easy to talk when we're working, and I get bored. I might not have noticed Carlos going somewhere."

Everyone nodded at her words.

Cap Guy directed them to the general area Carlos had been assigned to and then the rescue team let the crew get to work.

Greta glanced around, taking in the deeply forested area with its steep hills and hidden inclines. "Needle in a damn haystack."

At least there were signs that someone had been there. There was a stack of cut boughs and boot prints in the mud. A red and yellow knit cap lay at the base of a tree.

"We might need more people," Casey agreed.

"Fuck this, I'm radioing in and asking for all hands." Greta unhooked the sat phone from her belt and punched in a number she knew by heart.

"Jim? Yeah, it's Greta. We have a missing person."

All hands meant every local agency with trained search and rescue staff would get the call. Quickly, Greta explained what they knew about the missing person to the coordinator for the all-hands teams, Jim Reilly.

"Yeah, Tor's here already. One sec." She pulled the phone away from her mouth and asked Casey, "What are the coordinates again?" He told her and she repeated them to Jim.

"All right, hopefully this will be a quick one." Ending the call, Greta tucked the phone back into her backpack. "Let's get started."

Shoulder to shoulder, they began to slowly make their way down the mountainside in the direction they hoped Carlos had headed, looking for signs that someone had passed that way recently. Nothing like a rescue mission to reinforce the square acreage of the forest.

"Snowflake in a blizzard, eh?"

"I think we have a better chance of finding that needle in a haystack you mentioned, to be honest," grumbled Casey.

They started walking, and a steady, slushy snow began falling. Yay for precipitation, Casey thought, but maybe not today while they had a missing person. They were dressed for the weather, of course, but that didn't mean they wouldn't get cold. And so would Carlos Garcia.

"So, your new neighbor," said Greta as they moved along.

"Seriously, Greta? We're on a rescue."

"I can probe into your life and search at the same time," she insisted.

"No, you cannot. We find this guy and you can ask all the questions you want."

She grinned and Casey realized he'd fallen into her trap. "I'm holding you to that."

EIGHT

Gabriel

Tuesday morning

GABE WAS DRAGGED from a deep sleep into an irritated wakefulness by an impatient buzzing and raindrops thrumming insistently against the *Ticket*'s deck and the wooden pier. Sleep-addled, he blinked uncertainly up at the ceiling, forcing his brain to break through the crust of slumber. Overnights on the sailboat had been hit-and-miss so far, sleepwise, but he was going to have to get used to it. There wasn't an alternative.

Last night, or possibly this morning, he'd had a series of uncomfortable, murky dreams involving Peter. But now that his eyes were open, the images were quickly fading, and Gabe wasn't awake enough yet to know if he was glad that he wouldn't remember them.

Dammit, Peter, what the hell happened?

Yesterday's unfortunate discovery forced itself to the front of his mind. Peter was dead and Gabe had been the one to discover his body on the sailboat kitty-corner from *The Golden Ticket*. There wasn't even a frying pan to jump out of; he was in a whole potful of boiling water with no way out.

His phone started to buzz again.

"Fucking hell," Gabe rasped.

Rolling over but managing to keep himself mostly under the covers to avoid the chilly fingers of the morning, Gabe patted around on the window ledge for his phone.

"'Lo?" He cleared his voice and tried again. "Hello?"

"Mr. Karne, when you didn't answer, I thought you might have skipped town."

Unfortunately, he was now awake enough to recognize the smug voice that belonged to the fuck weasel, Chief Deputy Spurring. Gabriel wasn't sure who he disliked more, Deputy Spurring or Chief Rizzi. They seemed to have been cut from the same mold, just at different times.

"Nope, I told you I wasn't going anywhere."

"That's good. We need you to come in and go over your statement. This morning."

"Again?"

Gabe wanted to argue that he'd told them everything—and he had, mostly. Instead, he reluctantly agreed to show up at the station in an hour. After all, he had expected them to call him in again, but it didn't mean that he'd been looking forward to it. And the fact that he'd been there less than twenty-four hours ago didn't bode well. Ending the call, he immediately rang Elton.

"Since I promised I'd call you, I'm calling. They want to talk to me some more. I'm supposed to get down there as soon as I'm dressed. Might as well get this over with."

A black, spindly legged spider with a body the size of a dime emerged from wherever it and its hordes of relatives had been secreting themselves. Gabe looked around for something to smash it with. The only thing they seemed to understand was violence. He grabbed the paperback he'd set aside a couple of nights ago, but when he turned back, the damn thing had disappeared. Dammit.

"Did they say anything specific? And are you ready for me to call a lawyer?"

Not yet. He scanned the floor looking for the creature; however, he might need the services of a courageous spider killer.

"Sounds like they just want to go over my statement for the third time. Which, since I've told them the truth, won't be difficult." A flexible truth, but it had been the truth.

"I'll drive you over."

"Elton," Gabe said, "I appreciate the support, I really do, but you had a root canal yesterday, and they just want to ask me questions. I can drive myself. No lawyer yet." He was also tempted to add that he was forty-four, not five.

"I'll be there in ten minutes," the stubborn old man said, his words followed by the definitive click of the call ending.

"The fuck." Gabe groaned again as he sat up and pushed himself to standing. He'd never had someone so determined to look after him. Not even his mother. It unsettled him. He wasn't sure if he could allow himself to get used to it. What the hell did Elton see in him that no one else did? Ranger Man certainly didn't seem to find anything worthy about Gabe.

It's time to stop feeling sorry for yourself, Chance.

Fine. He didn't like Lundin anyway.

A FULL ELEVEN MINUTES LATER, Gabe shivered as he huddled into his parka and tromped down the pier toward the lot. He hadn't had time to shower but didn't want to make Elton wait. The new shower system in the boat was better than nothing, but the tank took a bit too long to warm up. The last thing he wanted that morning was a cold shower before spending time with his new friend Spurring and the rest of the gang. Besides, he couldn't possibly smell worse than the interrogation room.

Tugging on the lock and chain, Gabe ensured the gate was secured behind him before crossing to where Elton's truck idled. It was only then that he registered that Casey's Wagoneer was not there. Where was Ranger Man? Maybe he'd heard him leave very early, but if so, he'd slid right back into a deep slumber. Wonderful, the next person to be murdered would be him because he slept like the dead.

Bad choice of words, Chance.

Last night, after Elton had dropped him off, Gabe had considered knocking on Lundin's door, but *The Barbara* had been locked up for the night—and had a *don't bug me* feel to it. Instead, he'd climbed aboard the *Ticket* and spent the rest of the evening obsessively going over every memory he had of Peter, wondering what he'd missed that might point to why he'd shown up on Heartstone.

By the time he'd fallen asleep, he hadn't come up with a thing.

"I BROUGHT YOU SOME COFFEE, figured you might not have had the time to make any," Elton said as Gabe opened the passenger door and climbed inside.

"Bless the caffeine. I take back all the mean things I was thinking about you making me hurry," Gabe muttered. He clipped his seat belt and then accepted the twenty-ounce thermal mug like the sacred offering it was.

"You're the one who said they wanted you ASAP. Did they say anything specific when they called?" Elton checked the rearview mirror and began to back onto the roadway.

"It was that asshole Spurring who called and nope, nothing specific. He opened with the fact that he was surprised I hadn't skipped town. Which, I suppose, doesn't bode well."

"I'll wait for you again. It never hurts to have extra eyes and ears."

Since Gabe needed a ride back home, he chose not to argue. And besides, he suspected Elton had an ulterior motive.

WHEN THEY ARRIVED at the station, the same older woman—*Althea*, Gabe recalled—sat behind the desk again. She shot a quick glance at Elton, and Gabe thought he spotted the ghost of a smile. Elton's motive wasn't even ulterior.

"Gabriel Karne? I'll let the deputies know you're here."

Again, it was Deputy Eagan who came out from the back of the station and guided him to the same interview room they'd used the day before. It still smelled like old socks. Gabe noted that the deputy looked like she hadn't slept well. And possibly worse than a bad night of sleep, her lips were pressed into a thin line. Something was up.

"Chief Deputy Spurring will be with you as soon as he can, and possibly Chief Rizzi," she said. "Make yourself comfortable."

"Ah, I get the top brass two days in a row. Must be special."

Eagan didn't respond, but conflicting expressions on the deputy's face told him that she had something she wanted to say but either felt she shouldn't or had been specifically told not to.

"Don't worry about me," Gabe said with an eyebrow waggle and grin. "I'll be fine. And if not, Elton will call in the cavalry."

The deputy didn't return his smile; she just shook her head and stepped out of the room, pulling the door shut behind her. The shaking of a head wasn't new to him, but usually he could get people to toss him a smile. Maybe he should have been more worried than he was.

Chief Deputy Spurring made Gabe wait. Gabe wasn't shocked, and he was sure the delay was on purpose. It was obvious that the officer liked to think he was a big fish around Heartstone, second only to his boss.

Gabe had been sipping at his coffee and cooling his heels for about half an hour when Spurring decided to make his appearance. Unlike the sheriff, the chief deputy was on the heavy side, his potbelly listing over the belt that worked overtime to hold up his slacks. He was also fighting a receding hairline and losing. Genetics sucked, but that didn't stop Gabe from being secretly pleased that, regardless of the silver sparks, he had most of his hair.

You're welcome for that, Chance.

"Unfortunately, Sheriff Rizzi has other business. He won't be joining us this morning."

That at least seemed like good news. If they had something on him, surely the sheriff would make the effort to be there.

Like he had the day before, Spurring sat down at the opposite side of the table from Gabriel. The flimsy plastic chair creaked worryingly under his weight. Gabriel remained still in his seat, his hands in his lap, refusing to squirm or shift his position. He had nothing to be nervous about. He hadn't killed Peter.

"This interview will be recorded." Spurring tapped the voice recorder set into the table. "This is Chief Deputy Emmett Spurring interviewing Gabriel Karne. Mr. Karne, please acknowledge you are aware that you are being recorded."

"Yes, I am aware." He wanted to say something more, but on the way over, Elton had made him promise not to antagonize the deputy, as if the man were a bear at a zoo. Also, Gabriel hadn't had enough coffee to be a real pain in the ass.

He's not worth the effort, Chance.

Noted.

"Let's get right down to business," Spurring said, leaning forward and tapping a pen against the spiral notebook he'd set on the surface of the table. With a flourish, he opened the book and began to thumb through the pages until he reached a page only half filled with cramped notes.

"Tell us again about the victim, about Peter Vale. From when you met him to the last time you say you saw him."

It wouldn't do to show his impatience with the questions, so Gabe told the deputy exactly what he'd told him and Deputy Eagan less than twenty-four hours before. The rehashing of yesterday's statement continued, with Spurring asking questions in different ways to catch Gabe in a lie.

"You say you only saw the body after you returned from your errand?"

"Yes."

"You didn't hear or see anything before you left?"

"No."

"No strange cars?"

"No."

He looked down at his notepad. "You and the victim—"

"His name was Peter. Peter Vale." Gabe and Peter may not have been involved anymore, but he was a human with a name, not a faceless victim.

Spurring stared at him, his beady eyes narrow. "You say you met Vale at a networking event."

Statement or question? This guy was getting on Gabe's nerves. He was tired of repeating himself and wished he could figure out exactly what the deputy was trying to home in on.

"That is exactly where I met him. I can even give you the address if you like." Gabe kept his hands in his lap, his fingers wrapped around the go-cup so he wouldn't be tempted to strangle Spurring.

"You were involved in"—Spurring looked down at his notepad again—"investments."

Again, a statement. Gabe was certain this was an act on Spurring's part; the chief deputy was not looking at his notes, he knew exactly what questions he wanted to ask Gabriel.

"Yep. We had projects and found investors to help them get off the ground. Sometimes we worked with other groups, sometimes we invested our own money. Why?" he asked innocently. "Do you have cash lying around that you'd like me to invest?"

A sneer twisted his thin lips as the chief deputy leaned forward. He must not have realized how close he was to the table because it rocked and scraped forward a few inches across the vinyl floor. Gabe managed not to startle.

"Peter Vale was not the victim's legal name. How long had he been using a pseudonym?"

"Peter Vale was a fake name?" Gabe wasn't able to control his reaction; his eyebrows shot up, and so did his voice. The hell. He hadn't known Peter at all, had he? "How should I know how long? I didn't know he was using a fake name. It's not like I asked him for ID before we jumped into bed together. Why does it matter now how long he'd been using it? He's dead. You should care less about his legal name and more about who killed him."

"Maybe he was hiding from someone. Someone you know, and that's why he was using a fake name. Maybe you found out and used the information to have him killed."

Gabriel didn't bother to try and tease the logic out of what Spurring was saying.

"I'm sorry, what? I found out Peter was using an alias and had him offed? *No.* Peter and I were romantically involved when we first met, but the bloom wore off pretty damn fast, and by the end we were merely housemates. I had no reason to harm him. As I have said numerous times, when I left town, I hadn't seen or spoken to Peter—or whatever his real name is—in weeks."

"Why did you leave Seattle?" Spurring demanded.

Gabe hesitated a bit too long before saying, "Among other things, my mother died. It was time to move on."

Spurring's eyes narrowed. He wasn't stupid; he knew that Gabe wasn't telling him something.

"Can I ask a question?" Gabe asked. Spurring was slow to nod. "What was Peter's real name?"

The chief deputy stared at him, apparently trying to decide whether Peter's legal name was classified information or not. Eventually, he spoke. "Vale was the victim's mother's maiden name; his birth name was Peter Stevens. Does that change anything you've told us?"

Gabe ran through his internal address book and did not come up with anyone named Stevens. Maybe an acquaintance? He shook his head.

"Rings zero bells." Gabe had to admit that Vale was a much more interesting name than Stevens. "Peter did tell me he was estranged from his family. Maybe just his dad? He never clarified. The subject wasn't something Peter talked about, so I didn't pursue it. Have you located his relatives?"

Gabe had assumed Peter's story was one experienced by far too many, especially those of their age—that Peter's family had turned their back on him when he came out as gay. If that was the case, would they care that he'd been murdered? Fuck that. Rage at the stupidity of humans surged, and Gabe had to take a deep breath to tamp it down.

Damn those dirty socks.

Spurring ignored Gabe's question. For his part, Gabe tucked away the name *Stevens* for later. There were probably thousands of Stevenses in the state, but were there thousands of Vales? Maybe he could track down Peter's family himself. Surely if the TCSO knew Peter's identity, they'd have reached out to notify the family? On the other hand, Peter likely had valid reasons for using a different name.

"You know what?" Spurring smacked his pen down and leaned back in the chair. It popped and Gabe winced, but the chair held. The deputy tapped a meaty index finger against the tabletop. "You're not telling us something, Mr. Karne. And that something could be what led to Mr. Stevens's death. You've been on Heartstone for two weeks, and the murder rate has doubled."

He didn't rise to the bait Spurring dangled. No way was he getting into a discussion about Dwayne Perkins's death. The one thing he was sure of there was that neither he nor the Colavitos had anything to do with Perkins's demise.

And fuck, it really could have been Lundin who had unknowingly alerted them to Gabe's location when he did that damn background check. Gabe made a note to find out what service he'd used. Was it possible the long arm of the unlawful had stretched from Seattle to Heartstone?

"Don't you think it's wrong to call Peter by a name he actively chose not to use?" Gabriel asked. He was officially tired of the cop's attitude. Not enough coffee, no breakfast. Too much death.

Spurring shifted his weight, eliciting more protest from the furniture. "It's my job to get to the truth of what happened to Mr. Stevens. And your job is to tell me the truth about your relationship with the victim."

Gabriel forced himself not to ask if the deputy had a hearing issue. "Well, I had nothing to do with his death. I have stated, twice now, that our relationship was over. We weren't speaking. I'd moved out and have no idea how he came to be on Heartstone. As I told you last night, he showed up a week ago and I wasn't at the marina—ask Ranger Lundin if you don't believe me, or Elton because I was with him. Lundin talked to him briefly and Peter left of his own accord. I expected him to stop by again, but he never did. End of story. Surely, Lundin's security feed showed you that."

All he got for his trouble was a noncommittal grunt and a sour face at the mention of Lundin's name. Gabe figured that they'd watched the video several times already and wished it showed more. The tape was clear evidence that no one but Gabe and Lundin had entered the dock through the gate in the past week.

Abruptly, Spurring stood up from the table, bumping it with his thigh this time. "Don't leave town."

Gabe sucked in another breath, drawing upon a well of patience that was running dry. "You can't force me to stay in town without cause. If you call me in again, I'm bringing a lawyer along."

Gabe didn't want to play the lawyer card, but he would if he had to. So far, he'd been able to skate around the hard facts. And he'd learned that Vale was an alias. It was not a shock, not in their business, but Gabe felt oddly hurt that Peter had never told him.

"You do that," Spurring retorted with a mean smile. He lumbered to his feet and gestured for Gabriel to leave the room ahead of him.

That man is trouble, Chance, and not in a good way.

Gabe found himself nodding in agreement.

On his short trip back out to the lobby, Gabe heard Elton's voice. When Elton spotted Gabriel coming around the corner, he stopped talking and rose to his feet, both bushy white eyebrows raised in question. Gabe nodded but kept moving toward the exit. He didn't have anything to do with Peter's death, but being in the station made his skin crawl.

OUTSIDE THE STATION, the tail end of November weather was living up to its reputation. It had been a steady rain when he and Elton arrived at the station but now it was pouring, and it seemed that some of the precipitation was slushy snowdrops. The day had also gotten darker since he'd been inside. Gabe peered upward, and a drop of water fell into one eye; he blinked it away.

Needing some fresh air after the gym sock assault, Gabe waited next to the passenger door while Elton slowly climbed into the truck and scooted behind the steering wheel. The man seriously needed a step stool.

An older silver Mercedes pulled into the lot and passed by them, parking a few spaces away. Gabe understood the choice, Elton's truck *menaced*. It hulked, it was a beast. The vehicle lorded over two parking spots all on its own, and then some. Which was probably why Elton insisted on driving as much as possible, the thing was a tank.

Curiosity piqued, he watched an older-than-him-but-younger-than-Elton man emerge from the Mercedes sedan. For a moment, the stranger paused next to his vehicle, staring at the greenish-white building. He was average height and appeared lean under the fitted raincoat he was wearing. Gabe couldn't see his face, but he had the sense the man was steeling himself for something unpleasant. There was a reluctance in his stance.

Then the stranger's shoulders rose and fell as if he'd taken a deep breath to fortify himself, and he began making his way toward the front entrance, his steps slow and measured as he started around the corner. Just as he turned to push open the door, Gabe caught a glimpse of his profile and had the strangest sensation of familiarity.

"Back to the *Ticket*?" Elton asked after Gabe scooted onto the bench seat and shut the door.

Shaking off the twisted déjà vu, Gabe started to agree, but his stomach growled, overruling him. There was nothing decent in his mini-fridge. The rumble was loud enough to be heard over the rain thumping against the cab of the truck. Glancing across the bench seat, he caught Elton's amused glance.

"Hungry? Let's head over to the Geoduck Inn. They have breakfast until noon, and the burgers are good too."

Gabe's stomach rumbled again. "I think that's a great idea." He felt vaguely guilty about being hungry, as if his body needed to work harder than it was at mourning Peter. But on the other hand, maybe the best way to grieve him was to figure out who the fuck murdered him since the Twana County Sheriff's Office wasn't going to.

NINE

Gabriel

Around lunchtime, Tuesday

THE GEODUCK INN was a mile or so down the highway. The funky aging restaurant was housed in a long, low one-story building and had been constructed with lumber that had darkened to almost black over the years. Gabe vaguely remembered driving past it the day he'd arrived.

"Elton! It's been too long!" A slender woman with long dark hair, who looked to be possibly in her late forties, greeted them when they stepped inside out of the storm that had rolled in. "Hello, Elton's friend," she added with an engaging smile. "Sit anywhere you like. Coffee? Your usual or are you going wild today?"

Gabe smirked. Of course, Elton knew the host. The question was, who didn't he know?

"Always lovely to see you, Livia, it has been too long. Two

coffees and two standard breakfasts. Unless there's something you can't eat?" The last words were intended for Gabe.

"Nope. I'm hungry, a hot breakfast sounds amazing."

Except for Elton, Gabriel, and three damp bikers sitting morosely around a horseshoe-shaped bar that jutted from the kitchen out into the room, the restaurant was basically empty. There was a single retirement-age couple sitting at a tall table against one wall, enjoying pints of beer and a basket of fries, but it was too early to be playing pool or darts, and the jukebox was quiet.

The bare wood walls were hung with stuffed hunting trophies, mostly elk and deer—Gabe thought anyway. These shared the space with neon signs advertising lite beer and what appeared to be a signed poster of Wayne Gretzky. Huh.

Shrugging out of his damp parka, Gabriel followed Elton across the large space to one of several tables placed next to floor-to-ceiling plate glass windows.

"I bet this has a great view in nicer weather," Gabe commented.

"Eh, the view's not bad right now."

Elton was right, the view was stunning. Past the drop-off of a large outside deck, there was a marsh or wetlands. Disheveled cattails and drooping tall grasses grew in hummocks, and after one hundred or so feet, the land gently descended to the salt-water below.

"I suppose you're right."

"I know I'm right." Elton mimicked Gabe by taking off his coat and hanging it on the spare chair next to him. "Now, tell me what happened in there," he said when he was seated.

"Here's the coffee, food's on the way." Livia plopped two dark brown mugs full to the brim and a saucer loaded with creamers down in front of them.

"Thank you, Livia," Elton said as she started back toward the kitchen. "Now, tell me what Emmett wanted."

Gabe was tempted to tease him a bit, but instead he ran through the one-sided conversation he'd had with Deputy Spurring, finishing with the fact that Peter Vale was, in fact, not a Vale but a Stevens.

"Stevens?" Elton repeated, frowning and leaning back in his seat to stare outside for a second. "That's not an uncommon name. But ..." He stared hard at Gabe, the sides of his mouth pointing downward. His expression made Gabriel uneasy. Very uneasy.

"What about Stevens? What do you know about the name?" he demanded when Elton had paused for too long.

Setting his elbows on the table, Elton leaned in again, as if he was about to share a secret. Gabriel did the same.

"I had the sense that the dead man seemed familiar to me when I saw the body," Elton said quietly, "but it seemed far-fetched, so I dismissed it as an old man's imagination. But now I'm thinking I was right, and your Peter Vale was John Stevens's boy."

"Oh?" There was a twist Gabe hadn't seen coming. "Remind me, who is John Stevens when he's at home?" The name sounded familiar, but he couldn't place it.

"He's retired, was the Twana County Prosecuting Attorney for years. He was the prosecutor for Mickie Lundin's trial, among other things. He's the person I called to ask if he knew of a property lawyer, but he didn't."

Huh. Gabriel maybe have been the New Guy, but he was aware that John Stevens had been involved in putting Casey's brother behind bars. Casey had told him as much when Elton went missing and also had made it clear that his brother, and the case, were not up for discussion. The subject was not something

Gabe ever planned on bringing up with his surly neighbor—but he could get information from Elton.

"I think that was him just now," he told Elton.

Elton glanced around the restaurant. "Where?"

"Not here," Gabe clarified. "Back at the station, the guy in the Mercedes. I didn't recognize him, but now that you've connected the dots, I can see where Peter got his profile from."

"Huh. I didn't see him but you're probably right. I know he drives a flashy car."

Setting aside the flashy car comment, Gabe tapped his bottom lip while gathering his thoughts.

"Let me put this all together. Casey's brother is in jail for murder and was put there by John Stevens, who is the father of my ex, who was killed and dumped on a boat at the marina where I am currently living? Have I got this right?"

Elton shrugged. "A bit of a run-on sentence, but I think that sums it up."

"Begs the question, did Peter really show up at the marina to talk to me? Or to Ranger Man but chickened out when he saw him? Or was it for some other reason entirely? Additionally, why didn't Casey recognize him?"

"Peter's around your age. Left the island after graduating and I don't think he ever returned. Not that I know of anyway. Don't know if Casey ever met him."

"So that would've been over twenty years ago. I assume you mean graduating from high school?"

Elton nodded. "Stevens and I were never friends, so I don't know what happened between him and his son. But Mickie's arrest and conviction hit Casey hard."

"Obviously. I can't imagine."

"Mickie's about eight, ten years older than Casey? Something like that. When he was arrested for the murder of his girl-friend, Casey's whole world was turned upside down. The result is that Casey's not a fan of John Stevens or, as you know, Sheriff Rizzi. He—Casey—still thinks his brother's innocent."

Gabe had to ask. "Is he?"

Elton waggled his head. "In here"—he tapped his chest with two gnarled fingers—"I think he is. It's hard for me to imagine that twenty-one-year-old kid doing what they said he did. Mickie was a gentle soul from what I knew of him, but they had the circumstantial evidence to convict him. It also seemed to me that everything went almost too fast. Mickie's arrest, the trial—it all happened really quick."

The flutter of wings outside the window caught Gabriel's attention. A great blue heron rose into the air and flopped awkwardly across the marshy area before landing on a log overlooking a pool of water. Then the big bird tucked its wings in and hunched its shoulders upward, looking very much like a disgruntled old person caught out in the weather.

"Huh. So. Do we think Peter's murder has anything to do with what happened in Seattle? Or was he killed because of some ancient history here on Heartstone?"

What was that saying, *Something's rotten in the state of Denmark?* It sure seemed to him that Heartstone Island was not the happy-go-lucky place it was advertised as. It also nagged at Gabe that Peter had been related to someone Ranger Man hated. What were the chances? In his line of work, he didn't trust chance.

He wanted to ask Elton if he thought Casey could possibly have had something to do with Peter's murder. An eye for an eye sort of thing. He opened his mouth, intending to ask. But as luck would have it, Livia returned with two plates piled with scrambled eggs, pancakes, and thick slices of bacon. Gabe set the question aside for later—or never. He was fairly sure he knew what Elton's answer would be.

And Gabe would have to agree with him, even if it meant

admitting Lundin was a power for good. Ranger Man was not the type to resort to murder.

TEN

Casey

Tuesday

IN SPITE of the high-quality winter gear he was bundled up in, the cold was starting to get to Casey. His nose, fingers, and toes were feeling the windchill, and his voice was getting hoarse from calling Carlos's name again and again.

They'd been searching for much longer than two hours and so far, nothing. There was no sign of the missing man. The top-of-the-hour check-ins with Tor were depressing and short as the other search teams were also coming up empty.

The radio crackled right on time.

"Lundin here."

"Anything?" Tor asked.

"Nope," Casey replied. "We found a couple of footprints in a clear area underneath a tree, but they disappeared."

"Damn."

"Yeah."

The likelihood of Carlos's survival—if he was still alive—was plummeting with every passing minute.

"Keep on, touch base in forty-five minutes. There's not much daylight left and it's getting too cold to stay out much longer."

Yes, thank you, Tor. Casey was well aware of how much time they didn't have.

There'd been that glimmer of hope half an hour ago when Greta had spotted a set of footprints off the narrow path they'd been following. But if there had been more, they'd been washed away or perhaps covered up by the slushy half-rain half-snow that was falling.

"What do you think, keep heading this way?" Casey asked, pausing next to Greta under the protective branches of a Sitka spruce that had planted itself against the banks of a steep, rocky hillside and managed to not only survive but flourish.

Thankfully, the wind had died down to almost nothing, which was good, but the mercury still lingered around freezing and would drop below that overnight. He did not envy anyone who spent the night without proper gear.

Greta nodded, staring intently out at the landscape, as if Carlos might abruptly appear. "That's my instinct. We haven't seen any other signs of a human being coming through here. If it is him, he's heading downhill. We'll find him."

Greta always talked about rescues in the present tense. She said that it helped her stay positive, that negative energy didn't help search efforts. Was it a bit woo-woo for Casey? Yes. But there was no arguing with Greta's success record.

"All right, let's break for a few more minutes, then keep heading in the same direction until the next check-in." He glanced through the branches to the darkening sky overhead. "I think Tor wants us to hike out to the road."

Greta nodded but wasn't looking at him. Her attention was

aimed outward, on the faint path most likely created by creatures of the forest, not humans.

While being equally watchful for signs of the missing man, Casey tugged off his pack and pulled his Yeti travel thermos out to take a long sip of the still molten coffee, then groaned with pleasure. The hot liquid began to work its magic, thawing him from his insides out.

"Ahhhh," he groaned.

After shooting him a raised-eyebrow glance, Greta took a sip but did not groan.

"I think you need to get laid."

"Who says that kind of stuff anymore, 'get laid'?"

"Obviously, I do," she scoffed. "It sounds like you're having a carnal relationship with that java you're holding there."

"I do not need to get laid."

"Methinks the ranger doth protest too much."

"Do not even misquote Hamlet to me."

A small smile playing across her lips, Greta shrugged as if to say *I'm right and you know it.*

There was no way in hell Casey was telling her he'd had a dream about Gabriel Karne. More than once. The same drawn-out, sensual, suggestive dream, several times over the past week. And each morning he'd woken up sweaty, hard, and wanting. But he refused to give in, so he'd also been unbearably grouchy. Casey had never felt the need to get laid before in his life, and Gabriel Karne was not relationship material.

Casey pressed his lips together to keep himself from continuing the conversation. Not that it was one. Greta would only take any denial as a challenge. Damn her and her Spidey senses. Because yes, Karne was attractive. And sexy. Something undefinable about him had Casey's attention in a way very few ever had. But on the other hand, he was a dissolute grifter with the moral compass of an alley cat. It was beyond Casey's comprehension that Elton seemed to not only like Karne but also trust him. Charming Fucker he was and would remain.

For another couple of minutes, the two of them stood in place and listened to the sounds of the forest. What could it be telling them? The soft sounds that reached their ears were unremarkable. It was quiet, almost too quiet, but what they did hear was typical of a cold, snowy day.

A small creature scuffled in the salal and bearberry that grew on the hillside above them. Regardless of weather forecasts, the forest creatures needed to eat. Wet snow slid off a tree branch and plopped to the ground with an audible smack.

The critter squeaked again, higher pitched this time and a bit louder.

Greta cocked her head in the direction the sound came from.

"That doesn't sound like any bird call I know of," Casey said. He wasn't a bird-call expert, but he'd spent a lot of time in these woods.

In tandem, he and Greta turned to face the incline. It was a dirt-covered boulder that didn't quite qualify as a hill. There was just enough soil to allow the shallow-root shrubs to grow there, but no trees had found purchase.

"Carlos?" Greta called out.

For a moment, there was nothing but silence; the forest seemed to have inhaled a deep breath and held it. Then Casey heard a sound. Not a bird or a squirrel—a low moan. A human moan. He and Greta stared at each other.

"Carlos?" Casey said, making his voice gentle as possible. "We're here to help. Can you make another sound? We've been looking all over the forest for you, buddy."

The silence was amplified. As hard as Casey listened, the only things he could hear were the soft sound of Greta's breathing, the wind through the treetops, and the irregular drip of raindrops falling from branches overhead. If Greta hadn't heard the sound too, Casey might have convinced himself he was imagining things.

Leaning in a bit closer, Greta whispered, "Let me try."

Casey nodded. If Carlos was afraid for some reason, he might respond better to a woman's voice.

"Carlos?" she called out. "My name is Greta Harris, and I'm one of the park rangers. Casey's one too. Are you injured? We want to help you."

Whoever—if anyone—was out there, they were silent for so long that Casey was back to thinking they'd both imagined the moan of pain. Maybe it had been the wind or tree branches rubbing together, and they were wasting precious time. He peered up the steep hillside and glanced over at Greta. Her nose was pink from the chill. Casey knew that his was too.

"We're losing valuable time—" Casey began.

"Shh!" Greta clapped a mittened hand over his mouth and mouthed *be quiet*. Blinking, Casey nodded, and Greta dropped her hand.

Almost immediately, they were rewarded with a half groan and a ragged voice calling out, "Here, over here." And this time they were both looking in the right direction.

Greta pointed up and to their left. "Up there!"

Squinting into the quickly increasing shadows, Casey peered upward to where Greta had indicated. About halfway up the hill was an odd hollow space in the shrubbery. Greta flicked on her flashlight and shone the beam in that direction. A single, slender branch of salal appeared to move of its own accord.

"Yes," hissed Casey. "Let's go."

Side by side, they began to scramble up the rocky hillside, grabbing onto branches and vines and whatever they could reach to help pull themselves up. Leave no trace was thrown away in the hopes they'd found Carlos.

Halfway to where they thought he was, Casey stepped into a hole hidden by fallen leaves. If it weren't for his boots, he would have wrenched his ankle or worse.

"Shit." He let himself fall forward onto his knees instead of fighting gravity.

"You okay?"

"Yeah. I'll feel it tomorrow, but the only thing wounded is my pride." Casey surged to his feet and started climbing upward again, ignoring the vague pain in his right knee.

It took them about fifteen minutes to reach the spot. They'd had to detour around another hidden crevasse, this one much larger than the one Casey had tripped into. When they reached the general location, they took turns calling Carlos's name, but they didn't hear or see a response.

"I sure hope we're not climbing for nothing."

"We're not," huffed Greta. "He's here, I can feel it. Let's go a bit higher."

Casey knew better than to question Greta's hunches. More than once she'd proven to be right, and more than one person had survived due to her instincts.

Because of the crevasse, they had to cut across and up the slope. It was hard going due to the frigid cold and rough terrain, and Casey had to work to ignore whatever he'd done to his knee. When he got home that night, he figured he'd ice it and take it easy for a couple of days. No big deal.

If Carlos *was* up here, why? What could have made the brush worker climb part of a mountain that not even nimble deer or other larger animals crossed? At least, not this time of the year. Maybe, for once, Greta was wrong, and they'd climbed up the treacherous crag for no reason.

He started to suggest that they head back down, that Tor

and the rest of the team didn't need another couple of people trapped overnight on the mountain. But at that moment, Casey glanced a few feet ahead and realized that they were at the top end of the cut in the mountainside.

"Stay here," he told Greta. "No reason for both of us to fall in this thing."

Unsurprisingly, Greta did not listen, but hey, he'd tried.

Casey inched across to where he estimated the edge was; it was hard to tell with the tangled overgrown shrubs and woody plants that had found purchase. When he made it without a misstep, Casey flicked on his flashlight and shone it downward.

Wedged inside, about twenty feet down, was a man. A living man, but it was going to be a bitch to get him out.

"Carlos?" he asked.

The man managed a weak nod.

"Can't move ..." he whispered. "Leg."

Crouching next to the edge with his light, Casey did a quick visual assessment, swallowing as he noted how Carlos's lower body appeared to be twisted and caught in the fissure. Behind him, he could hear Greta making the call to Tor and the rest of the team. They would need a copter and more bodies to get Carlos out of the cleft in the mountainside and to safety.

Rummaging around in his pack, Casey located the emergency silver space blanket and began to lower himself into the crack in the earth. He was only able to get about ten feet down before it became too narrow. Fuck. Even if he took off his winter gear, it wouldn't make his shoulders any less wide.

"I'm going to swap places with my partner, Greta. She'll see what she can do to get you covered up."

Casey clambered back up so Greta could take his place. He couldn't imagine how Carlos had gotten so tangled up.

"Carlos." The man moved his head. Hopefully that meant he'd heard Casey. "What happened, how did you end up here?"

It was always a good sign if Casey could get the injured person talking. But Carlos looked bad. He blinked up at Casey but didn't reply, and one of his arms was also trapped underneath him. Casey'd seen injuries like this before, and right now the priority was keeping Carlos conscious.

"Are you thirsty? I think we can get you some water."

Greta had made it down to him and done what she could to tuck the blanket around his body. She glanced back up at Casey, and that one look told him things did not look good. Over Greta's shoulder, Casey saw Carlos's head move a bit, and Casey decided he was nodding.

He reached for one of the bottles of water he'd packed in and tied a short piece of twine around it. Then he slowly lowered the bottle down. Greta grabbed it and held it to Carlos's lips. Some of the liquid spilled out, but it looked to Casey that he at least got some down.

"Can you tell us what happened?" he asked gently as he tried to make himself comfortable on the rocky ledge.

"A wild man, a creature," Carlos rasped, "chased me."

Casey didn't like that it was difficult for Carlos to speak and that he wasn't shivering regardless of the below freezing temperature—that suggested hypothermia had set in. He dug into Greta's bag for the chemical heat packs. They could be tucked around Carlos to create a barrier between him and the cold earth, and they just might help his body fight off the chill.

What Carlos had said coalesced into something meaningful. "A wild man?" Casey repeated. Casey had been prepared for Carlos to tell them how he'd ended up stuck in a crevasse, not that he'd been attacked by someone.

"Came out of nowhere. Screamed." Carlos swallowed convulsively. "I ran, thought he was going to kill me."

"Someone from the crew?" Greta asked.

He moved his head from side to side. "Stranger. Didn't know."

His eyes drifted shut.

Crouched awkwardly next to him, Greta looked up again, her expression more concerned than before. They both knew there was no way that the two of them alone would be able to extract Carlos from the fissure without hurting him, and maybe worse than he already was.

"Hey, we need you to stay awake. The rest of the team is on the way," she told the injured man. "We'll have you out of there ASAP."

Casey knew speaking was taxing Carlos, but as long as he kept talking, he was alive. They needed to know more before he was medivacked out. If there was some nutjob loose in the forest, they had a problem in addition to a lost and injured worker.

"Yeah, stay with us, Carlos. Can you tell us any more about this man? What did he look like?"

The man's eyes closed again. For a tense fifteen seconds, Casey thought he'd slipped into unconsciousness, but he must have been trying to recall what had happened.

"The wild man was big. Crazy," he whispered. "Thought he was a demon at first. Charged at me, fire in his eyes. Screamed." Carlos's eyes drifted shut.

"Carlos, stick with us. Tell us more," Greta encouraged. "We'd like to find this man."

"I ran. He chased me."

"You said he was big. Taller than you? Heavier?"

"Yeah, both. Long beard, no hair, camo ... Face was green. Big gun."

The prickle that had been forming in the back of Casey's mind turned into a full-fledged rash.

"Sounds like that could have been Calvin Perkins," he said

to Greta. "I think this is the first sighting of him since Dwayne was found."

It had been Karne who'd discovered Dwayne's body but the fewer who knew that fact, the better. Gabe had just been unlucky enough to have the last known run-in with the two. Throw a rock anywhere in Twana County and you'd hit somebody who'd clashed with the brothers.

"I didn't kill no one!" Carlos wheezed, fear and anxiety overwhelming him again. He started to struggle against the crevasse's hold on him, using up energy he couldn't afford to lose.

"We don't think you did, Carlos," Greta assured him as she tucked the space blanket around him again. "Everything is going to be okay."

But was it? With the possibility of a rampaging Calvin Perkins, no one was safe on the mountain. Was he injured as well? Why was he chasing down innocent brush workers? Where the hell was he hiding out? The forest was over two million acres, he could be anywhere.

Greta caught his eye, and from her grim expression, he knew she was thinking along the same lines.

"We're going to have to talk to Rizzi," she said quietly. "And release a general memo to Fish and Wildlife so they keep their eye out. We don't want anyone else hurt."

Finally, from a distance but approaching quickly, Casey heard the sound of an approaching helicopter.

"Help's arrived, Carlos. We're gonna get you out of here."

ELEVEN

Gabriel

Tuesday afternoon into evening

AFTER THEY LEFT the Geoduck Inn, Elton dropped Gabriel off at the marina. It was late afternoon, and he had a full stomach and a lot to think about.

"I'll check in tomorrow," he told Elton.

Slush was falling, a gross mix of rain and snow. It wasn't pretty and it didn't hint at magical—it was cold. The world was wet and oversaturated, but just one look west told him that the white stuff was accumulating on the hills and higher peaks.

Aboard the *Ticket*, Gabe stomped around to get his feet warm again and then fumbled with the thermostat because his fingers were cold, but eventually he managed to fire up the old boat's heater.

He puttered around for a good hour, one ear listening for his neighbor, before starting to wonder where the hell Lundin was. Again, the Wagoneer had not been parked in its spot when he got to the marina. Gabe had questions about Casey's brother, like if Mickie might have known Peter. Or—a long shot, from what Elton had told him—if maybe Casey had. Thoughts swirled and danced in his brain like the tails of a kite. Gabe would mentally grab hold of one possibility, but then another would pop into his head and the first would fall to the wayside. There was a whole damn pile of them lying there waiting to be taken seriously.

Was there a deeper connection between Peter and Heartstone, one that hadn't been ended by Peter himself over twenty years ago? Gabe hated feeling like the odd guy out, which he totally was on the island. He was the new arrival. The social history of the island was a murky unknown to him, which put him at a disadvantage. If Gabe was going to figure out who killed Peter Vale before the cops decided Gabe had been the one to off him, he needed to act fast.

Know your audience, Chance.

How many times had his mother said that? Too many to count. Heidi had been incredibly successful because she *always* had done her homework. *Always*. Heidi Karne did not barge into a situation without knowing the net worth of everyone present, who they were romantically and monetarily involved with, and what their weakest points were.

Gabe had barged in. Admittedly, he'd been in a bit of a hurry. But still, he'd violated Heidi's rule number one. He did not know enough.

He glanced around the cabin; he desperately needed a notebook and something to write with. He was also wishing he'd bought a phone with more bells and whistles, but the one he'd gone with was basic and had no internet capabilities. Staring at the almost useless thing, he snorted.

"What was I thinking?"

He'd been thinking it was the best way to stay out of trouble.

And look where that got you. Still in trouble.

If anyone had told him that by the end of the year, Gabe would be living on a sketchy sailboat with no internet and no laptop, not even a fancy coffee maker, he would have laughed his ass off. And yet, here he was.

Pulling his parka back on and sliding his feet into his boots, Gabe stepped back out onto the pier. It was colder than when he'd returned; the slush had turned to snow and was starting to stick. It was postcard pretty, but being a Northwesterner, Gabe did not trust it. Maybe folks were used to snow around here. Maybe it wouldn't start to melt by morning and turn the roads into sheets of ice.

Carefully, he made his way down the dock and across the road to the store.

A GUY around his age was working the checkout counter. There were no signs of the younger folk who'd been working his last few visits.

"Evening," Gabe said. He got a nod in return.

"Can I help you find something?" the man asked.

"I'm in need of a notebook or pad of paper, and something to write with," Gabe replied, making his way down the aisle toward the checkout.

The guy narrowed his eyes and bit the inside of his lip, clearly thinking. Now that he was close enough, Gabe could read his name tag: *Barry*.

"Ah, you must be the new guy," Barry said, coming out from behind the counter.

"That's me, the new guy." Funny that he'd had that thought before making the short trip over from the marina. "I'm Gabriel Karne."

And no angel.

Thanks, Mom.

"Barry Dawson," Barry replied, extending his hand. "Welcome to Heartstone."

After quickly shaking hands, Barry directed Gabe toward the VHS and DVD library. "I think Mercy might have some stuff like that stocked over there. I've seen coloring books. For game nights and the like. In general, locals don't shop here for school supplies."

"Thanks."

And that was how Gabe ended up with a glitter-encrusted Hello Kitty notebook and matching pink pen.

"Pretty sure Mercy ordered those when Brooklyn was wild about that cat. Everything in our house was pink." He shook his head. "They've been on the shelf for a few years. I'll give it to you half off."

Since he was there already, Gabe grabbed a quart of ice cream from the freezer and a couple of apples for the morning. Why not live it up a bit? Lonely Street, a black cherry double-chocolate brownie ice cream – part of Jewel Creamery's new Angsty and Emo series — was a much better choice than the six-pack of IPA he'd turned his back on. Except for a couple of times the last week or so, he hadn't craved alcohol much since he stopped drinking, at least not enough to give in. Previously, he'd tried The Licorice Experience, which had been amazing, and fancy-as-fuck ice cream, he'd discovered, was better than getting drunk.

"Thanks, Barry."

"Any time. You know where we are."

GABE MADE his way back across the road, unreasonably irritated that Casey and Bowie were still not home, as evidenced by the lack of Casey's Wagoneer.

Their absence made the marina feel more desolate than it was normally. Gabe wasn't made for desolate—he could admit that without losing his man-card. He liked being around people; this whole *hiding out from the Colavito family* thing was cramping his style.

You have no idea, Chance. Why do you think we moved states and not just towns?

More than once, Heidi had complained that Gabe made friends wherever they landed—even in the middle of the desert, where no other children lived. It was a superpower.

Hanging the bag with the ice cream, notebook, and pen on one arm, he dug into his coat pocket with his other hand for the gate key. Even though he'd only been across the street for a short time, he'd made sure to lock everything up. Gabe wasn't going to be responsible for, say, someone dumping a dead body on one of the boats while he was gone.

The gate opened with a raspy squeak, and Gabe angled his body so he could squeeze through the gap. No reason to open the thing all the way when it screeched like the back gate to hell. Someone needed to oil the hinges, which probably meant Gabriel should step the fuck up.

Before he could push the door shut again, something small, fuzzy, and wet streaked past his feet and shot down the dock.

"What the fuck?"

Whatever it was, it darted past the *Shangri-La* and the fluttering crime scene tape looped around it. Pausing for a second, the critter seemed to look back over its shoulder and stare directly at Gabe. Then it scurried across the pier, leaped onto the *Ticket*, and disappeared from view.

"Seriously, *what the fuck?*" Was he going to have to call animal control or whatever passed for that out here to evict a stray cat? What was a cat doing out in this weather anyway? At least, it sort of resembled a cat. He hoped to fuck it wasn't a raccoon.

Making sure the fence was closed and locked behind him, Gabe hurried down to the *Ticket* and climbed aboard. The boat rocked under his weight, and he half expected the cat to panic and abandon ship, but the creature seemed to have found a place to hide. He glanced around but couldn't see anything in the dark, not even glowing eyes.

With a sigh, he stepped down and opened the cabin door. There were more pressing things for him to worry about than a stray cat, like melting ice cream and trying to make sense of what was going on around Heartstone. Maybe Casey knew something about the cat; he seemed like the type to have a soft spot for strays.

Except when it came to Gabriel.

Not everyone who meets you is going to like you, Chance. And you're not going to like everyone you meet. Sometimes you'll just have to fake it 'til you make it.

Ugh. He hated when Heidi was right.

SETTLING on one of the benches at his retractable dining table with the heat turned up again, Gabe snagged a spoon and pried the lid off the ice cream. He'd already decided he might as well eat it out of the container. To save on dishes, of course. Setting his dessert to one side to soften up, he flipped open the garish notebook and began making a list.

The *Ticket* rocked a bit as the wind blew and waves rolled in, the movement almost comforting. Gabe was starting to get used to the sounds the boat made, so very different from what he was used to. The creaking of the mast. The way the boat rubbed against the rubber thingies that protected the dock. Or maybe they protected the boat? It was probably something he should know, but his learning curve had been steep over the last few weeks.

He hadn't gotten much past writing *Peter Vale/Stevens, why?* on the first page of the notebook when a vibration or something alerted him that someone was on the pier. Half crouching, half standing, he lifted himself to look out the window behind him, the one that opened out onto the dock.

Backlit by the single security light fixed to the shed, Gabe recognized the form of Ranger Man moving slowly. His shoulders were slumped as if he were exhausted—or worse, defeated by his day. Bowie, on the other hand, practically skipped down the planking, his nose pressed against the boards to follow a scent. Or the trail of a cat. The dog came to an abrupt stop at the *Ticket*, pointing his snout at the deck.

"Not tonight, Bowie."

Even Ranger Man's voice sounded different to Gabe's ears. Tired. Gabe glanced at the tub of ice cream he hadn't dug into yet and tapped on the glass. Ice cream wasn't the top of the food pyramid, but in his experience, it went a long way toward fixing a tiresome day. And, truthfully, Jewel Creamery's stuff was real-life magic.

He tugged the window ajar and called out, "Lundin, you're out late tonight."

Casey stopped walking. Gabe could see muddy boots and the bottom of his Carhartt work pants. Bowie trotted over and stuck his whole face into the open window, his entire body wiggling back and forth. At least the dog was happy to see him.

"It was a long day, Karne. And I just had a run-in with the sheriff. Do you need something?"

A run-in with the sheriff? What had happened? Was that why he was so much later than usual?

"I have some dark cherry chocolate ice cream from across the way. You look like you might need it more than I do." It was only after the words were out of his mouth that Gabe realized how ridiculous he sounded.

For fuck's sake, Chance.

"Never mind," Gabe said hastily when Casey didn't immediately reply. "But just so you know, we learned something interesting about Peter. Stop by tomorrow if you can."

Gabe could interrogate him about the sheriff then too.

"Did it come with a wooden spoon?"

Gabe frowned. "Excuse me, what are you talking about?"

"Did the ice cream come with one of those flat wooden things that are supposed to pass for a spoon?"

"Uh, no? But I could probably whittle you one if that's what you need."

"Whittle me one, that's funny. Let me change out of these clothes. I'll be right back."

Gabe was so stunned by Casey's response that he didn't ask if he needed any help choosing an outfit. A wasted opportunity, there. Although this was progress, so he'd take it. Who knew it would take murder for Ranger Man to lighten up?

Gabe shoved the ice cream into his tiny freezer so it wouldn't soften any further, although he probably could have stuck it outside, it was cold enough.

"SO, WHAT HAVE YOU GOT?" Casey said thirty minutes later.

Gabriel didn't answer right away, he just stared. Changing clothes had turned out to mean taking a shower. Casey's auburn hair was artfully mussed, and he'd slipped into a pair of Levi's worn thin enough that there were probably laws about wearing them in public spaces. The black-and-white striped sweater he now wore molded to his shoulders and chest and was made with alpaca yarn or some other soft textile.

He had to physically stop himself from reaching out and petting Casey's chest. It was the sweater. Anyone would want to touch that.

"Charming!"

Gabe blinked. "Uh, right. What have I got. Er, have a seat. Where's Bowie?"

"He's sniffing around topside, he'll be down in a minute."

"That's right. A cat or something—god, I hope it was a cat— ran in through the gate earlier." He was having trouble focusing his thoughts on something that wasn't how *good* Lundin looked.

Come on, Chance, you're on the wrong side of forty, you shouldn't have this problem. Breathe.

There was just room enough for Casey to squeeze in at the end of the table, but barely. Whatever shower gel he used, Gabe was going to have to buy his own bottle just so he could sniff it.

Good god, Chance, you always were sniffing people.

So he liked good smells, not a crime.

There was another thump from above.

"Bowie, that's enough. Get down here."

A few seconds passed and then they heard Bowie clacking down the breezeway. Gabe moved to slide the door open. And stared. The running dog was preceded by a soggy cat who was running even faster. The cat paused, its gaze flicking around the room before it darted past Gabe and into the stateroom.

For the shortest of seconds, Gabe was too stunned to react.

"Dammit," he sputtered, coming to life and chasing after it.

"Let me," rumbled Casey, squeezing—again, how did the huge man live on a boat?—past Gabe and into the spartan bedroom. "Bowie, sit-stay."

Reluctantly, the dog did as he was commanded and Gabe kind of wondered if he should too.

"Hand me a towel, will you. I've had my eye on this beast for a few months, but she's been wily. I think she was abandoned by someone who moved off the island. If I figure out who it is, they're getting a shit-o-gram."

Wordlessly, Gabe leaned into the head, grabbed the towel hanging on the doorknob, and handed it to Casey. He watched while Casey knelt down on the wood floor and morphed into the cat whisperer. Within a minute, the cat was wrapped up in Gabe's towel and cradled in Casey's arms.

"I understand, cat, I understand," Gabe murmured.

Was the beast purring now?

Casey rose to his feet, keeping his head bowed so he didn't knock it against the ceiling.

"We'll get you warmed up, sweetheart."

Casey looked up from the cat and caught Gabriel watching him. The glimmer of a smile crossed his lips, and he shrugged.

"I like animals. They like me."

"I can see that. Are we going to deal with this now? Is there a veterinarian close by?"

"Not one that's open late, but we can take her in the morning. I have a friend who'll take a look at her."

"Ah, so." Gabe waved at the dining table. "Do you still want to know what I found out today?"

The cat, filthy as it was, looked like a tabby of some kind. Possibly it was orange. Its greenish eyes peeked over the towel, shooting Gabe a dangerous and skeptical look.

"Yes, I want to know what you learned." Casey perched with the cat on the edge of the bench seat. "And I still want some of that ice cream."

TWELVE

Casey

Tuesday night

MAYBE IT WAS a mix of the long day, the iffy rescue, and the confrontation with Rizzi when he and Greta had stopped in to report what Carlos had told them before losing consciousness, but Casey was in an odd humor.

Twitchy. Too aware.

He toyed with the idea that it was the presence of Charming Fucker on what Casey considered his dock—even if they were currently aboard the *Ticket*. It was a shock to realize he was glad that Gabriel had stopped him and offered ice cream.

They didn't know yet if Carlos would survive his injuries. Only time and good medical care would tell. When they'd gotten him loaded up, he'd been slipping in and out of unconsciousness, always a bad sign, and he hadn't spoken again.

The cat squirmed his arms. "You want to get down now? Alright." He glanced at Gabe, who shrugged. Casey knew that

Bowie wouldn't do anything; his best dog was nothing if not well-behaved. Giving the cat one last squeeze and a final wipe with the now filthy towel, Casey set it down on the floor. It immediately began to explore the cabin while keeping to the perimeter of the room.

"Don't clam up on me now, Karne. I'm not used to you being quiet."

Gabe had retrieved the ice cream and was busy splitting it between a cereal bowl and a coffee mug.

"I do have more than one spoon, don't worry," he said, setting the bowl in front of Casey and taking the mug for himself before passing him a spoon from the dish drainer.

"Anyway, the wild news is that Vale wasn't Peter's name. He was a Stevens, and he grew up here on Heartstone. His father was the county prosecutor you talked about the other day."

Casey blinked comically, a spoonful of ice cream halfway to his mouth.

"What?" he said, jamming the sweet dessert into his mouth and letting the chill of it against his teeth ground him.

"Peter's last name was, in fact, Stevens," Karne repeated. "At least, that's the name he was born with."

Casey swallowed and then popped another spoonful of frozen deliciousness into his mouth, giving himself time to process what Gabriel was telling him. After swallowing that bite, he scooped more into his mouth, managing not to make a single inappropriate sound. He was pretty sure that having Jewel Creamery ice cream in stock single-handedly kept Norskland General Store in business over the slow months.

"You're not kidding around, are you?" he finally managed to say.

Karne shook his head. "Nope. Not kidding, not even joking."

A megawatt smile had Casey blinking. Could a frozen dairy product be an aphrodisiac?

"Good ice cream, huh?" Karne said with an added eyebrow waggle.

Casey forced his thoughts back on track. The right track. Not only was Charming Fucker's ex originally from Heartstone, but the ex was also related to the man who'd ultimately been responsible for his brother going to prison. Was, in fact, the asshole's son. Sure, Rizzi had supplied the so-called *evidence*, but the Honorable John Stevens was the one who'd manipulated it to lock up Mickie.

"The fuck."

"Yeah, mind-blowing, huh? Do you think you knew him? Peter, I mean. If he was from here originally, then maybe he didn't show up here the other day because of me."

"You're the only person he asked about."

"How the fuck did he know I was here, then? For the life of me, I cannot figure out how he could have traced me to Heartstone."

"Does it matter?" Watching him closely, Casey scooped the last bite out of his bowl. "Your dessert is melting."

Karne shot him a glance before answering. He stirred the softened ice cream and spooned some into his mouth. A little bit ended up on his top lip, and he stuck his lip out and licked it off. Slowly.

Not sexy, Casey reminded himself. His reaction was ludicrous. After years of no serious sexual interest in another human, he did not need his libido coming online for a sketchy con man. Lucky for him, the cat chose that moment to startle and jump back into his lap, clawing his thigh in the process.

"Colavitos." The word came out so fast Casey almost missed it.

"Say again? Slowly this time."

"The Colavitos," Karne repeated through gritted teeth.

"Yeah, you've mentioned them before."

Gabe's eyes rolled up to the ceiling for a second.

"Is there more I need to know? *We* need to know?"

Casey was the recipient of a dirty look before he got his answer.

"I mean, *they* are who Peter and I pissed off, remember? *They* are why I'm here—them and my mother's letter." He tapped his chin and looked thoughtful. "Actually, that letter had more to do with my arrival here specifically than the Colavitos. If not for her, I would've headed south to Venice Beach or the border."

"So, the Colavitos followed you here. Or, possibly, they followed Peter?"

"I don't know what to think. Maybe they did follow Peter. But, and I ask you this in all seriousness, what the fuck? Nothing makes sense! If they followed him, offed him, and dumped him on the *Shangri-La*, why didn't they kill me too? I mean, I was literally thirty feet away!"

"You weren't here when Vale was dumped," Casey felt the need to point out.

"No, I wasn't. But they *still* left the *Ticket* alone. If the Colavitos are behind this, it seems they—at the very least— would have ransacked my boat. They're pissed. Only offing Peter alone wouldn't be enough. They said they want to destroy both of us if they catch us on their turf, and they don't care how they do it. This is why I'm starting to think maybe it wasn't them. If Larry Colavito and, or, his henchmen were on the island, I think everyone would know it. Larry does not believe in the word subtle."

"Noted. What else did you find out?"

Gabe was peering inside his mug. He frowned, apparently disappointed that his ice cream had disappeared. Karne lifted his head and caught Casey watching him—and grinned. A full-on, no-holds-barred grin that was almost blinding. No doubt about it, that grin was going to be a problem. Charming Fucker as a whole? Also a problem.

"What else?" Gabe blinked at him. "Oh, you mean from my super fun session with the cops today. They don't have a suspect other than me to focus on, and they don't plan on looking that hard. At least, that utter toad, Deputy Spurring, isn't looking anywhere else. I didn't get to experience the joy of Rizzi this morning. Which means it's up to me to get myself out of this mess—again."

Casey pressed his lips together for a second. Footage of Gabriel Karne wreaking havoc across Heartstone and elsewhere as he turned every stone looking for a killer streamed across his mental screen. What he imagined was not so much the turning of stones but tossing, throwing, and lobbing, and not caring where the rocks landed as long as he wasn't the one in the hot seat. He also wasn't shocked that the Sheriff's Office had wanted to interview Charming again.

"Did anyone aside from Spurring question you this time?"

Casey and Greta had stopped by the station after coming down the mountain. It was their duty to let the officers know what Carlos had said about a possible sighting of Calvin Perkins. Rizzi had been less than thrilled to see them and had half-heartedly jotted down notes while a wet-behind-the-ears trainee deputy had watched him. But maybe his attitude had more to do with Gabriel Karne than Casey's appearance at the station.

"Nope. He smells like dirty gym socks. Or it was the room, could've been both."

What was Rizzi up to? Casey had expected him to at least display some kind of interest over the fact there'd been a possible sighting of his nephew.

Instead, the man had stared impassively at Casey and Greta from behind his gunmetal gray desk and dismissed them with a curt "Thank you" and then picked up his phone, but he'd waited until they'd turned to leave to punch in a number. Glancing back over his shoulder, Casey'd seen an almost calculating expression cross the sheriff's face, but it went blank when he realized Casey was watching him.

"Was that weird?" Greta had asked him on their way back to the truck. "I think that was weird, even for Rizzi."

Casey agreed with her. As far as he was concerned, Rizzi was a misfortune the citizens of the county were forced to suffer through until the man decided to retire. Unfortunately, Casey's opinion was not the popular one, considering Rizzi ran unopposed every four years. The man was dirty, and Casey just hadn't figured out how to prove it yet, not even with the shooting of Deter Nolan.

The Sheriff's Office released a public statement almost immediately after the "self-defense" shooting of the deputy. It hadn't gone into detail, only stating that Nolan had drawn first with intent to harm and Rizzi had reacted. The sheriff was cleared of any wrongdoing—easy to do when you were the one in charge.

Karne and a freaked-out Gordon MacDonald were the only witnesses to the shooting, and Nolan had been abducting MacDonald, so maybe Rizzi had been justified. But damn it had been fast. And Casey couldn't help but think he'd arrived at the hospital prepared for violence.

"Deputy Eagan seems okay—for a cop," Gabe said thoughtfully, bringing Casey back to the present. "But once Deputy Spurring showed up, he pretty much shut her out. I was lucky enough to get him to myself today. Not."

That wasn't a shock. Spurring probably wanted to be the

one to solve Vale's murder. It would be a feather in his cap, and maybe he'd get a pat on the head from Rizzi.

"Back to this. Peter Vale is—was—John Stevens's son? Huh. I'm still having some issues wrapping my head around that, to be honest." Casey thought back to the day Vale had stopped by and asked about Karne. There'd been no spark of recognition for Casey; as far as he knew, they'd never crossed paths in the past.

"Elton told me a little more about John Stevens prosecuting your brother."

Oh, Elton. Casey sort of wanted to strangle his old friend. Mickie being still behind bars was an open wound. Greta would say it had festered.

"Half brother, but yeah, he did. Based on evidence provided by the Sheriff's Office, of course. Which I didn't believe then and I don't believe now."

"What happened? If you don't mind me asking."

He did mind him asking, but Charming Fucker could just as easily find out what happened from the internet. Or from a longer conversation with Elton.

"It was August and there was a heat wave going on. Mickie and his girlfriend, Maya Crane, were drinking at the Pizza Joint, they argued, and Maya left. Mickie stayed behind, drinking more before he decided to walk home to his new place. No one ever saw Maya alive again. Her body was discovered at the point by some kayakers. She'd been strangled and raped."

Maya's murder had punctuated the end of the terrible summer before Casey started high school. In many ways, Maya's murder marked the end of Casey's childhood.

"Witnesses saw them arguing at the Pizza Joint, and Mickie didn't make it home that night after all. He passed out on a friend's patio, so no alibi. Only came to our place because he didn't have food at his apartment yet. The crazy thing is, I thought I saw Maya. Maybe I was the last one, but, well—"

Even with all the time that had passed, it was hard for him to talk about Maya's murder and the fallout from it. His family, already crumbling that summer, had been obliterated, their lives forever changed with Mickie's arrest and the subsequent trial. There was life before Mickie's arrest—not perfect, but good enough. Then whatever the fuck afterward.

He wasn't sure he'd ever forgive their parents for imagining Mickie could have done something as evil as raping and murdering his girlfriend. Worse, because he'd been barely fourteen, no one believed Casey had seen Maya later in the evening, still alive. And Mickie never would say what his and Maya's argument had been about. Just that it was personal.

"Mickie wasn't lying. I snuck out of the house and saw Maya on my way to the summer's end bonfire." He'd been too excited to stop and say hi, exhilarated by the thought of hanging out with the cool kids and, maybe, sneaking a beer. "Most of the island kids used to show up at the Senior Sneak at least once before becoming true seniors. I even saw Gordon MacDonald there that night, and he's a good four years younger than me."

The clink-clink of Gabe scraping his spoon against the side of the ceramic mug in a fruitless search for more ice cream distracted him. Casey watched him for a second, then shook his head and blinked, realizing he'd lost his train of thought.

"My mom and dad—well, that was a shitstorm and still is." Casey pursed his lips, fighting off the distraction that arose from having Gabriel's undivided attention, "Having Mickie accused and convicted of murder tore them apart. Within a couple years of the trial, as soon as I was eighteen, they sold their property and moved as far away as they could afford. And then they split up. I can't relate to either of them, their utter lack of loyalty. They abandoned both of us and then each other."

"I'm sorry that happened to you," Gabe said, bringing him back to the present—again.

"Yeah, me too." Mostly, Casey was sorry that Mickie only had him fighting for him. Mickie deserved more. Casey could only do so much with how the cards were currently stacked.

The cat chose that moment to come out of hiding—Casey'd forgotten it was there—and rub up against Gabe's legs. Moving away again, the beast stared up at Casey and meowed.

"I have some cat food on my boat." Because he was a sucker and had planned on luring the cat inside with it before the weather got too horrible.

"Oh, good, you can take the cat with you when you leave."

Casey laughed. "Yeah, no. It picked you. Damn thing has terrible taste, but here we are. I'll take Bowie and go grab the food for you. My friend who's a vet lives near Greta and Abby, he might be willing to do an exam for you."

The expression on Gabe's face was comical, and Casey couldn't help but laugh again. "I'll be right back."

While Gabe was sputtering about "cats" and "what did he know?" Casey climbed off the *Ticket* and jogged over to *The Barbara* for the spare food. Privately, he thought it was hilarious that the cat had chosen Gabe and was looking forward to seeing how it all played out. Regardless of his tough talk, Gabriel Karne was a soft touch.

THIRTEEN

Gabriel

Tuesday, Night of the Ever-Loving Cat

"HOW THE FUCK did I end up with you?" Gabe asked the scrawny cat after Casey had returned with a can of wet food and a plastic container of dry and then departed again. He'd wanted to protest that he was not a pet person. But maybe he'd never been a pet person because he'd never been allowed one. Moving in the dead of night did not lend itself to pets of any kind. Not even goldfish or lizards.

But something told him that this was sort of a test, that he needed to pass if—

If what, Chance?

Fuck off. If lots of things.

If he wanted to gain anything close to respect from Casey Lundiṇ. Which he did. Which irritated him but also meant that the filthy and probably flea-ridden cat horking down dry kibble was staying with him for the immediate future.

"You need a bath."

The cat looked up at the sound of his voice and gave him a look that telegraphed *You and what army?*

"It's gonna happen. Not tonight, but it's gonna happen."

While the cat ate—looking a bit like a dragon hunched around its hoard, guarding it against hairy-footed creatures—Gabe dug around for something soft for it to sleep on. It wasn't as if he had spare blankets sitting around, but he dug up one last bath towel and decided that the sacrifice was worth it. The thing could be washed or burned later. Folding it into a thick square, he set it by the food dish and then pondered a cat box before deciding it had lived outside for a while and knew what to do. Hopefully.

"Good night, cat."

It was going to need a name if it decided to stick around. Because there was that too. The cat had an air of arrogant independence that told Gabe anything it did—eat, sleep, pee in the right place—was its choice and had nothing to do with Gabe's approval.

"Fine, I get the message. We'll see how this goes." Talking to a cat was probably some kind of slippery slope to madness, but at this point, who was going to know? He was a bachelor living aboard a rickety sailboat with no "visible means of support" and only Elton Cox at his back. Who cared if he talked to a cat.

The ice cream he and Casey had shared maybe didn't count as dinner, but after the past day and a half, Gabe was exhausted and too tired to make anything. Not even on the stove he hadn't had a chance to use yet.

Leaving the cat to its own devices, he ducked his head, stepped into the cabin, and changed into a pair of thick cotton sweatpants and a long-sleeved shirt. He left his regular clothes on one of the closet shelves with a note-to-self that he needed to do a couple loads of laundry.

Glancing out the window again, he saw that it was no longer snowing. Good. Maybe the temperatures would warm up a bit because even with a working heater, the temperature on the *Ticket* tended to vacillate.

"Goodnight, cat."

Crawling into the bunk, he lay back and listened to the sounds he was starting to get used to—ripples lapping against the hull, the crack of the lines against the mast, the creak of the lumber that had been forced into boat shape. His brain, too busy for immediate sleep, kept going over what had happened that day and what he'd learned about his ex.

Had Peter grown up playing in the island's parks? Had he run barefoot across the rocks, barnacles, and oyster shells that seemed to be what Heartstone had to offer when it came to beaches? Gabe imagined a younger Peter at the grocery store, waiting in line for soft-serve ice cream or hanging out at the Pizza Joint with high school friends. Did he have siblings?

Gabe had no idea.

The awful truth was that he'd never known Peter at all. They'd been two stupid ships in the night that anchored close together for a while but never bothered to share anything real about themselves. On Gabe's part, not sharing was a lifetime habit. Growing up under Heidi's influence meant he knew better than to share much personal information even when he wanted to. That was how you got burned. That was how people found you after you'd dumped a con. He snorted and rolled onto his side.

Likely, when he and Peter had bumped into each other at the networking event, Peter had recognized Gabe as a like-minded soul. He'd correctly figured Gabe would be safe because he wouldn't ask any uncomfortable questions. Say, questions about his childhood, etcetera. And Gabe hadn't. He hadn't bothered to ask any fucking thing, not even a question where Peter's answer would've been a lie.

"Fuck, I'm an asshole."

Out in the main cabin, there was a heavy thump, and after listening for a second, he realized it had been the cat. It must've jumped up on something, maybe the bench seat or windowsill. Was it sitting on the sill, peering out into the night, being a watch-cat? With thoughts of feral cats and the events of the past couple of days swirling in his head, Gabe finally fell asleep and into uneasy dreams.

At first, he was back in the Central District of Seattle, running from the growling watchdog and its handler. But then, as dreams inexplicably do, Peter was calling to him from the other side of a short fence, not the chain-link he'd been racing for. There was an open gate at the far end and Peter was mouthing *This way*. Gabe veered Peter's direction and then the dog was gone. Now they were running down the Riddle Bay dock as if the gate had led right to Heartstone and the marina. Peter was moving fast, and it was Gabe's turn to call out for him, to tell him he needed to stop, that the dock was slick with snow and ice and he would slip into the cold water. But also, as is the way with some dreams, he formed the words but couldn't make a sound. Peter couldn't hear him and was going to go into the icy water.

"Stooopp," Dream Gabe hissed. Fear forced the words out just as something heavy landed in the center of his chest. His eyes popped open, and he met the panicked emerald gaze of the cat. It mewed and clawed at his chin as if ordering him to wake up.

"Wha—?" But the rest of his question went unasked as Gabe's nose twitched and the acrid scent of smoke filled his nostrils.

Fire.

Fuck. The dock was no place for a fire, too much flammable shit. It was almost winter, so it couldn't be chalked up to some tourist having an illegal bonfire on the closest beach. This time of year, it was only Casey and now, Gabe out here.

"Shit."

The cat made to dart off, but Gabe managed to grab it. Quickly, he wrapped the squirming animal in his blanket so it couldn't claw him to shreds. He'd ask forgiveness later. Tucking the animal against his chest, he ran into the cabin and peeked out the dockside window.

"Shit, shit, shit."

Across the way, the *Shangri-La* was already fully engulfed in flames. And if that wasn't terrifying enough, footprints in the crusty snow led over to *The Golden Ticket*. A creaking sound alerted him to a shadowy figure dockside lurking near the stern. Thankful he'd left his work boots where they were easy to find and hard to trip over, Gabe jammed his feet into them and popped open the window.

"Hey!" he yelled. "What the fuck! Get the hell out of here!"

The figure—or was it two people?— paused, then lurched, and something heavy landed on the deck with a thud. The cat was doing its best to claw its way out of the towel, but Gabe held on tight, risking disembowelment. Flames shot skyward caused by whatever the asshole had tossed aboard the *Ticket*.

"Motherfucker!"

There was no time. Gabe rushed up the causeway and out into the cold night. Somehow still managing to hold on to the cat, he jumped to the pier and, instead of running after the men, headed the other way, toward *The Barbara*. He risked one look over his shoulder. Even with the flames lighting up the night sky, he couldn't quite tell if it was one or two people racing down the dock. Then, instead of going through the gate, the shadow veered to the left and jumped into a waiting boat. The sputter of the outboard motor had Gabe running faster.

"Casey! Fire!"

Just as Gabe neared the end of the dock, the pier rocked under his feet from the percussion of an explosion. He staggered but caught himself before he fell to his knees. The cat yowled. Gabe blinked and coughed as burning fragments fell into the water around him. A light came on inside *The Barbara* and then Casey was there in front of him, dragging Gabe and, by association, the cat onboard.

"Stay here," Casey ordered.

He disappeared outside again. Gabe heard his footsteps thumping around on the deck overhead.

"What the actual fuck? What the fuck just happened?" he whispered.

Within a minute, Casey was back, and Gabe figured he must have been untying the lines that held *The Barbara* to the pier; they were floating away from the flames and to relative safety.

"You saved the cat."

"Of course I saved the cat! I'm not a monster!"

The cat wiggled and this time Gabriel set it down, blanket and all. It was hard not to laugh at the bedraggled beast. Gabe was shocked when, instead of finding someplace to hide or scratching the hell out of him, the cat jumped up next to him and started to purr.

Then, for the second time in less than forty-eight hours, he heard sirens screaming as emergency vehicles raced toward the marina. The cat hissed and ran into Casey's bedroom. Clearly had good instincts.

"Ugh, the cops again."

"At least the fire department is less shitty than Rizzi or

Spurring," Casey said as he stood at the window watching the red and white lights get closer. "You still deciding this isn't the Colavitos?"

Gabe wasn't sure of anything, so he shrugged. "Believe me, it's hard to consider letting them off the hook. But this seems a bit dramatic for them. They aren't the arson type. And if it was them, why would they go for the *Shangri-La* first?"

"What happened? Did you see or hear anything?" Casey asked, his attention still on the emergency vehicles.

"Can't say for sure. I was asleep. The cat woke me up and less than sixty seconds later, I was running your direction."

Casey's cell phone rang. "That'll be Elton," he said before he picked it up off the sill and pressed Accept.

"Yeah. We're both fine. Pretty sure we'll be awhile, no doubt there will be questions. *The Barbara* is fine, but the *Shangri-La* is totaled for sure. We don't know yet about the *Ticket*, but I suspect it's also a goner. We're out in the bay, Gabe's with me and Bowie. As soon as we end this call, we'll row in. Yeah, I love you too, old man."

AN HOUR OR SO LATER, it was clear that the *Shangri-La* and *The Golden Ticket* were both lost causes. The *Shangri-La* was reduced to merely a few boards floating in the dark water. The *Ticket* had taken less of a hit, but even if he could get it back to a livable state, Gabe knew he'd never feel safe aboard it again. Maybe it hadn't burned to the waterline like the *Shangri-La,* but it wasn't from lack of effort on the *Ticket's* part. It was obviously a sign from somewhere that *The Golden Ticket* wasn't the place he was meant to be.

And why throw good money after bad?

Once the fires had been put out, Casey moored *The Barbara*

at a buoy meant for visiting boats and rowed them to shore, away from the emergency vehicles. Bowie came with them, but the cat had declined, glaring its disapproval from underneath one of the bunk beds in the second cabin. "It'll be fine," Casey said, locking the cabin door behind him.

Elton was waiting for them in his truck, because of course he was. No one was going to tell Elton he couldn't park off to the side of the emergency vehicles. And he wasn't accepting Casey's word that they were all okay.

"Can Bowie hang with you while Gabe and I answer questions?" Casey asked.

"That's a stupid question." Elton patted the seat next to him and Bowie leaped into the cab, settling next to Elton, one paw across his skinny thigh. "We'll be right here."

"We still need to look into a dog for you."

At that, Elton just rolled his eyes. "We can share Bowie."

THE FIRE CHIEF was a solid-looking man in his late thirties, five o'clock shadow or whatever it's called after midnight, and bright blue eyes. His name badge declared him to be Simeon Greery. Compared to Deputy Spurring standing next to him, who looked like he'd sucked a lemon and then eaten it rind and all, Greery was a saint. Even better, his presence seemed to discourage Spurring from his normal role of asshole cop, although only by a little.

"I'm getting a bit tired of seeing you, Karne."

"That makes two of us, Deputy."

Greery shot them both warning looks, and Gabe bit his lips together to stop himself from pointing out that Spurring had started it. Was he twelve at heart?

Was that ever in question?

. . .

THE TWO OF them interviewed Gabe first.

Gabe felt oddly guilty that he didn't have anything worthwhile to tell them about the shadowy figure or figures he'd seen throwing *something* and then running away. He'd been dreaming too deeply and hadn't heard the motorboat arrive or anyone walking on the pier.

Greery was nodding and taking notes while Spurring scowled at him and, Gabe realized, noshed on a fat wad of tobacco.

"That stuff causes cancer, you know," Gabe said, earning himself an extra toxic glare from the deputy. "Just saying."

Under the red, white, and blue flashing lights, Spurring's face looked odd, like something out of a cartoon, puffy and strangely shadowed. On the other hand, he sort of always looked that way, so maybe it wasn't the lights.

In response, Spurring leaned over and spit onto the ground, leaving a gross brown mark on the already melting snow. Gabe wrinkled his nose. He wasn't sure if he could like a person less without actively hating them. But he was tired, and the deputy wasn't worth the effort hate took.

"You can go. Do you have somewhere to stay tonight?"

Gabe glanced at Elton's truck, lurking on the edge of the scene. At that moment, Bowie popped up to look out of the windshield and Gabe figured Elton had said something to the dog.

"Yeah, I have a place."

After they were done with Casey, Greery called Gabe back over and spoke to them together.

"Lucky for you that your cat was around," he told Gabe, a serious expression on his face. "The explosive the perp threw onto your boat was most likely some kind of modified Molotov cocktail. It appears to have hit the far edge of the deck and engaged, but it rolled off into the water before it could really get a fire going. Likely, you surprised whoever it was."

"He surprised me, too, I have to admit."

"If we have any more questions?" Greery looked at Gabe. Because, yeah, Casey was not hard to track down.

"You can reach me through Casey or Elton."

A month ago, he'd never heard of either of them, and now his life depended on their kindness. What the hell was up with that?

I wouldn't get used to it, but you do you, Chance.

Gabe hadn't accumulated many belongings in the two and a half weeks he'd been on Heartstone, but what hadn't been burned to a crispy was drenched and would not be worth the effort of saving. Currently, he wore a parka Casey had loaned him, a pair of sweats that had seen better days, and the long-sleeved t-shirt he'd donned only a few hours ago. No undies or socks. And he smelled like smoke, ash, and fear. The coat was doing its job keeping him warm, but he also now knew just how broad Casey's shoulders really were.

Fucking broad. Support-the-world broad.

Finally, around O-dark thirty, which was around four in the morning in winter months Pacific time, they were allowed to go home.

The last of the emergency vehicles pulled away, heading back the way they'd come. Gabe narrowed his gaze at his mom's car.

"Goddamn fucking car keys are vaporized. And my fancy new notebook, dammit all to hell." For a moment, Gabe felt a stab of true despair. A weird grief he hadn't allowed himself, not even when Heidi died.

A surprisingly warm hand landed on his shoulder, startling him as well as anchoring him. How was it possible that he felt the heat of it through the fabric of the parka?

"It'll be fine, Charming."

Gabe wanted to believe Ranger Man, and it was a bit easier to when he called him Charming.

"Let's go. Elton is waiting up for us."

FOURTEEN

Casey

Tuesday, maybe Wednesday, too close for comfort

"THAT WAS CLOSE," Elton said quietly. "Too close. What the hell is going on around here?"

They were in his living room while Gabe took a shower. He'd said he needed to get the smell of smoke off his skin, but Casey figured he also needed some time to himself to process what had almost happened. If not for the cat, he'd probably have died. Casey didn't appreciate the way his stomach twisted at that thought.

"It was."

"What are you thinking?"

"I'm thinking Charming is damn lucky that cat chose tonight to come in from the cold."

Shifting back in his recliner, Elton raised a single bushy snow-white eyebrow. "He does have a dash of charm, doesn't he?"

Casey ignored Elton's comment as he leaned against the back of the couch, his leg stretched out to accommodate his banged-up knee, his head angled to stare at the ceiling, and let the events of the night replay. He'd gone to sleep early, physically and mentally exhausted from the rescue. Under normal circumstances, he'd like to think he would have heard a boat in the water and trespassers on the dock.

Maybe he'd gotten too used to the sound of watercraft and whatnot at all hours. But maybe the perps had floated in on the current from wherever they'd come? That would be much quieter than using a motor and would explain why Bowie hadn't alerted him.

"As much as I hate to admit it, I don't think we can blame this on the big city creeps that Gabe is hiding from," Casey finally said. Gabe had hinted that he thought the Molotov cocktail assault was further than the Colavitos would go. God, he still had a knee-jerk reaction to agreeing with Charming Fucker; it went against every cell in his body. "Too many things point to local knowledge and not just from chatting up Barry at the store, who we know cannot keep a secret to save his life. Whoever is behind this must be familiar with the marina and the dock itself. And they went for the *Shangri-La* first, where Vale was either killed or dumped. Why? Not that I'm a criminal mastermind, but it seems to me that if Gabe was the intended target, they would've hit the *Ticket* first, make sure they succeeded."

"Maybe they didn't know which boat was which? But what you're saying makes sense. Was Gabe an afterthought? Is it possible they were trying to get rid of evidence?"

"What evidence? The *Shangri-La* was already sinking. The marina board was planning a vote at the spring meeting to declare it derelict and have it towed away if the owner didn't come forward."

Who owned the *Shangri-La* was one of the things Casey felt

he should have known, but he was not on the board and had never thought to ask when one of them was around.

"Maybe they *think* Gabe witnessed something? He says he didn't see anything out of the ordinary before he left for town, but maybe he did and doesn't know it?"

"Maybe," Casey agreed. "But if he doesn't know what he saw, why would someone try and kill him for it?"

"Because they don't know that he doesn't know what he saw."

"Christ, I can't even follow that."

They were silent for a moment. The shower was still running, but the small house was otherwise quiet. Bowie had made himself comfortable tucked in between the couch and the recliner, where he could keep an eye on everyone.

"Who does own the *Shangri-La*?" Elton asked.

"Pardon me? The man who knows everything and everyone on the island doesn't know who's responsible for the *Shangri-La*?"

Elton scowled at him, his eyebrows drawn together tightly. "No, I don't. I've done some research, but I'm not good with the internet, you know that. And the computer at the library is usually reserved before I can get there. And I didn't have a reason to want to know."

Down the hall, the sound of the shower stopped, then they heard a few thumps and a muttered *fuck me*.

Casey snorted but quickly wiped the grin off his face. "It didn't seem important to me. They obviously pay the moorage, or the board would've done something about it before now." He blew out a sigh. "I'll reach out to my connection in Olympia and have her do a search. The one time I poked around, I only got as far as an LLC and a post office box. But there must be a legal name somewhere."

· · ·

A FEW MINUTES LATER, Charming emerged from the shower, a towel slung over his bare shoulders, his dark hair damp. Somewhere he'd found long underwear bottoms that left zero to the imagination unless Casey had been curious about any tattoos. Which he was not. He didn't want to be noticing anything about Gabriel Karne.

And yet, here he was, noticing. And Charming Fucker did not appear to have any tattoos.

Gabe realized they were both watching him and grinned. Casey quickly schooled his expression to appear unaffected, while Elton seemed amused. How the man could summon a smile after a night like they'd had, Casey couldn't imagine. Did he take nothing seriously? The thought immediately pissed Casey off because his dad had constantly told him he was too serious. *"Laugh a little, son, it's no big deal."* But neither his dad nor mom had laughed much in recent years. Not that Casey spoke to them often. Or ever.

"I'm not sleeping in jeans, and for some reason I threw these in my bag when I was leaving Seattle." Gabe lifted one leg, twisting it to show off the moose-festooned pj's. Setting his foot down again, he said, "No idea why I did, but they're coming in useful tonight. This morning. Whatever."

Sleep. Casey needed that too. Gabe's rambling speech had him pushing to his feet.

"I'm taking off, I'll call about the *Shangri-La* first thing in the morning."

Casey left, returning to the marina and rowing Bowie and himself out to *The Barbara*, exhausted and beyond ready to hit the sack once more. He didn't bother to do more than strip off his jeans before falling onto his bed.

The resulting yowl was nearly the end of him.

"Goddamn, I forgot about you," he growled after levitating back to standing now staring at the indignant, still-needing-a-bath animal glaring at him from the mattress. "But I do not have the spoons. Scoot the fuck over, fleabag."

HIS PHONE RANG AFTER LESS than two hours in bed, jerking Casey from sleep.

"For fuck's sake, what does a guy have to do?" Glancing at the screen, he saw the call was from Olympic Rescue headquarters. His stomach sank. There was only one reason Tor would call this early.

"Tor, please don't tell me we have another missing person," he rasped.

"No can do, big guy. But heard you had some excitement last night, so you're second string today. Consider this a courtesy call."

"Who is it?"

"It's two people, actually. A couple day hikers didn't return from Big Bear last night. We got the call an hour ago. The team is getting ready to head up, but I thought you'd want to know. Sounds like they have decent equipment and whatnot, so hopefully it's just that they took too long and decided to stay over."

"Is the team aware that Calvin Perkins has possibly been sighted?"

He wouldn't put it past the sheriff to keep that information to himself.

"Yeah," Tor confirmed. "Everyone who can be is armed. And those who can't probably are as well."

That at least was good news. Even with no proof, Casey decided it had been Deputy Eagan who'd made sure word got around.

"Any news on Carlos?"

The medivac had flown him directly to the closest trauma hospital, which was in Seattle.

"We haven't heard anything."

Casey hoped they would hear from the brush worker—mostly because it meant he was on the way to recovering—but also maybe they'd learn more about the interaction with Perkins, get a clue that would point to where he was hiding out.

"Damn."

"So, what happened with you last night?" Tor asked. "Sounds like you had a close call."

Of course Tor had already heard about the fire. Of course he had, the man slept with a police radio near his head and Simeon Greery in his bed. Maybe it was Simeon's bed, Casey didn't know, and it wasn't his damn business.

"There isn't a lot to go on yet, but someone torched two of the sailboats moored here. The guy who's been living aboard one of them managed to get out—and with his cat, but it was close."

Too close for Casey's comfort. He swung his legs out from underneath the bedcovers and rose to his feet. There was no way he'd be able to fall back asleep anyway, not with his imagination working overtime. He'd shut his eyes and see the *Shangri-La* burning, or Charming racing down the dock, sheer panic on his face, and sometimes Casey wasn't there to save the day. It was too early, but it wouldn't be the first time he'd had to function on only a few hours' sleep.

With his phone pressed against his ear, he padded out to the galley and flicked on the generator and then the Keurig. He needed coffee stat. Bowie licked at his empty food bowl, reminding Casey that he hadn't eaten yet.

"The perps got away in a small watercraft. I didn't see it, too busy getting *The Barbara* to safety."

"Damn. Well, keep your phone close by in case we need more bodies searching today. Hopefully, we'll find these two quickly. From what we've been told, they were prepared for inclement weather, so at least we shouldn't be looking for popsicles."

Ah yes, because morgue humor was not just cops standing around staring at dead bodies. Enough missions and a searcher learned to compartmentalize. The missing weren't always uninjured and simply waiting for rescuers underneath the comforting boughs of a tree like something out of *Snow White.* Yesterday's rescue was a perfect example. There were times when Casey hated how unforgiving the forest was, but whenever he had that thought, he also realized that was one of the things he liked about it. A person had to respect the forest; it was a living, breathing entity, and it was perfectly willing to kill those who disregarded its power.

"I'll have my phone with me."

Clicking off, Casey snagged the plastic container of dry dog food from under the sink and dumped a serving into Bowie's dish. One last can of wet cat food was hiding at the back of the cabinet, so he opened it and spooned half onto a saucer. The cat appeared out of nowhere, sniffed the food, glared at Casey, and began to delicately eat.

Casey grabbed his waiting coffee and inhaled the scent of it deep into his lungs—the smell was almost as good as the real thing—then sat down at his table. Setting the cup to one side, he scrolled through his contacts until he found the number he wanted, his college friend who now worked in Olympia.

"Hey, Casey." His friend sounded out of breath, as if even at this relatively early hour she was already headed out somewhere.

"Marlene, sorry to call you out of the blue like this again. Is there any chance you can do me a favor and look up a registration? It's for one of the sailboats at the marina. There was a fire last night, and we're having a hard time getting hold of the registered owner."

"Ugh, I would, even though all you ever do is call for favors," she teased. "One of these days I'm going to call in a biggy. But I can't today. There's a family emergency and I'm on leave for the week, not in the office at all."

"I'm sorry, is there anything I can do to help?"

"Fix my dysfunctional family? Ha." She sighed and Casey heard a car door being beeped open in the background. "My estranged cousin was killed last week, and my asshole uncle just got around to telling me. I know it's because he's grief-stricken and alone, but fuck, the man brought it on himself. He's the one who couldn't handle the gay. Now he's dead and there's no chance for them to reconcile, and I think Uncle John wanted to reconnect. I'd been talking to Pete recently about it, and I think he was coming around to the idea. God, humans are so monumentally stupid."

At the name *Pete*, icy invisible fingers crawled down Casey's spine.

"Marlene, your cousin's name was Peter? Did I hear that right?" Casey grimaced as he forced himself to ask the next question. "Did he use the same last name as you? Was he on your mom's or your dad's side of the family?"

"My mom was Uncle John's sister, so we don't share the same last name."

Marlene and Casey had been study-buddies in college who'd bonded because neither one of them had been big partiers or into the recreational drugs that were readily available on and around the campus. They had a running joke that school officials might as well have invested in drug vending machines; at least then they would have gotten a kickback, maybe been able to fund a few scholarships.

Still raw from Mickie's trial and incarceration, Casey hadn't mentioned his family situation and Marlene had taken the hint and hardly ever talked about hers. He had known that she'd grown up in Westfort, that her mom had died of breast cancer while she was in high school, and that her dad owned a fishing boat. While Marlene knew that Casey was from Heartstone, had a soft spot for rescue animals, and spent his summers hiking the backcountry trails. That had been enough to form a connection that had persisted past college graduation.

"And no on Pete, too," she said, like Casey'd known she would. "After Uncle John kicked him out, he started using *his* mom's maiden name, but I didn't know that until later. He is—was," Marlene corrected, "older than me. We weren't super close growing up, but I ran into him a few years back. Why?"

Instead of answering her, Casey asked another question. "I know this is going to sound weird, but had you talked to your cousin lately?"

He heard the thump of a car door shutting, the clatter of keys, and the hum of an engine.

"Funny you should ask that. He called right after you did the other week. Had a question about the same person you did, Gabriel Karne. Said he had something of his and wanted to return it. Maybe I shouldn't have, but I mentioned your request. It just seemed so odd." She was quiet for a moment. "Why are you asking me these questions, Casey?"

"I'm not sure yet," he said honestly. "Does your uncle happen to own a sailboat?"

"My aunt did. Sailing was her dream. She was such a goof, she named it *Shangri-La* after that moldy old book. It was moored at your marina last I heard. Pete and I thought that was kind of funny too, such a small world. Seriously, Casey, tell me what is going on."

"I can't. For one, I don't have a good grasp of it all yet. But also, the less you know the better. I think anyway."

Marlene huffed, clearly not pleased with Casey's response.

"I'm driving up to Westfort now to help my uncle organize

Pete's memorial." It sounded to Casey like she was choking back tears. "Which is really just me because my uncle didn't know anything about his own son and my dad honestly wants to smack Uncle John every time they're in the same room. I generally run interference, it's cheaper than a visit to the ER. Keep an eye out for me. I'll be in your neighborhood as soon as I can and I'm going to want some answers. None of this evasive bullshit. You're my friend and I expect better from you."

There was a click and then Casey was listening to empty air.

"Dammit." Then he added, "Fuck," for good measure.

An ominous feeling in the pit of his stomach was warning him that shit was *possibly* about to hit the fan. But at least now Casey thought he'd figured out how Peter Vale had known to ask for Gabriel the other day.

It was Casey's fault.

He gulped the rapidly cooling coffee, making a face as he did so. The exchange with Vale had been short and sweet. Casey had just returned from the Weird Gabriel Karne Family Reunion at Elton's after detouring through the park to walk Bowie and trying to reclaim his sense of equilibrium. He'd parked at the marina and was unlocking the gate when a stranger had pulled up in a flashy white BMW, effectively blocking in Casey's Wagoneer.

Casey'd been about to tell him to fuck right off and get his damn car off private property when the driver stopped him by asking about Charming Fucker.

What had Casey said? "He's not here." Seemed straightforward, and even better, it had been the truth.

"But he is staying around here?"

By this time, he had gotten out of his car and was approaching Casey. For his part, Bowie had ignored the stranger and was instead sniffing around for the stray cat—some guard dog he was. Casey, on the other hand, had immediately been irritated by the man's manufactured perfection. The short, tidy, blond hair, the khaki slacks that showed no signs of wrinkles, the pink oxford-style shirt that peeked out from his high-end parka —it had all bothered Casey for reasons he still wasn't willing to think deeply about.

"If you say so." Not one of his better responses, but he had a natural suspicion about sharing information with strangers.

"Sorry, my manners are terrible," the man had said. "My name's Peter, I'm a friend of Gabe's. If you see him, will you pass a message along for me?"

"I'm not Karne's personal secretary. Come back when he's here."

Nice, Casey.

"In that case, I won't bother giving you my card," Peter had responded with a sneer. "Thanks for nothing." Less than a minute later, the man had driven off, going too fast down the road like most BMW drivers did. Casey had resisted shaking his fist; he wasn't really an angry old man. Not yet anyway. Then he'd let himself onto the dock and immediately called Karne.

Shaking off the memory, Casey took a last swallow of his coffee and scowled at the mug's contents, which were no longer tepid but in fact stone cold.

"Gross."

Standing up and crossing to the sink, he rinsed out the mug and set it in the drainer.

"Come on, everybody," Casey said to Bowie and the as-yet-to-be-named cat. Bowie jumped up in excitement. The cat narrowed its eyes in suspicion. "Yep, you're coming too." He grabbed his parka and slipped it on, then made sure his gloves were in the pocket.

. . .

A TANGLED KNOT was starting to break up and reveal secrets, or at least some of them. For undefined reasons, this was not a comforting thought. Maybe it was more like a giant iceberg calving and sending the consequences out into the universe—no control, no steering, just crushing everything in its path.

"All fucking hell is going to break loose," he said to Bowie as he tugged his toque onto his head. "Come on, might as well get the day started."

Casey left the rowboat pulled high up onto the shore and turned to examine the pier, analyzing the damage he could see. The fire department had cordoned it off with DO NOT CROSS tape, which didn't do anything except add to the general air of despair lingering around the marina.

He made a mental note to check in with Greery. The two sailboats were a loss; he didn't need to be an inspector to know that. Even though the weather was cold and damp, the flames had fulfilled their purpose. What Casey needed to know was how severely the dock had been affected by the fire. Would he have to search for a new berth? As it was, getting through the red tape to get the dock repaired—if repairs were needed—was likely going to be a fucking nightmare. He sent a little prayer up to the yellow-tinged clouds that the pier was relatively undamaged.

With that last thought, he scooped up the cat, tucked it under one arm, and started toward the parking lot with Bowie, as usual, trotting along at his side.

"BEFORE ANYTHING, we need to drop the cat at Pedro's. He has time right now," he told Elton and Charming not too much later. "Then we have things to talk about."

"I'm impressed you managed to get both Bowie and the cat to shore," Elton said.

"The cat must have had some experience as a boat cat because it didn't try and jump out, even stuck around when we bumped onto the beach." Maybe it had been because the air still smelled like smoke. Or maybe the creature recognized a good setup when Gabe had wrapped it in a blanket and saved it from flames.

"I have cash," said Gabe, patting his back pocket. "I'll pay for the exam."

They'd decided to meet in the Norskland parking lot. Casey had hoped to grab more coffee, but Pedro Morales, the island's only veterinarian, had returned his call sooner than Casey'd expected.

"All right, let's get going, moneybags."

"I'm gonna let you two go on your own. There's no reason to take two vehicles."

Casey decided to ignore the smirk accompanying Elton's statement.

FIFTEEN

Gabriel

Wednesday

"IT TOOK two of you human brutes to bring this beautiful gal in?"

The veterinarian, Pedro Morales, was adorable. He was probably in his late thirties and was Gabe's height but slender. And unless Gabe's radar was broken beyond repair, he was gay. Bi at the very least, considering the way he caught Gabe's amused glance and shot him a flirty grin in return.

Gabe smiled back even harder and added a wink. Next to him, Casey cleared his throat, and Gabe knew without looking that he was rolling his eyes. Didn't the man know there was nothing wrong with a little harmless flirting? Apparently not. Could he be jealous? Food for thought.

"She's a survivor, that's for sure. I love the orange girls. I think they control the shared brain cell." The vet continued running first the electronic wand and then his hand across the cat's body. He glanced at the wand and frowned up at them. "No chip."

"Good. That means Keith is meant for me," Gabe said. Until that moment, he hadn't known he wanted to give the cat a home or a name. But now that he'd said the words, he wasn't taking them back.

"Keith?" Casey sputtered and coughed.

"Yep." If Casey's reaction was anything to go by, it made Gabe even more certain that Keith was the right name. "Look at Keith Richards, he's still hanging around after all these years. If Keith is good enough for him, it's good enough for the cat that saved my life. Besides, your dog is Bowie. They can both be rock stars."

"And how is my best doggo?" Pedro asked, forestalling the inevitable bickering that would normally follow Casey and Gabe's exchange. Gabe was just a tiny bit sad about that.

"Good, he's good," grumbled Casey.

Twenty minutes later, they were back in the lobby and Gabe was peeling off several hundred dollars in cash for vaccinations, a microchip, the exam, and everything else the cat needed—he was marking it down as go-bag expenses. Keith was unhappily loaded into a carrier and made her displeasure known with hearty yowls.

Picking up the box and the rest of the supplies—which put him back another couple hundred—Gabe headed to the parking lot. Once they were all tucked inside the Wagoneer, Gabe said, "Okay, spill. What did you learn this morning? And how? The fire was less than twelve hours ago, did you not sleep?"

"I promised Elton, and I don't want to have to repeat myself."

"Oh my god," Gabe huffed, crossing his arms over his chest. "Fine, Step on it."

"There is literally no traffic on the island this time of year," Casey told him.

"Which means you can step on it."

Casey ignored him. "What was that with Pedro?" he asked instead.

Was Ranger Man jealous? The man was a puzzle—Gabe loved unraveling puzzles.

"What was what that?" asked Gabe, blinking at Casey. He knew perfectly well what *that* had been. And he'd do it again just to get a reaction out of Casey.

"The smiling and"—he lifted a hand off the steering wheel and waved it around—"glinting shit."

Gabe snorted. "Glinting shit? What, it's illegal to smile now? Pedro is a nice guy, why wouldn't I smile?"

Casey growled. "It is not illegal to smile. It's the *way* you smile, and you know it."

Because he couldn't help himself, Gabe smiled again. But he directed it away from Casey.

"I bet you have a great smile, not that I've seen it. Hold it, maybe I have, but it was so fleeting that it didn't make an impression."

He was gifted with another deep-chested growl. The raspy sound had Gabe's fucking heart doing a weird flip-flop. Worse than the flip-flop, it made him want to poke the bear even more. If flirting with the cute veterinarian made Ranger Man cranky ... it meant there was something here. Gabe wasn't imagining it.

Of course, it could also mean that he hadn't gotten enough sleep or enough coffee in the past two days, but Gabe was choosing to believe this particular brand of Casey Lundin grumpiness originated from a different source. One that had nothing to do with sleep or trespassing and everything to do with one Gabriel Luke Karne. *Note to self.*

Gabe allowed himself a smirk and enjoyed the rest of the short, un-trafficky drive to Elton's, checking out the houses and small businesses they passed by. Maybe right now wasn't the time to test *whatever this was* between them, but it would be soon enough. If there was one thing Gabe was good at, it was being patient. There were few impatient con men, it tended to cut their careers short.

And if there was another thing Gabe was certain of right this minute, it was that his radar was not broken, and it was telling him that Ranger Man's antennae—vibe, whatever—was angling toward Gabe. Oh, he was fighting the draw, but with every growl, grump, arms crossed over that broad chest, Gabe knew he was closer to something.

You'd better figure out what you want before you jump, Chance.

He blew out a sigh and snuck a glance at Ranger Man out of the corner of his eye. Solid. Stalwart. Smart. Damaged.

Want.

Gabe had a private theory that everyone—even the poor little rich kid—was damaged one way or another. They just all wore their scars differently. When he'd floated the idea past Peter during the course of a rare conversation that hadn't been centered around money, his ex had scoffed and told him to stop already with his wanna-be psychology bullshit. Which had told Gabe he was onto something.

Casey Lundin was unlike anyone else that Gabe had been even remotely attracted to over his lifetime, but Heidi's voice was right—Ranger Man wasn't fuck-around-and-find-out material. Luckily, before he said or did anything outlandishly stupid, they arrived at Elton's.

.   .   .

"KEITH?" Elton's eyebrows rose close to his hairline. "Whatever floats your boat, I suppose."

Keith had been released from her box and was currently stalking the perimeter of Elton's living room.

"I had the vet put your address on the microchip, just until I get myself sorted out."

"About that. Not that I'm not happy to have you here." Elton sat forward in his chair. "I know it's not the Ritz, or whatever else you're used to, but Bill has an opening at Smitty's, and I can put in a good word for you."

"Beggars and choosers. I'd appreciate that," Gabe said lightly, knowing he would accept. He wasn't too proud to accept help or live in a mobile home park; it wouldn't be the first time. "I need coffee."

"There's a fresh pot, help yourself. But also, you know you're more than welcome to stay here with me, of course, for as long as you need."

Gabe dismissed Elton's offer. With Peter dead—murdered—and the *Ticket* reduced to floating rubble, not to mention Gabe and Keith barely escaping with their lives, he wasn't about to place Elton in more danger than he already had, even if it hadn't been on purpose.

"Do you need a warm-up?" he asked Elton.

"I think I'm fully caffeinated. I'll pass."

"That is crazy talk, old man."

The day was shaping up to be a three- or four-cup day. Hell, maybe even a fiver. In the kitchen, two clean mugs sat next to the coffee pot, so he filled both of them and headed back out to the living room. He was ready to learn what Casey had discovered.

The irritating man had made himself comfortable on the couch, which forced Gabe to sit at the table. He smirked. Gabe shot him a mischievous glance.

"Casey's got space for us on that big boat of his."

Casey'd been lifting the full mug to his lips, and Gabe's outrageous statement had him jerking his arm and splashing some of the liquid onto his hand.

"Gotcha," Gabe said.

"Am I going to have to separate you two?" Elton chuckled. "Quit screwing around, Gabriel, I want to hear what Casey has to say."

"LET ME GET THIS STRAIGHT. Your 'contact,' who did the background check on me—illegally, I'm just gonna point out—told Peter enough information that he sussed out I was here on Heartstone. On top of that, the *Shangri-La* is his dad's boat. Was his dad's boat." Gabe frowned. "Or rather, was his mom's boat that his dad paid for. Boy, that's really a lot to wrap my head around."

Gabe sent a raised eyebrow Casey's direction and was rewarded with a glower and a flicker of guilt. Not undeserved. Gabe could have died last night, maybe Casey too. Whoever firebombed the marina wasn't fucking around. On the other hand, it wasn't a target difficult to hit, so maybe it had been a crime of opportunity. But Gabe knew the fire had been a message. To whom was the question.

Gabe was working to process the information Casey had shared with them. Dammit, he'd been concerned that a background check would lead the Colavitos to him, but this was—he didn't know what this was. An attempt on his life or a message to John Stevens? Maybe both.

"Okay, so who the fuck killed Peter?" Gabe asked. "And why dump his body on a boat they just turned around and burned to the waterline anyway? Seems a bit extreme."

"Maybe the killer and the arsonist aren't the same people?" Elton suggested.

"And let's not forget that Peter's father is the prosecutor who put your brother behind bars. That might not give you motive to kill Peter, but what about tossing a match on the sailboat? I know you didn't, Casey, but none of this makes sense, and the cops are surely going to want to find someone for this. We're missing something important, something big."

A humming interrupted him, the buzzing of a cell phone. He stared at Casey; it had to be his since Gabe's newest was at the bottom of the bay along with his car keys, and Elton didn't have one. Although Gabe was going to take care of that as soon as he could. It was a two-way street, he could take care of Elton too.

With a frown, Casey dug into the pocket of the parka he'd slung over the arm of the couch. "It's Tor, I have to take this." Grabbing his phone, Casey stepped into the kitchen.

"Tor?"

"Olympic Rescue," Elton told him.

Gabe was perfectly happy to eavesdrop on Ranger Man's conversation, but someone knocked on Elton's front door.

"Expecting someone?"

"No." Elton pushed himself to standing and started across the room to open the door.

An older man, probably younger than Elton but not by much, waited on the tiny porch, and it only took one glance for Gabe to know exactly who he was. John Stevens, Peter's father. Ranger Man's mortal enemy. He was definitely the man he'd seen in the parking lot at the sheriff's the day before.

"John, this is a surprise."

Gabe had never met Peter's father, had never seen a picture, had no idea he existed. But Peter had looked just like him.

Stevens was saturated in grief. A man who wished he was the one who'd died. As if it had taken almost the last vestige of his strength to curl his fingers into a fist and bang on Elton's door.

He looked over Elton's shoulder to Gabe, who rose to his feet. His mouth opened and closed as if he couldn't force whatever words he needed to say past his lips.

"Come in." Elton stepped back. "Casey Lundin is here. He's in the kitchen talking on the phone."

"I know, I saw his Jeep. I shouldn't be here. I'm supposed to be meeting someone, family, but I don't know where to turn. What to do."

"Well, come inside, Gabriel won't bite. But I can't guarantee Casey's reaction."

"I've been a fool, Cox."

Gabe recognized the sound of defeat, of futility, practically dripping from his words. Why had Stevens come here, to Elton? When Elton had mentioned Stevens to Gabe, his tone hadn't been one of admiration. The Elton approval meter clearly pointed toward scorn and disgust, not friendship and acceptance.

"No doubt you have," Elton agreed. "Are you going to come inside or are you going to make me hold this door open and let the heat and the cat out?"

"Dammit," Gabe muttered under his breath as he spun back around. He'd forgotten about Keith *and* Bowie, but neither of them were in plain sight. Bowie must have been in the kitchen with Casey while Keith was somewhere plotting murder, or whatever it was cats did most of the day. He turned back to the door.

One last hesitation, then Stevens bowed his head and stepped over the threshold. Peter's father was a thin man who had once been tall but was now stooped with age or illness. He looked like a plant desperately in need of watering. Still, it was easy to see where Peter had inherited his thick hair and prominent straight nose from.

"Have a seat." Gabe gestured in the direction of the couch.

The one-sided conversation in the kitchen abruptly ended and Casey appeared at the archway, his head down as he looked at his phone. Nodding, he tucked the phone into the side pocket of his cargo pants. Then he looked up and saw Stevens. Always implacable, Casey's expression stilled to something scary, something *other*.

"What's he doing here?" he asked, his tone stony.

"We don't know yet," Elton said. "Do you have time to find out?"

Gabe had an inkling of an idea. They'd seen Stevens at the station earlier. He must have recognized Elton or maybe one of the deputies had said something.

"No, I don't." Casey turned his flat dark gaze on Stevens. The disdain he felt for the man oozed from every pore. "What are you doing here?"

"Let the man sit down, Casey. Before he falls down."

Stevens shuffled across the room to take the spot on the couch that Casey had occupied before the phone call. Having experienced Casey's frustration and irritation firsthand, Gabe knew what his glare felt like, and at the moment, Ranger Man's emotions were so strong they made the air feel thick and almost difficult to breathe.

Stevens's shoulders rose and fell. He seemed to gather himself before looking at Elton, then Gabe. His gaze skittered past Casey and turned back to Gabriel again.

"You're the one who moved onto *The Golden Ticket*. You knew my son."

Gabe's suspicion that it had been one of the deputies who

had had loose lips, or perhaps the sweet old gal at the front desk, intensified.

Never underestimate small towns.

"Yes, I briefly lived on the *Ticket* until somebody decided to torch it and a neighboring sailboat. And I don't think Peter let anyone know him, not really."

"That's my fault, I –"

"It's a little too late to apologize, and we're the wrong audience—at least I am," Casey interrupted, his tone laced with impatience now. "I learned you kicked your son out when he told you he was gay and now you have to live with the consequences. The one person who should have had his back, and you turned on him."

"Yes," Stevens agreed, cocking his head, "I deserve that. It's the truth, I have no excuse."

"So why do you suddenly care?"

Obviously, Casey was not planning on letting this go. And, frankly, Gabe was curious too. He might have gone about asking in a different way, but this was Casey. Ranger Man was front and center.

"It's not sudden—look, I don't have to explain myself to you," Stevens retorted with a burst of arrogance. "The sheriff says that Peter talked to you just last week, Casey. What did he want? Did he say anything? Please."

The man was grieving, possibly ill; his son had been murdered, but the lawyer in Stevens was alive and kicking and looking for any answers. It was easy for Gabe to see why he'd been a successful prosecutor. He'd also said *please*.

"Don't call me Casey like you know me. Why should I tell you anything? Why would you believe anything I say?"

Elton winced, caught Gabe's quick glance, and pursed his lips.

"You're right, of course. You don't have to tell me anything. I just—" Stevens's voice broke again. He looked down at his hands for a moment, then, clearing his throat, he looked at Elton, probably his safest choice. "Peter's dead. He deserves justice. I owe him that much."

"That's rich coming from you. I'd say you owe him a great deal more than that, but as you pointed out, it's too late."

"Casey." Elton said his name quietly, but there was a warning there. Or an admonition. Gabe was impressed.

Slowly inhaling through his nose, Casey held the oxygen for a moment, rolled his shoulders, and blew the breath out.

"Your son stopped by the marina, Sunday a week ago. I didn't recognize him, didn't know who he was, and he just identified himself as Peter, nothing else. He asked about Gabe, Gabe wasn't there, so I sent him on his way. That was it."

"Nothing else?"

"Nope." The pop on the *P* was final. Extra final. It was clear to Gabe that Casey had nothing else to say. "I need to go. Two hikers are still missing." He turned to Elton. "Can Bowie hang here, or should I drop him at Greta's? Not sure when I'll be back."

"He can stay. Bowie is always welcome. If you're late, I have some kibble for him."

Casey left without saying goodbye, the door slamming behind him with calculated finality. John Stevens wasn't receiving forgiveness or anything close to it today—or maybe any day—not from Casey.

"Why did you come here, John?" Elton asked, breaking the silence once they heard Casey's Jeep start up and the crack of gravel under his tires. "What did you mean, you'd been a fool? Because you didn't accept your son for who he was, or something more? Not sure there's anything worse than not being accepted by your parent."

This time it was Gabe who winced. Elton wasn't pulling

any punches either. There was other history Gabe was ignorant of, and he had the feeling whatever it was, it was going to be a lot.

"There's always something more, Cox," Stevens said quietly. "A long time ago I wanted something and made a deal with the devil. I was young and arrogant, didn't see what I'd agreed to as inherently wrong."

"What did you do, John?"

"At first, not much. And it stayed low-key for years. But the agreement did bring me connections. In exchange, I guess, I was invited to be part of ... various groups that had money or the means to get it."

"And?"

"And?" He looked away from Elton, staring out the front window or perhaps at nothing at all. "As Twana County Prosecuting Attorney, I ... sometimes looked the other way. Not often. I did have a reputation as a tough-on-crime prosecutor, after all."

Gabe snorted. He could see what was coming a mile away. This may have been a long con, a long bait before the switch, but John Stevens had been conned. And by the time he realized he was a mark, it was too late. They—whoever they were, although Gabe had a pretty damn good idea—had enough to destroy Stevens, so he'd been theirs to control.

"Classic," Gabe muttered, recalling what he'd heard so far about Casey's older brother. "Let me guess. After you'd looked the other way enough times, they threatened to expose you if you didn't cooperate when Mickie Lundin was arrested. And they wanted him charged with murder."

Remorse with a heavy splash of guilt flitted across the old prosecutor's face. That was all Gabe needed.

"Mickie Lundin wasn't the first or only innocent person who got the shaft, was he? Who else has suffered from your particular brand of justice?" He shifted so that he was standing directly in front of Stevens, effectively blocking his view of the window. "I never bartered human lives for money. I've conned people all my life, I won't deny it. But my soul is my own. People like you disgust me. Are you trying to get some kind of absolution from Elton? You'll never get it from Casey. Just a guess here, but I'd bet my go-bags that putting Mickie Lundin behind bars for a crime he didn't commit destroyed a family and several lives. And what did you get in return?"

Stevens stared up at him.

"There's something else," he said, his voice hoarse.

"More? Worse than what you've already confessed to?" Gabe crossed his arms over his chest and wrinkled his nose at the guy like he was a bug. "For fuck's sake, how fucked up can a fuckup fuck?"

The man winced. Gabe was just going to assume it was a pretty major fuckup.

"I did see Peter last week, briefly." Again, he didn't appear to be seeing Gabe or Elton as he spoke. Maybe he was looking to his past, wishing for something different. "He showed up at the house. I was in my office looking over some paperwork."

"I take it you didn't have the joyous reunion you'd imagined. Not a shocker, seeing as you kicked him out. Peter never was good at forgiveness. I see where he got it from."

Stevens narrowed his gaze at Gabe before continuing. Gabe ignored it; that stare was child's play.

"He got a look at some documents I was working on. I'm a paper-and-pen man, too old to trust everything to computers." His laugh was weak, self-mocking.

"Did he figure out what you'd been doing all these years?" Gabe asked.

"No, nothing like that. He thought he might be interested in investing in a project, getting involved. We talked for a while, buried the hatchet so to speak, and decided it might not be a bad idea to have more than one pair of eyes on it."

"And?" Elton asked.

Stevens shook his head. "And? He left. Said he'd be in touch with me soon. A week later, the sheriff was calling to say that Peter had been found dead."

"You don't know where he was last week? He didn't tell you anything?" That wouldn't surprise Gabe, Peter had liked to keep his movements during a con under wraps. "Why are you here? How do you think Elton can help you?"

"I don't really know, you were the only person I could think of, Elton. And I knew from island chatter that you were here too," he said to Gabe. "It was foolish of me to think you might have an answer or a solution I haven't already come up with."

With a grimace, the man pushed himself to his feet and started for the door. Halfway across the room, he twisted around to look at Elton and Gabe. "For what it's worth, I am sorry. My own son was dead to me for many years, and now he really is dead. Children aren't supposed to die before their parents, and I have no one to blame but myself."

"John," Elton said his name quietly, a plea with an edge of anger.

Stevens didn't answer him—or simply had no more to say. With a shrug, he pulled the front door open and slowly made his way to his car, the same car Gabriel had seen in the Sheriff's Office parking lot earlier.

Gabe started to say something to Elton, clear the air of the stench of remorse, but the phone rang before he could come up with anything remotely appropriate.

"Casey?" Elton said into the receiver.

The words were muffled, but Gabe recognized Ranger Man's deep grumble on the other end of the line.

"Yeah, Stevens is gone. Put you on speaker? Crikey, as if I

know how to do that sort of thing." Elton poked around on the handset for a minute. "Aha," he said triumphantly. "Casey, you are on speaker. Damn, I'm good. What were you telling me?"

"Why the hell did Stevens show up at your place, Elton? What did he want?" The tinny sound of Casey's voice filled the room.

"Let's skip back to why the hell did you blab my location to some rando?" demanded Gabe. "That's the issue I'd like to better understand."

An audible sigh reached their ears before Casey spoke again. "It's one of those six-degrees-of-separation things. As it turns out, my friend who did the background check on Gabe is Peter Vale's cousin. Stevens is her uncle on her mother's side, so I never suspected a connection there. Apparently, Vale had the same great idea I did and called her to see if she would look up Karne. She thought that was a remarkable coincidence and mentioned she already had done so when she talked to Peter."

Elton made an *I told you so* face at Gabe.

"Are you fucking kidding me?" Gabe said.

"Do I kid around, Karne?"

Yeah, no, Ranger Man did not fuck around.

"Elton wondered if that was how he'd found me. That explains how Peter tracked me down, but it doesn't explain why his body was dumped at the marina. Or why the boats were torched."

The fire, Gabriel now had the feeling, somehow belonged squarely at the feet of John Stevens and whatever no-good shit he was involved in.

"Nope, it doesn't. I gotta go, I'll check in later. Don't do anything stupid today." With those uplifting words, Casey clicked off.

"Don't do anything stupid? That's like waving a red flag in

front of a bull. Too bad he's off doing important ranger stuff, leaving us to our own devices."

Gabe briefly envisioned Casey behind the wheel of the banged-up Forest Service truck bumping up The Valley, heading into danger, ready to help search for a couple of hikers who'd gotten themselves into trouble. Even if the trouble was the hikers' own fault. Casey Lundin may act tough, but Gabe was starting to figure out that there was a soft center to the man. Maybe one he didn't want people to know about.

Elton snorted.

"Lundin is nothing if not economical with language," Gabe griped, steering himself out of his *kind and soft Ranger Man* train of thought. "I'd still like to know more about this *friend* of his who blabbed my existence."

"I'd like to know what the hell is going on around here. A missing person yesterday and two more today? The mountains are no place to mess around but this is a lot for the time of year."

"Add in Peter's murder. And the fires. Dwayne Perkins too." Gabe shuddered. He did not want to think about his last sighting of Dwayne.

What the hell was going on around Heartstone? Christ, was it only two weeks since he'd had that run-in with the Perkins brothers? Was it possible that there was more to the killing of Dwayne Perkins than the also-dead sheriff's deputy supposedly "going off the rails"? New guy to the island or not, he couldn't help but connect dots that faintly led from the Perkinses to the Twana County Sheriff's Office to the retired Twana County Prosecuting Attorney to Peter and possibly beyond.

Had Gabe's discovery of Dwayne's body only been the tip of the iceberg? What would have happened if he hadn't gone on a failed mission to find Gordon that day? Maybe Dwayne would've just disappeared. His questions were piling up like traffic on I-5 during construction season and a Mariners game, and a Taylor Swift concert was happening somewhere in there too.

At the hospital, when Deputy Nolan had almost managed to force Gordon into his cruiser, Gabe's impression had been of a man at the end of his rope. The thought had been fleeting, and the next thing Gabe knew, the deputy was dead, shot by Sheriff Rizzi. And Nolan had been an unknown, so he hadn't said anything when he'd been questioned. But what if—*what if*—Rizzi had murdered Nolan in cold blood to keep him from …

From what? From talking about what? In Gabe's mind, everything kept coming back to The Valley.

Questions started flowing out of his mouth. "Did you ever hear back about the land around Gordon's property? I mean, the brain trust is still AWOL, but could there be a connection between what's going on now and what happened with Gordon, Dwayne, and the deputy? Not sure how that would involve Peter, though. But what if he saw something else in Stevens's paperwork, more than Stevens thought he did?"

Even in his head he wasn't going to call that sack of water and oxygen Peter's father. He doubted the claim that they'd buried the hatchet. More likely Peter'd had an inkling of what Stevens was up to and wanted to derail it or direct the proceeds to himself.

Elton was quiet for several minutes, clearly going over what Stevens had told them and probably trying to figure out what he hadn't. Gabe sipped his too-cold coffee and waited.

Finally, Elton spoke. "What do you think about going to have a chat with Kelly Perkins?"

"Who's that?"

"Calvin and Dwayne's mother, Rizzi's sister. I should probably drop by and give her my condolences anyway, even if I always knew those boys would come to a bad end. My thinking is that if the brothers were somehow involved and Dwayne's death is related, she might have an idea about what it this all is, or she might not. Hard to tell with her sometimes."

"Let's do it. We're just spinning wheels here anyway."

Elton slowly rose to his feet, and Gabe could almost hear his joints popping. Bowie scrambled out from behind the recliner and headed for the door.

"You too?" Gabe said to the dog.

Bowie just looked at him with a decidedly *duh* expression.

SIXTEEN

Gabriel

Wednesday afternoon

IT WAS a five-minute drive from Elton's to the Perkinses' homestead. Elton spent every mile of it telling Gabe he needed to be on his best behavior. And when he veered right onto an overgrown gravel driveway, he said it one more time just for good measure.

"Fine," said Gabe, raising his hands in surrender, "I get it. I'll practice being seen and not heard."

"She's ... volatile."

"I never would have guessed," grumbled Gabe, "considering the way her sons are so calm, cool, and collected."

Obscured by trees and shrubs at first, the driveway opened up after about five hundred feet to reveal not a single house, but a compound of three. Closest to Gabe and Elton squatted a mid-century single-story home, overseeing the other two structures.

The owners had missed the memo about regular maintenance, not a surprise after the *Deliverance*-style driveway. Two older mobile-ish homes had been squeezed in on the back of the property, and they didn't look like they were in any better condition. Dingy was the nicest word that came to mind. One of them had a motorcycle parked out front, and from the parts strewn around it, Gabe figured the bike didn't run.

Most of the time, Gabe knew better than to judge a book by its cover, but damn, these folks were making it difficult. Very, very, difficult.

"Tell me this is one of those beauty-is-on-the-inside situations."

Elton stopped his truck next to a shiny white Lexus and set the parking brake.

"Remember what I told you," he said, giving Gabe a hard stare.

"*Behave, Gabe,*" he parroted. "You'd think I was twelve, not coming up on forty-five. Did Casey get to you when you went to the dentist the other day? Honestly, what have I ever done that indicated I can't behave myself? When it's absolutely necessary, I can."

Elton stared at him again, longer and harder this time. "Just behave. She's not going to make it easy for either of us."

It occurred to Gabe as they crossed the lawn toward the front door that he hadn't asked what their approach would be or how they were going to go from *condolences on your son being found shot dead* to *do you know what the hell is going on around here and why* or *there's an epidemic of death and could it have anything to do with the current fuckery.*

"Fine, I promise that I'll follow your lead."

"See that you do."

The door opened after the first knock. Gabe figured Kelly must've heard them coming and been watching them through the drab curtains that effectively kept any natural light from making its way inside the house.

The woman in front of them was likely in her mid- to late-fifties. The phrase "rode hard and put away wet" came to mind and had nothing to do with sex and everything to do with life in general.

"Elton Cox, what are you doing here?" Her somewhat bleary gaze moved to Gabriel, assessing him in a way he found distinctly uncomfortable. "And who's your friend?"

Without answering, Elton stepped inside, moving past Kelly Perkins as if she'd invited him in for tea. Gabe followed. When in Rome and all.

"This is a friend of mine, Gabriel Karne." He gestured Gabe's direction. "He's the son of a gal who used to work for me during the summers, back when I was still doing sculpture. Heidi Karne. I don't know if you ever met her."

Kelly tapped her bottom lip with her index finger, then shrugged. "The name doesn't sound familiar, but I was a kid back then. Uh, have a seat. Do you want something to drink?"

Blinking, she looked around the dim living room as if only just realizing two men had essentially barged into her house and the furniture was covered with bulging and overflowing bankers boxes. There were also dozens of smaller boxes stacked around the furniture and against the walls.

"We don't need anything, thank you. We're not here to get in your way, I know you're busy."

"Well, I need a drink. I don't know how I'm supposed to keep up with everything when one of my sons was murdered and the other is nowhere to be found. Calvin is just gone, out there somewhere, helpless in the wilderness."

A lone tear slid down one cheek, but Gabe wasn't sure if it or the grief were genuine. A literal lifetime as a grifter meant he was uniquely talented at parsing people's emotions. Something was off about Kelly Perkins. He was also fairly sure that Calvin Perkins was not helpless.

Almost robotically, she turned and walked toward a door at the back of the room. Elton and Gabe followed her and found themselves in a large kitchen that had gone through an unfortunate remodel in the late eighties. Whoever'd been the lobbyist for dark faux oak cabinets had to have made a killing on the stuff and deserved to burn in a circle of hell that also had the shag carpet salespeople. Gabe hated both; they reminded him of all the places he and Heidi had lived in when she was "on a break."

"All those boxes need to be sent out to my customers, and they're just sitting there." She sucked air in through her nose and released it. "Every time I go into the living room, they're still there, just waiting. Did you know that Dwayne used to help me get them to the post office?" There was a bottle on the counter. She grabbed it and filled the glass sitting next to it over halfway full. Raising the tumbler, she mock-toasted them and knocked the amber liquid back, drinking it down without wheezing.

Nothing acted as a deterrent to keep Gabe away from alcohol as well as witnessing another person spiral.

"Why are you here?" she demanded, abruptly switching off the emotional faucet. "It's not like we're close, Elton. You didn't like Dwayne or Calvin. And what did they ever do to you anyway? Just boys having fun, living their lives."

Elton didn't appear to be phased by her change in demeanor. Maybe Kelly Perkins was always like this. If so, it could go a long way toward explaining Calvin's and Dwayne's takes on life.

"I'm truly sorry about your boy," Elton said. "No parent should have to bury their child."

Maybe those were the only words she wanted to hear, Gabe didn't know. But they worked. It must have been hard having most people not at all sad when your violent, creepy son was murdered in cold blood.

"What do you think about Gabe and me taking those boxes and dropping them off at the post office for you? We'll go right past it on our way back to my place."

"You'd do that?" she asked with another sniffle.

"'Course we would."

Gabe knew that Elton's offer was sincere. He may not much like the brothers or Kelly Perkins, but he would lend a hand when it was needed. And it was clearly needed.

Tears sprang to Kelly's eyes again, and this time Gabe thought they were the real thing. There was a roll of paper towels next to the sink, so Gabe grabbed it and tore one off, handing it to Kelly.

"Thank you, kind sir," she said, dabbing at her cheeks and eyes before using the paper to blow her nose. "This whole thing has been awful. My worst nightmare. Are both my boys dead?" She started to sob. "I-I just don't know. No one knows. Goddamned Deter Nolan. I'm glad Eli killed him."

Gabriel wasn't entirely sure why Elton had dragged him along, especially after being told to behave himself. Did Kelly Perkins know that he'd been the one to find Dwayne? And if she didn't, would learning so be a good thing or a bad thing? In spite of his natural tendency to butt into pretty much any conversation, Gabe kept his mouth shut. He entertained himself by wondering what Casey was up to and if they'd located the hikers who hadn't returned from their trek.

"Kelly," Elton said softly. Softly enough that he immediately had Gabe's attention. "Can I ask you a question?"

"Sure," she said around her sodden paper towel.

"Do you know what Dwayne was doing up The Valley when he was killed?"

Her dark, red-rimmed eyes darted to Gabe and back to Elton.

"It's fine, we both know the boys harvested here and there. Everybody does it, don't they?"

"Yeah." She sniffled, leaning her butt against the edge of the counter. "Casey Lundin had no business taking it away from them. About a week ago, both boys sure were fired up that the ranger had stolen everything."

"So, they came home that morning and then went back to The Valley?"

Gabe knew the brothers had to have at least driven to the gas station on the other side of the isthmus because he'd had that lovely interaction with them there.

"They came home for lunch, they almost always did," Kelly confirmed. "They were both madder than hornets. Calvin was yelling all sorts of nonsense and promising he'd get even with Ranger Lundin. I was glad when Eli called with an errand for them. He's such a good uncle, making sure they get extra work when they need it."

"What did Eli need?"

"Oh." She waved a hand dismissively before swiping at her nose again. Gabe really wanted to hand her another, less damp, paper towel. "He needed them to do something up at that development of his, Snowcap Estates. They didn't tell me what it was, they never wanted me to worry. Such good boys." She sniffled again.

"Snowcap is going to be a beautiful place when it's all said and done," Elton said with false enthusiasm. "Eli's lucky to be a part of the investment team."

"Our sheriff's a dark horse, isn't he? Eli's been part owner of that land for ages. I think he bought into it back in the nineties. He's just been waiting for the right time to develop it. Honestly, I thought they'd have built on it by now."

"Snowcap Estates was owned by an LLC. Trillium, I think?" Elton said casually.

He was good. Very good. Gabe had to give the old man credit where it was deserved.

He's a keeper, Chance. Smooth like a Chuck Mangione song.

"Oh, it is," Kelly confirmed. "That's the main company, although there are others involved. I don't know all the details, but like I said, Eli owns more than just some lots at Snowcap Estates. He's got some property along Icicle Creek and further south too. One of the things Calvin and Dwayne do is keep an eye on everything for him. If somebody trespasses, they run them off or whatever." Her odd eyebrows drew together. "I don't know who all is involved, but I'd bet Emmett Spurring is because if Eli jumps, so does Emmett. Thinks Eli hung the moon. Calvin got himself arrested a while back, but Emmett smoothed it over before Eli even showed up. Whatever happened, it was just a misunderstanding."

Neither one of them corrected Kelly to the past tense when it came to her younger son. Thank fuck, because Gabe wasn't sure he could handle her breaking down in tears again if she didn't have a fresh tissue. He eyed the disaster she clutched in her fist, willing her to throw it away.

"It sounds like both boys have been a great help to you and Eli," Elton said. "Now, can we be a help to you and take the boxes to the post office for you?" He looked at his watch. "We should get over there. They close soon, I think."

SEVENTEEN

Casey

Late afternoon, Wednesday

"AT _EAST THEY aren't injured, or worse," said Greta.

Her voice was tinny. The signal was weak, which meant the connection could drop at any time. But Casey had his partner on speaker so they could bitch about most of a whole fucking day wasted, searching for people who hadn't wanted to be found until they were ready. But since their families hadn't been in on the plan, they'd reported them missing. Worse, when they were found, they were in a somewhat compromising position. Why couldn't it have been Tor or one of the other searchers who happened upon them? Casey had the worst luck.

"If I'd known what we were walking into, I would never have kept going. I'm not a prude—"

"You kind of are," Greta interrupted.

"—but I don't need to see somebody's ass and definitely not

two somebodies' bare asses. It would serve them right if they sat in nettles or worse. Sadly, it's too cloudy and dark for sunburns."

Greta snorted, agreeing with him.

What a waste of resources, that was what enraged him the most. They'd lied about where they were going to be, lied about their return plan, and consequently had wasted time and resources that could've been spent on a real emergency. He wished he could see their expressions when the fine landed in their mailboxes. It was going to be a significant sum.

The not-missing hikers were "social media influencers," a term Casey hated with a passion just on general principle. What did that even mean? The two had deviated from their original course and hiked out to a bridge that had been built back in the 1930s by a now defunct timber company. It was one of just a few of its kind in the country, as well as the fourth highest bridge on the West Coast, almost four hundred feet above Icicle Creek. So, yeah, it was dramatic, beautiful, awe-inspiring. Casey loved it up there, just standing on the bridge deck and taking in the natural beauty that surrounded it.

The bridge was popular for many reasons: the view, the drama of the creek running below it, its remote location. At night, it was one of the darkest places on the peninsula, so it was also great for astral photography. During last year's auroras, the Forest Service had been forced to station a ranger up there just to keep too many people from crowding onto the bridge. Which he entirely blamed on the aforementioned influencer types that he hated. Those people were why it often felt like there was nowhere sacred, nowhere peaceful and truly quiet anymore.

The area around the bridge was not, as far as Casey understood, a place to strip naked and fuck the bejeezus out of each other in a snow-covered field. Or to pose stark naked, backlit only by moonlight, pressed up against the railings. All on video for private subscribers. At least, that's what one of them had admitted once Casey and Greta caught up with them. After they'd gotten dressed.

"It's winter and with the snowfall, we figured no one would come up here."

Some things Casey would never understand.

"Oh, but the stories we have to tell our grandchildren," Greta said, her evil snicker carrying across their cell connection.

"Not having kids so can't have grandkids." He steered around a crater-sized pothole while managing to avoid a tree trunk that leaned perilously over the road.

"Come on, you'd be a great dad, Casey. Speaking of which, when do I get to meet Gabriel?"

The change of subject was uniquely abrupt, but Casey shouldn't have been shocked by it. Greta had been building up to this. For some reason, she was dying to meet Charming Fucker and had convinced herself that Casey had finally found someone who would hold his attention for longer than a day or two. She wasn't wrong, but not for the right reasons.

"Er, Gabriel?" He still tripped over his new neighbor's name. "We haven't done anything, we aren't ... anything. He irritates me, full stop. Why are you talking children when what I really want to do is drop him in the bay?"

Unbidden, the fire from the night before drifted into his thoughts. Gabriel's panicked pounding on the side of the sailboat waking Casey up from an R-rated dream. Then finding the subject of his dream with the stupid cat wrapped up in a blanket and clutched to his chest, two boats in flames behind him. Recalling the scene made Casey's heart shudder and skip several beats. But that would've happened to anyone. Right? Fire was scary and when you lived on a boat, it was terrifying.

"What is that Shakespeare quote?" Greta teased. "The grumpy man doth protest too much? You can't tell me you haven't thought about *it*. With him. And by it, I mean *it*, it."

He was certain she was making a lewd gesture with one hand. Why was he allowing this ridiculous conversation to continue? Because this was Greta, his closest, oldest friend. And because of that status he let her get away with shit no one else did. Hell, no one else would even try.

Except for Charming Fucker, a little voice murmured.

Goddammit. No.

"For Christ's sake, why would I think about Karne that way? He's a drifter and a con man. I've already told you he infuriates me daily, hourly even. Did I remember to tell you that not only did he name that stray cat *Keith*, but it's a girl cat? The cat clearly has no survival instincts because when she finally decided to come in out of the rain, she chose him! Of all the people, she chose him." He shook his head, disgusted. After feeding Keith half the summer, she chose Charming. "And besides, I don't need anyone."

Greta ignored his protest and focused on the cat instead.

"Apparently Keith has recognized the good in your guy. And I think Keith is a great name."

Gabe was not his guy, but Casey didn't bother to correct her. When she got going like this, nothing would stop her. He just had to let her run out of steam or find a subject that was not Gabriel Karne and distract her with it.

"Greta, you've never met the man. When you do, you're going to hate him."

"I don't think I'm going to hate him. I think I already love him. Big Guy, Elton has accepted him. I'm not saying run off to Costa Rica together, I'm saying maybe see if there's something to explore, maybe you'll be surprised. And I didn't say you needed someone, I said you're protesting too much."

"Frankly, I'm surprised we're having this conversa—what the fuck?"

Something just down the road caught his attention, something that, if it was what he thought it was, would distract Greta from this awful conversation. She wasn't going to like it; Casey already didn't like it.

"What? What's going on?" she demanded.

Greta had taken an alternate route, one that led toward Westfort instead of through The Valley. She'd drawn the short stick and had to drive all the way into town and help Tor fill out the damned paperwork. The idiots had wisely chosen to ride with Tor, likely to avoid the rest of the lecture Greta was spoiling to give them.

"I dunno for sure. I'm going to hang up and call you back in a few."

"Casey, don't you dare!"

He peered into the dark past the truck's headlights, trying to parse out what he was almost sure he was seeing. Something that was unwelcome. Maybe, if he was lucky, it wouldn't be what he suspected, and he'd be able to continue on his merry way.

Luck rarely took Casey's side.

The glow intensified.

Dammit, it was midafternoon and only a month out from winter solstice, but it was close to dark in the east-facing valley. Even the creeping shadows had withdrawn into the surrounding forest. Or maybe it was that they'd swallowed it. Casey found that it was easy to get fanciful about the forest. With no streetlights and only a few outside lights, it was fucking dark. Except for that flicker every human was wary of.

"If you don't hear from me in twenty minutes, call the cavalry," he told Greta. "I'm about a half mile northeast of Gordon MacDonald's place and I'm seeing what looks like fire."

There were few structures on the north side of this fire road, not as high up The Valley as he was now. The only place he could imagine it being was Gordon's. If it hadn't been so damn dark, he might have spotted smoke first instead of the glow of flames, not that he would've been able to respond any faster. Thankfully, Gordon was on the mend and currently visiting some car-buddy friends in Skagit.

If it was his place, he was going to be devastated.

"Shit."

"Yeah. You know what? Put the call in for the water trucks anyway, and if it's nothing, I'll take the heat, ha, ha."

"I'm on it. Stay safe and call me back as soon as you can."

Casey knew the way down The Valley like the back of his hand, so even with the deepening dark, he hadn't been concerned about the drive home. A possible fire was not what he'd been anticipating this time of year, but at least the snow and rain had stopped for the time being.

Tapping the brakes, Casey eased the truck down a steep incline. The glow he'd seen disappeared, but only because the road curved to the south before again heading east and angling north. As soon as he was around the corner, he saw the blaze again.

"One damn switchback after another," Casey grumbled, downshifting to take yet another corner.

When he rounded the last curve before Gordon's place, the glow increased in intensity. Casey was certain that he was seeing an active fire. Which, considering just how wet everything was with the recent snow and rain, was remarkable.

"Arson, has to be," he muttered, wishing Greta was there and not miles away on a different road heading in a different direction.

He arrived at the access to Gordon's property and maneuvered the truck onto the road. Because of the emergency vehicles that had driven in and out after Dwayne's death, much of the brush and scrub had been beaten back. Branches did not scrape along the side of the truck as he bumped closer to the dancing light, and in that instant, he thought he saw a figure carrying something large dart behind the red-orange glow. But it happened too fast for him to be positive.

What he did know for sure was that the shed was engulfed in flames. For now, the stand of trees closest to the tiny structure did not appear to be involved, but if the wind changed, all bets were off.

Next to him, Casey's phone lit up, illuminating the cab with an eerie glow. Assuming it was Greta, he reached over and tapped the screen to accept the call. He'd just assure her everything was fine and see if she had an ETA for emergency services.

It was not his partner.

"Casey." Elton's voice boomed. "Elton here on Gabe's phone—Gabe's listening in too."

Dammit, he didn't have time to shoot the shit with Elton. Or Karne.

"Sorry, Elton, I was on my way back to your place, but now there's a situation up here in The Valley. A fire at Gordon's shack. But there could be something else, maybe," he spoke quickly. "The blaze is too big for a campfire and who the fuck would be burning brush this time of year? Gotta check it out."

He eased the truck to the side of the road so that it hugged the gravel drive and would be out of the way of the emergency vehicles, which were still miles away. Forty to forty-five minutes by Casey's estimate, no less than thirty.

A lot could go wrong in half an hour.

"Wait, Casey," Elton said, "this is important. We figured out who—"

Again, Casey thought he saw a figure on the other side of what once had been Gordon's shed, its outline darker than the shadows. Whoever it was definitely had a similar shape to Calvin, but he couldn't be positive.

"Sorry, Elton, I really can't talk." Without waiting for his reply, Casey tucked the phone away into his side pocket. Leaning over, he grabbed his service weapon out of the glove box and tucked it in his holster, then snagged the flashlight. If it was Calvin Perkins doing some kind of weird *Picnic at Hanging Rock* thing—thanks to Mickie for the reference and for making Casey watch some of the oddest movies ever made—he wasn't stupid enough to approach the man unarmed. Especially if it had been Calvin who'd attacked Carlos.

Whoever was out there had to have seen him arrive. Casey hadn't bothered trying to be sneaky, but it was likely they couldn't hear much over the pop and crackle of the burning wood and if they were under the influence of something, he'd deal with that once he assessed the situation.

Popping the door open, he hopped out and stood next to the truck for a second, adjusting to the cold after the warmth of the cab. If he was right and it was Perkins, instinct told him he didn't have long.

"Hello! This is Forest Ranger Casey Lundin. I've called emergency services!" he shouted as he crossed toward the flickering remains of the shed, deciding to leave the flashlight off for the moment. "What's going on? Is anyone injured?"

Over the years, he'd had to take a few continuing ed courses, and several had been on how to negotiate, but he'd never had to use them before. He remembered that it was good to try and start from the position of offering help rather than assuming people were breaking the law, even if you knew they were. Did it always work? No, but he might as well try. He waited for a count of ten, but there was no answer to his question.

"I'm approaching the structure. Make yourself known."

Nothing. But he saw movement again, a bit further away from the fire this time.

"Calvin Perkins, is that you out there?" He was glad to have the weighty flashlight in one hand—he did not want to draw his weapon.

Something was off about this. Instinct was telling him to take care. Not just the fire, which was obviously as wrong as the possible Calvin sighting, but Casey didn't know what that something was yet. He took a few more steps forward. Again, his instincts shrieked *NO*, but Casey forced his feet to step further away from his truck and toward the small inferno.

"Don't come any closer," a distant voice shouted. "One more step and you're done too."

Too? What the hell did that mean?

"Calvin, is that you? It's Casey, Casey Lundin, you know me. What's this all about? How can I help you?"

"Get out of here, Lundin." Calvin's voice was hoarse, as if he'd been shouting for hours, days maybe. Casey remembered what Carlos had told them, that his attacker had been a screaming wild man. "This is tainted land. This land killed my brother. My brother, man. *My brother.*"

Casey thought Perkins was trying to still scream, but the words were coming out in a rasp—his vocal cords were totally blown.

"It's gonna kill you too. It's killed before and it will kill again. So much killing."

Rambling was not a good sign, even for Calvin Perkins, who was not the sharpest tool and with whom Casey'd had plenty of run-ins over the years. This behavior did not bode well for talking him down before emergency services arrived.

Casey stopped moving, tucked his flashlight under one arm, and raised his hands slightly, facing his palms outward. If Calvin was paying attention, he'd see that Casey wasn't carrying a weapon. Not in his hands anyway.

"I'm sorry about what happened to your brother, I really am.

Tell me what's going on here. I can't help you if I don't know the facts."

"Facts," Calvin spat. "Nobody cares about facts. Nobody cares about anything. It's all lies. Dwayne and me, we just do what we're told and have a little fun on the side. But when something goes sideways, we're nothing. Less than nothing. It's all burning down, all of it!"

Calvin had moved again, and for a second, Casey could clearly see a partial silhouette of him. In the firelight, he looked like a beast, barely human, worse than someone who'd been living rough for weeks or even months. Backlit by the flames, he looked like the wild man Carlos had described. Then Calvin started moving, jumping around and flailing his arms, and Casey started to worry that he was under the influence of something. If he'd had something in his hands, Casey couldn't see it now.

The wooden roof of the shed crackled and popped, then fell inward in slow motion, sending sparks shooting up into the night sky. A different kind of stars and not ones that Casey was overly fond of. The one good thing about this weird-ass situation was that it had started to snow. At first, he'd assumed the flakes landing on his clothing were ashes, but it seemed that nature had a different plan.

Unfortunately, the wind also started to pick up. Even with the precipitation, it wouldn't take too much for the scraggly cedars growing just feet from what was left of the shed to catch and go up like poorly made candles.

"Calvin." Casey tried to reach him with words again, even though he figured it was a lost cause. He scrambled to come up with another tactic. "You started the fire? Why?"

With what he hoped looked like casual ease, Casey started moving to his right, around the outside of the fire, away from the still burning pile of lumber. He figured he maybe could catch Perkins by surprise and disable him.

"Dwayne died there. It's one of those things." Calvin stood still while he thought about his answer. "A pyre. I'm releasing his spirit, it's trapped in there."

Briefly, Casey shut his eyes. Seriously? Calvin Perkins was going to make Casey feel sorry for him? After all these years of despising the man and his dead brother almost more than anyone else on Heartstone?

"Gotcha." His laugh was maniacal, and the sound had Casey's eyes snapping open and his stomach clenching. "Dwayne would've hated that fucking woo-woo bullshit. I'm burning this whole place down because it's haunted. It needs to go. I'm done with this. Then I'll take care of the rest. I'll take care of it all, there'll be nothing left."

"Er, Calvin, seems to me you're going a bit too far. This isn't your property—" He wasn't going to get into a who-the-land-belonged-to conversation since Casey had strong pro-Indigenous opinions about land rights. "This is Gordon's place, and I think he's going to be sad that you've burned it down."

"Gordon? You mean that namby-pamby man-boy? Everybody is all *poor Gordon*. What about me? What about Dwayne?!"

Ah, there it was, the world-revolves-around-me argument. Calvin had probably managed to convince himself that Dwayne's death was Gordon's fault—not Deter Nolan's.

"For fuck's sake," he muttered.

Slowly, Casey continued to ease around the blaze, not wanting to alert Perkins, although the guy didn't seem to be paying attention to him. Was he alone? Where was his massive truck? Casey peered into the dark, his flashlight in his hand once again.

The fire snapped violently, sending more sparks upward,

and again Calvin was briefly visible—if anything, he looked worse than Casey's initial impression, his clothing ripped and shredded, barely holding together. And whatever Calvin had been carrying now sat on the ground not far enough from the flames, just an odd lumpy shape. *Shit.* What was it?

"I wouldn't come any closer if I was you, *Ranger*." The last word was said with a familiar Perkins-style sneer.

The snowfall began to thicken, and visibility was diminishing. Fat flakes swirled in the dark and wind—except in the radius of the fire. From far away, Casey thought he heard the call of a siren, but he couldn't be sure.

"They're here," Calvin whispered in a singsong voice, "and they're going to get you next. You really shouldn't be here, Lundin."

Well, *that* wasn't creepy at all, Calvin sounded like he'd been taking lessons from Jack Nicholson. "Who are you talking about?" It was a good thing Mickie had made Casey watch quirky horror-adjacent shows as a kid. *Salem's Lot* and the *Chuckie* remake had left an indelible impression on young Casey. He pulled out his Glock.

Behind him was a crunching sound, and it wasn't the fire consuming fuel. A twig? A footstep? Shit. Casey started to spin around, but it was too late. Something hard slammed against the side of his head. Dropping the flashlight, he stumbled forward, trying to pick his feet up so he didn't lurch closer to the flames.

"What the fuck!?"

Blinking away tears of pain, Casey swung his gun hand around, weapon out, as he spun to fend off the attack. But his assailant lunged again, kicking this time, and the booted foot smacked hard against Casey's wrist. His service weapon flew out of his grip into the dark, and Casey stumbled backward, trying to get a better look at the person in the flickering light.

Whoever it was appeared to be average size and was

bundled up in cold winter gear, a baclava covering most of their face. All he could distinguish were unremarkable eyebrows that were just a dark slash above the fabric.

Casey was at a distinct disadvantage, reeling from the blow to the head, his weapon and flashlight out of reach. He was glad that at least he'd had the hood of his jacket pulled up over his toque. It had provided a small amount of protection, but he didn't know if he was bleeding or not.

"Stand down," he shouted, automatically raising his arms to protect himself. "I'm an officer of the law!"

His back was to Perkins now, and any second he expected Calvin to start raining blows on him. Casey had to assume these two were working together. The knock to his head was making him feel slightly nauseous, which was not good.

When is a head injury good, Casey?

The attacker remained silent and didn't back away. Instead, they moved into Casey's space, and with one shoulder dipped forward, they charged him. They were moving fast, and he'd already been caught off guard once and was now slightly dizzy.

He wobbled and lost his balance, landing on the frozen ground, a pained grunt escaping him. Casey's already tender skull banged against an exposed rock, or maybe just frozen earth, and he saw stars.

He struggled to stand up, but his head was throbbing. Instead, he grappled for the attacker's pant leg but couldn't get a good hold on the fabric because his fingers were too cold.

Greta was going to kill him.

They roughly pushed him onto his front and held him down with a foot on his back while they fastened something—zip ties, maybe—around his wrists so he was effectively immobilized.

All without a word.

What the fuck? Again, he heard the wail of a siren—closer now, but still not close enough. Whatever was going down, the responders weren't going to arrive in time to help him. Worse, Calvin had gone eerily silent too. Where was he? Had he fled the scene, or was he in cahoots with whoever this was?

A heavy-booted foot slammed into his ribs not once but twice. Crying out, Casey tried to curl up, to protect himself, but it was no good.

Everything hurt, and he shut his eyes for just a second.

EIGHTEEN

Gabriel

Wednesday evening

"HERE." Elton held his keys out to Gabe. "You drive."

Gabe accepted them with a raised eyebrow—two could play that game—and veered to the driver's side, wondering what had brought on the change of heart.

They'd exited the post office, having dropped off Kelly Perkins's mountain of boxes, much to the chagrin of the man behind the counter. Gabe was itching to know what she bought and sold while also actively realizing that probably he didn't want to know at all. He decided to imagine that she traded in rare Beanie Babies or Furbies.

Conveniently, the store of oddities that doubled as the island's post office carried a few cheap cell phones among its stock of inexplicably obscure hand tools, plastic beach toys, puzzles, and barbecue supplies. Who would've guessed? This was the best-kept secret on Heartstone, and Gabe had immediately set about picking a phone out for himself and getting it set up. When Elton hadn't been paying attention, Gabe had added a second phone for him but left it in the packaging for now. They could argue about it later.

"Gimme that phone. We need to talk to Casey a-sap and I have his number memorized," Elton said once he was settled in the passenger seat.

Case in point.

With a shake of his head, Gabe handed over the phone he'd activated.

"DRIVE FASTER," Elton demanded. He had his left hand tucked underneath his thigh, almost as if he was resisting the urge to shove Gabe out of the way and grab the wheel.

"Old man, I'm driving as fast as I fucking can. This may come as a shock to you, but Wheel Man has never been my specialty. Not once."

"I didn't get a chance to tell Casey what Kelly told us about Snowcap," Elton grumbled, continuing to hold the phone to his ear. "We're still connected, I'm not hanging up."

"Hanging up," Gabe teased, trying to lighten the mood. "We aren't living in the eighties anymore."

Sure, Casey had intended to click off, but he hadn't.

"He must have been distracted and slid his phone into his pocket and—"

"And we're eavesdropping on the longest butt dial in the history of butt dials."

It wasn't a butt dial, but he couldn't think of what else to call it.

And, Gabe reasoned, neither of them liked what they were hearing.

The connection wasn't particularly clear, and a couple of

times Elton claimed they'd lost the connection only to hear Casey's voice again after a few seconds. What they were listening to was fucking disturbing, and it was taking too long to bump their way up the road to where they assumed Casey was. When Gabe jammed his foot down on the accelerator, the truck's engine screamed in protest. The steep, winding, pothole-filled roadway was not designed for fifty miles an hour, and he was not one of the Fast and Furious guys.

"Dammit, I can't hear anything again. I think we lost 'em."

He was focused on the road, but Gabe still saw Elton jab a gnarled finger against the cell phone's screen with vigor.

"Don't break that thing. It's the third one I've bought in less than a month, I'm not made of money."

"We need to go faster."

"Seriously, Elton, I'm driving as fast as I can. The last thing we need is a breakdown or worse. Then we'd be the ones who'd have to call someone to come get us out of a jam."

Since when had Gabe become the voice of reason?

"No, I hear 'em again. Sounds like Calvin has finally lost his tenuous grip on reality. Goddammit!" With his focus one hundred percent on the road, Gabe imagined Elton was pressing the phone against his ear as if that might make it easier to hear what was being said, even though Casey was already on speaker. And did they really need to hear what was being said at this point anyway?

Habit had Gabe glancing at the rearview mirror as they bounced along. Red lights flashed in and out behind them.

"Hey, I think there are cops or some kind of emergency vehicle behind us."

Elton twisted around to peer out the back window. "Fire truck, I'd say. That glow we're seeing must be fire." He turned back around, his profile tense. "We're getting close to Gordon's place. Drive faster," he repeated. "Old Bessie can handle it."

Gabe pressed harder on the gas pedal and the truck lurched forward again, the Snowcap Estates sign appearing and disappearing.

"Old Bessie? Really?"

Not the time to get distracted, Chance.

"No, but I had to give her a name just now."

It had started snowing when the road turned from county to Forest Service and thus paved to dirt and rocks. It wasn't sticking, not yet. But it was falling faster now and the tiny blizzards in the truck's headlights made it hard for him to see the road or anything else. Gabe's grip on the steering wheel was tight enough that he knew his hands were going to hurt tomorrow.

They had to get to Casey in time. Ranger Man was not made of steel.

Elton pointed. "There it is, the turn."

Slowing back down to a crawl, he wrestled the truck past a boulder and a tree stump and onto the access road. It wasn't that late, but everything looked different in the winter's early dark. If Elton hadn't been there, he would've missed the turn.

His head hit the roof of the cab. "Fucking fuckery."

The sense of urgency was stifling. Gabe was scared for Ranger Man—he was more than scared, he was terrified. If Casey was in trouble, or the fire was out of control, what could Gabe and an eighty-year-old man do? They weren't firefighters or cops, and as far as Gabe knew, they had no weapons. Although he wouldn't put it past Elton to have a gun stashed somewhere in the truck. Gabe wasn't terribly worried about his safety, but if Elton got hurt on his watch—or worse—he'd have to move to Siberia or Mars. And even Mars might not be far enough.

But he was also painfully aware that nothing and no one was going to stop Elton from racing to Casey's assistance. Or

Gabe, for that matter. Which meant what? Casey didn't even like him.

Really, Chance, cons shouldn't try and con themselves.

"I see taillights," Elton whispered.

"Why are you whispering?"

Elton ignored him. "That's Casey's. Pull in behind it."

Gabe did not point out that he was perfectly aware the Wagoneer was Casey's.

"Now what?"

"Now we figure out what the hell is going on. Leave the headlights on so we can see what we're doing." Twisting to reach underneath the truck's bench seat, Elton pulled out a battered tire iron. The thing had to be an antique—just like Elton. "There's a pipe wrench in the toolbox in back. And we have Bowie."

At the appearance of the ancient tool, Gabe winced. Dammit, he should've convinced Elton to stay at home. He sighed; the attempt would've been unsuccessful. That was his final thought on the matter, and he was sticking to it. There was no turning back now.

Gabe turned around and eyed the dog in the back seat. He'd been quiet for most of the drive, but now that they were stopped, he'd popped up on all fours with a low whine. Bowie knew something wasn't right. His doggy expression was serious and intense as if to say *My person needs me.* Staring back at Gabriel, he released a little huff of impatience and stomped his feet.

"Right. Okay, there are *three* of us. I stand corrected. Let's do this. But when it's done, we're going to have to come up with nicknames for our crime-fighting gang. And maybe Keith wants to be a part of it too."

He opened the door, not expecting Bowie to leap over the seat and his lap and dash into the darkness. The headlights and the flickering glow from the remains of Gordon's shed hardly made a difference. Had Gabe ever experienced dark like this? An almost complete lack of light? He didn't think so.

"Dammit, Ranger Man is going to kill me with his bare hands."

And Gabe would let him if bare hands meant that Casey Lundin was alive and uninjured.

"He'll find Casey," Elton said as he eased himself off the seat and down to the ground, the tire iron gripped in one hand.

Trying to imagine Elton actually whacking someone with the tool—and failing—Gabe fished around in the truck bed's toolbox for the wrench. He would be the one to do any necessary thrashing. It was a big one, around two feet long, and weighed maybe three pounds. If he walloped someone with it, they weren't going anywhere, for a little while anyway.

"Okay, let's do this."

Was he nervous? Fuck, yes. Running cons and grifting marks seldom required violence. Gabe wasn't a violent person, having learned early that force rarely achieved the desired results. Which, thinking about it, was why he was in this situation—maybe the Colavitos would have left him alone if he'd responded with violence instead of running.

But neither Larry nor his idiot nephews were in The Valley. This situation had nothing to do with Seattle. Even Gabriel couldn't imagine a scenario in which the family were at all involved with Rizzi's game. He and Elton were sure it had to be Rizzi, and perhaps some unknown partners, someone like Spurring, who were behind recent events. They hadn't yet come to a conclusion as to the exact reasons why Dwayne had been killed, Deputy Nolan assassinated, and Peter murdered, but the eight-ball had been queried and it had indicated *signs point to yes* when it came to Sheriff Eli Rizzi.

The driving force, the main theme, had to be money, of

course. Greed and money. Or power. But likely all of the above. When tonight was in the bag, they could all work together figuring which combination of the three it was.

It's always money, Chance. Follow the money. Power and greed follow the cash.

For once, Gabriel wished his inner Heidi was wrong.

THE FIRE APPEARED to be dying out. However, it proved too soon to think that as they slowly approached what had once been Gordon's shed. Something major shifted in the center, and the conflagration whoofed and snapped as it was fed new fuel. A plume of flame and sparks shot upward, lighting up the area around the blaze. Embers caught in one of the lurking trees and began to smolder.

"Fuck, that is not good," Gabe said, watching the flames start to crawl up the tree.

"A water truck is on the way. We need to focus on finding Casey and Bowie."

Right, focus on finding Casey.

Stopping well away from the flames, Gabe peered around, hoping to see Casey or the dog, but neither were visible.

"Casey," Elton called out. He had the tire iron up and ready; he must have been formidable when he was younger. Hell, he was formidable now.

There was no answer to Elton's call. Gabe stopped walking for a moment, thinking he'd heard something, just not words. He walked faster, heading into the dark.

There was a crash followed by the sound of quick footsteps, but they were moving away, not coming closer.

"Someone's out there! Casey!" Elton yelled again, and—again—got no answer.

But then, maybe, a groan.

Gabe never would've expected Elton to move that fast, but the old man did.

Whoever else was out there wasn't trying to be quiet as they stumbled through the brush and brambles that grew after clear cuts. A few muttered curses and grunts and then silence. Did they have a vehicle? Casey's truck was the only car Gabe had seen.

Bowie yipped: *Get over here already!* Gabe quickened his pace, wary of the uneven terrain, the wrench a comforting weight in his hand. A just-in-case weapon. He didn't make it far before spotting Bowie and a still form on the ground. His heart rose in his throat, nearly choking him.

Scratch that, *not* still. Casey rolled onto his side, a groan escaping him as he forced himself to a sitting position. Bowie was wagging and bumping against him, the doggy version of *Jesus Christ, you scared the fuck out of me.*

And me too. But Gabe wasn't about to say that out loud.

"Ranger Man, you scared the crap out of us."

Or maybe he was.

A large silver flashlight lay a few feet from Casey, its fading beam spearing the dark beyond him. Grabbing it off the ground, Gabe shone the light over him and had to stop himself from gasping.

"Your head's going to hurt in the morning." Gabe had to force himself not to pat him down, to prove to all of them that he was alive and breathing. "Do not get up."

Remarkably, Casey stayed seated, which only meant that he was in real pain. Bowie sat on his haunches next to him, his furry body pressed against Casey's larger one. Gabe glanced at Elton, whose expression said the person who got away was damn lucky. Probably matched Gabe's.

Gabe blinked at the sight of the blood trickling down the side of Casey's face and into his beard. Goose bumps popped up over his entire body, and a rage he'd never experienced began to crawl through his veins. He'd never understood the phrase *seeing red*. He did now.

"I'm okay, I'm okay," Casey insisted. "Head wounds bleed, we all know that. Hurts, but I'm okay, not seeing double."

"How can that mean you're okay?" Gabe wanted to know. "It's fucking dark out."

"What happened?" Elton asked. "Who attacked you?"

"Asshole caught me by surprise. Snuck up on me, didn't they?" Casey shifted to his knees and twisted around, looking for something or someone. "Is Perkins still hanging around? It wasn't him who hit me," he was quick to add.

Gabe couldn't begin to process the thundercloud of emotion that was close to choking him. He simultaneously wanted to beat the living daylights out of whoever had done this and wrap Casey up in cotton. So, like a normal male person, he ignored it. Wasn't easy.

"Who was it?" Elton repeated. "Did you get a look at them at all?" He put his hand on Gabe's shoulder and squeezed it, as if he somehow realized Gabe was a heartbeat away from losing his shit.

"Dunno," Casey mumbled, rolling his neck. "Never got a good look at them and they didn't give me their name."

With a grunt, Gabe knelt in the muddy snow next to Casey, ignoring the pounding of his heart. The panicked thumps had zero to do with adrenaline and everything to do with Casey's irritating self, which, regardless of his personality, had managed to become important to Gabe. With care, Gabe eased the hood of Casey's coat off his head and removed the wool cap he wore.

"Con man and EMT? That's quite a skill set."

"Fuck off," Gabe said mildly. The reality was, if Casey could snark, he wasn't on death's doorstep. Gabe's heartbeat slowed to a reasonable pace. "I'll have you know, I'm qualified.

Mom bought me a doctor's kit for my eighth birthday. Definitely qualified enough to say you are one lucky fucker. That hideous hat must've absorbed a lot of the impact."

"My toque was given to me by a friend."

"A friend with no fashion sense."

"I work for the Forest Service, not *GQ*."

"Focus, you two," Elton interjected. "What do you think you were hit with?"

"Whatever it was, it was hard and heavy. Maybe firewood, a branch, something like that. Did you see Perkins?" he asked again.

"No. Did you see him, Elton?" Gabe pushed to his feet and glanced around. Still dark, still nothing that he could see. Only the pile of snapping embers that had once been Gordon's shed, and the single tree that had caught.

"Nope. But the fire truck's finally made it."

Elton gestured toward the Forest Service water truck that had rumbled past Casey and Elton's vehicles and parked as close to what remained of the fire as they could get. Two people in full gear jumped out and presumably began to drag hoses from the tank toward the blaze.

"I had Greta call it in. Help me up." Casey had one hand raised Gabe's direction.

"No."

"Gabriel," Casey said with a sigh, lowering his hand. "Calvin had something with him—I didn't see what it was before the attack. Is it still over there?" He pointed generally toward the emergency responders. "Kind of to the right, I think. If it's still there, I want to know what it is before it gets hosed off."

"I'm on it." Gabe gingerly made his way to the spot Casey had indicated. Elton could watch over Casey.

Sure enough, there was something sitting on the ground twenty or so feet away from the flames.

"It's still here," he called back to Casey. "Should I be worried? This is Perkins, after all."

"Just—can you grab it and bring it over here?"

Rolling his eyes, Gabe darted around the spray of water from the fire hose as the responders doused the cedar tree. Hoisting the black bag off the ground, Gabe carried it back to where Elton and Casey were impatiently waiting.

Whatever was encased in the black plastic bag wasn't excessively heavy. The bag itself had been wrapped with what appeared to be silver duct tape, but the adhesive had dried and cracked so it no longer stuck to the plastic.

"What do you think's inside?" he asked as he set the bag down again.

"Dunno. I think we're going to have to open it to find out. You got a knife in your pocket, Elton?"

Gabe couldn't read Casey and Elton's thoughts, but technically, they were disturbing a crime scene. But no one had come to check on them yet, so was it an official crime scene? And who knew what side the cops were on in this scenario. Gabe's experience thus far did not have him rushing to put his trust in the TCSO.

Elton stuck a hand in his pants pocket and brought out a penknife with a bone handle. "Always prepared."

It seemed there were some ethical lines Ranger Man would cross. Noted.

Flicking open the knife, Elton bent down and swiped at the tape a few times. Casey held the flashlight so Elton could see what he was doing. The ancient plastic bag began to fall apart on its own, and Gabe reached down to tug it further open.

"This is like when Geraldo Rivera was opening Capone's safe."

"It's not."

"Not a speck of romance in your soul."

"There was nothing romantic about Al Capone. He was a vicious killer."

Gabe had a clever retort ready, but the bag was fully open now.

"What is that? A backpack?" he asked. "Why would Calvin have a backpack in a bag?"

It looked old, at least to Gabe, who was not an expert on outdoor gear. The brand was North Face, which he did know was fairly pricey. A tag attached to a rusty beaded chain hung from one strap. Gabe flipped it over in case there was a name on it.

"What does it say? Whose was it?" There was something in Casey's tone that had the hair on Gabe's forearms rising and the goose bumps returning.

The ink was faded but not so much he couldn't read what had been written there. *"Property of Suzie Warner.* There's a phone number, address too." Gabe looked at Casey and then Elton. "On Heartstone."

NINETEEN

Casey

Wednesday night

ONE OF THE two emergency responders half-heartedly tried to get Casey to go to the hospital and get his head checked out.

"Jeremiah, I'm good to go, just like I told these guys." He gestured toward Elton and Gabriel. "I'm fine. My head hurts and I won't be able to brush my hair for a few days." He shrugged. "But I'm okay."

"I don't want to get in trouble with Greta."

"I'll cover for you if something goes awry. Everything good here?"

Jeremiah didn't look convinced by Casey's argument but all he said was, "Yep, we got it all. A few of the lower branches of that tree didn't make it. All in all, it's a good thing you had Greta call us in. It probably would have burned itself out without doing much more damage, but you never know, do you?"

"Thanks for coming out."

"Yeah, sure, hope not to see you soon." Picking up his first aid kit, Jeremiah sketched a wave and ambled back the direction he'd come, heading for the water truck and his partner, who was finishing putting the hoses and whatnot away.

"We're all freezing," Gabe announced, "and you're not driving, so here's the dealio. I can drive your truck and you can ride shotgun with me, or I can drive your truck and you can ride with Elton."

Going by the expression on both their faces, Casey knew he wasn't going to be able to pitch that he could drive perfectly well. Elton may have been as old as the hills, but he knew the road better than anyone. Charming Fucker, on the other hand?

"My place," Elton said, his tone uncompromising. "In fact, I'm transporting this."

With that, Elton picked up the backpack and started for his truck, not sticking around for the argument.

Casey caught Gabe's amused glance and shook his head—then winced, regretting the move. "I guess there's no debating with him."

"TELL ME ABOUT THAT PACK. Why did you look like you'd seen a ghost?"

Gabe was doing his best to avoid the worst sections of the roadway, but Casey's head throbbed, and he sort of wanted to vomit every time they hit a bump. But not as intensely as when Gabe had read Suzie Warner's name off that tag.

"Suzie Warner is a ghost. I mean, if we're finding her backpack up here after she's been missing for twenty years." He paused as he tried to think back and come up with a timeline.

"Keep talking, Ranger Man. Do not go silent on me now."

"It's just, she was supposed to have left on a hiking trip, and as far as I know, her family has always believed something happened to her on the trail, not close to home. Sorry, my memory is muddled because this all happened around the same time Maya Crane was murdered. I was fourteen and the only thing I was focused on was my brother and the fact that no one would listen to me when I told them I'd seen Maya alive after everyone else claimed they had. They thought I was covering for him."

"But you weren't, of course you weren't. What happened with this Suzie person?"

Casey shrugged again, and pain made him regret the movement. He hadn't thought about Suzie Warner in years, not since she'd left the island.

"Elton probably remembers better than I do. Suzie had graduated from high school and planned to hike around before starting college. No, that's not right. She decided she didn't want to go to school, at least not right away. Her plan was to hike, maybe the Pacific Crest Trail? And then—well, I don't know if she had much of a plan after that."

Casey tried to think of what else he remembered from that time. The headache was not helping.

"Honestly, there aren't many other details coming to mind. It seems like she was just gone and never heard from again. It's not as if people, especially women, don't disappear on a daily basis."

"Her parents thought she left the island?"

"I think so, yes. No one ever saw or heard from her again."

"And yet the pack would indicate that she did not."

"Yep," Casey said to his reflection in the passenger window. "It would seem that she did not."

"YOUR PLACE IS STARTING HAVE that special Batcave

feel to it, Elton. All we need is a bank of computers, an elegant butler, and maybe a fancy cologne."

Elton had forced Casey to lay back in his recliner.

"Stay still while I clean this up again. That kid up there did a half-ass job. Pfft."

"Is it half-ass or half-assed?"

"Gabriel," Casey sighed. It had been a fucking long day.

Gabe stopped pacing to stand at Casey's feet.

"Deal with it," he said. "Humor is a coping mechanism I can afford, a bottle of whiskey is one I cannot." Gabriel had his hands jammed deep into his jeans pockets, as if he was just barely holding himself together. They hadn't spoken much after Casey had shared what little he knew about Suzie. The rest of the drive had been silent. A quiet Charming Fucker was unnerving.

"What do you remember about Suzie Warner, Elton?" Casey asked, wincing as Elton swiped the cut on his hairline with hydrogen peroxide.

"I think it was a few months before the Warners began to worry that something had happened to her. As I recall, they eventually hired someone to retrace her steps, but there was no sign of her."

"Because she never made it to the trail and no one was looking in this neck of the woods because she wasn't supposed to be here."

They were silent, the hum of the refrigerator seeming to expand and fill the quiet along with their own breathing. What the fuck had happened and why was it coming to light now? Bowie was curled up at the base of the recliner, clearly not letting Casey out of his sight. The cat had even emerged and was perched on the windowsill, supervising the goings-on.

"What do we do with her bag?" Gabe asked. "It's not a body, it doesn't prove anything. She could have changed her mind, left town with someone else. We all know that's not true, but—"

"Two girls, one dead, one assumed dead, presumably within days of each other ..." Casey winced again. "Knock it off, Elton, the cut hurts more now than it did when it happened."

With a sigh, Elton paused his aggressive cleaning and set the cotton swabs and antibiotics down on his side table. Casey released a quiet sigh of relief.

It was Gabe who sucked in a long breath, stared at them intently for a long moment, and then said the thing they had to all have been thinking.

"What if the backpack isn't the only thing up there?" His hands landed on top of his head as if he was trying to keep all his thoughts inside his skull but they were escaping against his will anyway. "Think about it. The business with Gordon getting busted earlier in the year, which kept him out of the loop, then Silent Bob—Dwayne Perkins, I mean—and now finding this. Smacks of somebody trying to keep something hidden. Maybe more than a backpack."

"That thought did cross my mind," Elton said, turning and heading toward his kitchen. "Whatever they're hiding, it has to do with Gordon's property, Snowcap Estates, or both. I'm heating up some soup for us."

Since it was a statement and not a question, Casey kept his mouth shut. Elton was in mother-hen mode, and nothing was going to stop him. And he was also starving.

"Yeah, Snowcap Estates. Let's assume that something happened to Suzie Warner before she left for her hiking trip, something bad." Gabe walked toward the hallway, then turned around and headed back toward the kitchen as he thought out loud. "It's a bad thing, she's dead. The murderer takes her remains up"—he waved—"that way. And her pack too? No.

Seems more likely she was killed there. That would make more sense."

"Panicked and then what?" Elton said from his spot at the stove. "But we don't know that Suzie was ever up The Valley."

"Stands to reason, though, doesn't it? She wouldn't be parted from her backpack. It would've had everything she needed in it."

Casey's headache was diminishing now that Elton wasn't scraping the skin off his skull, and he thought Gabe had the right idea. Which, considering the source, made Casey grimace.

Gabriel Karne was a bit like an escaped ping-pong ball that Casey couldn't quite grab a hold of, but he wasn't stupid. He encouraged people to think he was flighty and a mess, and no doubt it helped when the man had his Charming Fucker act going. But he was smart, aware, and had good instincts. Sexy.

Dammit again.

"It stands to reason," Casey reluctantly agreed.

Gabriel blinked and his eyebrows rose toward his hairline.

"It does," Casey said, knowing he sounded mildly defensive. "I think it's fairly safe for us to assume that Suzie Warner and her backpack made it up The Valley together, one way or another. Could be she was lured up there, maybe she was dead already."

A long-buried memory from the one and only time he'd attended the senior bonfire popped into his head. He hadn't thought about the celebration in years, maybe not since that night, because of what happened afterward.

"What?" demanded Gabe, his eyes narrowed. "What are you thinking?"

"I'm not sure. All this happened a long time ago." He could hear Elton shuffling around, getting out bowls and spoons. "It's possible Suzie might have disappeared the same night that Maya was murdered. Did anyone see her after the bonfire? Would anyone on Heartstone have known to look for her?"

Casey and his family had been too wrapped up with Mickie being arrested and accused of Maya's murder for him to remember much of anything else.

Elton returned with two bowls. Steam rose off the hot soup, and once again Casey realized just how hungry he was. "Not homemade, but we won't go to bed hungry," Elton said, handing each of them a bowl before returning for his own.

"I don't think anyone would have known to look for Suzie Warner," Elton said as he sat down on the couch, his bowl cupped in his hands. "But there is someone we can ask."

"Mercy," said Casey, nodding.

"Mercy?" Gabe parroted.

"Mercy Dawson," Elton confirmed. "She owns the store and is Suzie Warner's sister."

"Whoa." Gabe set his spoon back into his soup. "Whoa, we can't just willy-nilly go asking people. What if we're wrong? As reluctant as I am to actually talk to cops, that's what we need to do."

Casey ignored him, forcing himself to think back to the night of the bonfire while he spooned just-hot-enough chicken soup into his mouth. As an incoming high school freshman, he'd been an outlier and very nervous about getting in trouble with his parents. As it turned out, his parents never learned he'd been at the beach that night. Maya's death had eclipsed everything.

All the older island kids had been there, including Calvin and Dwayne Perkins. Even Gordon MacDonald, who hadn't been in high school yet either. And Greta, of course.

"Greta." He set his empty bowl down and shoved his hand into his side pocket, searching for his cell. When he pulled it out, the damn thing was dead. "Shit."

"Yeah, you forgot to end the call—that's how we were able to hear the fuckery that was going on. Not an experience I want to repeat, thank you very much." Gabe's cheeks reddened and he avoided eye contact with Casey, as if he'd unintentionally admitted ... *something*.

Huh.

"Here, use mine." Elton handed over the cordless receiver to his landline.

Dismissing thoughts of Charming Fucker in any capacity other than irritating neighbor, Casey quickly punched in Greta's number and put her on speaker.

"Elton!" she exclaimed. "Do you know if Casey is okay? I've been trying to reach him since I got back from Westfort, and his phone keeps going to voicemail. I know the fire was put out up there because I talked to Jeremiah, who told me he'd been hurt. Attacked? When I get my hands on him, I'm going to kill him. If he's dead already, I'm going to revive him and kill him again!"

"Greta—" Casey tried.

"I very clearly told him to call and let me know he was okay —wait, what? Casey? That you? You okay?"

"Yeah, a few bumps and bruises, but I'll be fine. Look, before you kill me, we have a question for you. It's about the senior bonfire the year Maya Crane was murdered. You're on speaker. Gabriel and Elton are here too."

Casey could picture Greta changing gears from full-on pissed off and scared to curious.

"Okay, sure, I'm intrigued."

"You knew Suzie Warner, right?"

"Suzie Warner," she repeated. "Now that's a name I haven't heard in years. I knew her well enough, I suppose. She was a couple of years older than me. You know how it is in high school. Heaven forbid you associate with underclassmen. But yeah, I knew her."

"Think back. Can you remember if she was seen after the party? Did she have plans to leave the island right away?"

There was silence while Greta thought back two decades.

"I don't have a steel-trap memory like you do, Casey. But I don't recall seeing her around. I mean, she was saying her good-byes at that party, so one would assume she was at least leaving soon. Why?"

Casey looked at Gabe and Elton, his eyebrows raised. Were they telling Greta what they'd found? They both nodded.

"We found her backpack tonight, on Gordon's property."

She was silent for a heartbeat. "The fuck you did."

"The fuck we did. Calvin Perkins was there, admitted to setting tonight's fire. Something to do with his brother, but honestly, I don't think that detail matters. But he had the pack, or he found it there, or something along those lines. I don't know if he was planning on trying to burn it too or what. He may not have had a plan. Before I could learn more, someone attacked me—hit me on the head pretty good—and now Calvin is in the wind again. And so is whoever whacked me."

"Damn."

"Yeah, the attacker disappeared when Gabriel and Elton showed up. They ended up leaving the pack behind."

"And you're sure it's Suzie's?"

"There's a tag attached with her name on it. We haven't opened it. The less we screw around with it, the better."

"Are you planning on taking it to the sheriff?" she asked carefully. Greta was fully aware of Casey's innate distrust of the Twana County Sheriff's Office. And of Sheriff Rizzi in particular.

"We haven't talked next steps yet."

Turning the bag in was the right thing to do, but sometimes the obvious right thing was all wrong. Casey was thinking that the Westfort PD would be the better choice. Technically, the sheriff had jurisdiction over the entire county, which included The Valley, but Casey didn't want Rizzi getting his hands on the bag too soon. Too easy for it to get "lost." It wouldn't be the first piece of evidence to conveniently go missing.

"This is going to blow up the island," Greta eventually said.

"There's more," Elton interjected.

Casey cut over to him, surprised. What else could there be, wasn't finding a missing girl's backpack where it wasn't supposed to be enough? Shit, it had been a long day. It was almost—he glanced down at his watch—nine p.m., but it felt closer to midnight. Or he was getting old.

"What is it?" Greta asked.

"Remember how John Stevens was here earlier? That's what we were calling you about, Casey, to go over what he said and what Kelly Perkins told us when we stopped by her place."

Elton started speaking and when he was done, Casey was ready to tear somebody's head off, starting off with Stevens and ending with Rizzi. Twenty years ago, no one had believed him, and it was because the sheriff and the prosecutor had a deal.

"Holy fuck," muttered Greta.

"But who killed Peter and why?" Gabe asked. "Not to make it about me or anything, but Peter is the most recently murdered person. His death fits in with all this somehow, but he would've left Heartstone before Suzie Warner's or Maya's deaths, right? Which means that Stevens is a key player here because that's the only way Peter relates to all this. He prosecuted your brother, right? Using evidence provided by the sheriff, with whom Stevens was in a partnership?"

"I cannot wait to meet you in person, Gabriel," said Greta. "You're thinking Rizzi had—has—Stevens by the balls, and I totally agree. Fast forward twenty years, his son's murder changes everything, and now Stevens regrets his entire life, as he fucking should. Now what?"

"I'm guessing Stevens is telling the truth about wanting to reconnect with his son. He tried to end, or at least retire from, the agreement, and Vale's death was the result." That was Elton.

"He admitted that Peter got a look at some documents," Gabe said. "Maybe Peter saw something or maybe Stevens said something to him that tipped him off. I guess we'll never know. Did Peter confront Rizzi? Did he go up to see what Snowcap Estates was and, I dunno, end up seeing something he shouldn't have?"

Casey eyed Gabe. He suspected that, had Gabe been in Peter's situation, he would have snooped around.

"If he did drive up there, he could have run into Rizzi or whoever else is part of the investment group," Casey said. "Maybe he wasn't killed on purpose, but they"—now he used finger quotes—"decided to leave his body at the marina as a message to Stevens."

"Why not at Stevens's house?" Gabe asked.

"Stevens doesn't live on the island anymore. It would be a bit of a drive with a dead body in the back of a car," Elton pointed out.

Casey scowled at no one in particular. "Not if you're the sheriff."

"We know that Stevens ultimately was the owner of the *Shangri-La*, so killing Vale and dumping his body there was a message."

"A direct threat, I'd say." Greta said. She'd been silent for so long he'd almost forgotten she was on the line.

"Still can't figure out why they came back and firebombed the *Ticket* as well as the *Shangri-La*."

Gabe had returned to pacing between the kitchen and the hallway, his hands clasped over the top of his head as they brainstormed. Casey felt a sharp ping in the center of his chest —like the pull of a muscle that hadn't been used much before now—

that he was starting to realize had everything to do with Charming. He felt a bit dizzy, and it had nothing to do with the knock on his head.

"*If* it was the same person." Greta sounded thoughtful. "But who else would it be?"

"There's coincidence and then there's the ridiculous," Casey said, struggling to his feet. He had to move even if every cell in his body screamed for him to sit his ass back down. "For now, we assume it was the same perp. They must've thought Gabe saw or heard something he shouldn't have."

He looked over at Gabe, a complicated expression flitting across his face as he watched Casey try, and fail, to hide the pain he was in. His ribs weren't broken, but there was going to be a hell of a bruise.

"Maybe they didn't expect you back so soon, or at all," Casey continued. "Who besides Elton and me knew for sure that you were living there? If Keith-the-cat hadn't alerted you, maybe the arsonists would have torched *The Barbara* too. Did Vale know you were living aboard? Or did he assume that I could find you because of what my friend Marlene told him?"

"My bet is Peter didn't know I was living there and just figured you might know where I was if you were asking about me. He was always good at recon."

They were all quiet now as they realized just how narrowly Gabriel and Casey had avoided serious injury or death. Casey winced as he moved slightly, reminding himself that he hadn't avoided getting hurt entirely.

"Well, what are we doing now?" asked Greta.

"Nothing tonight, but tomorrow we ride," said Gabe. "Or something like that anyway. I'll drive Casey and Bowie back to the marina—and don't argue with me, Ranger Man, I'm not having it tonight."

"*Ranger Man*," Greta repeated, laughing, although she tried to hide it with a cough.

The call ended with a promise they'd touch base first thing.

Casey released the groan he'd been holding back since Gabe mentioned the marina.

"What?" Gabe asked as he collected the now empty bowls and walked them into the kitchen, rinsed them out, and set them on the counter. "What else could there possibly be?"

"As far as I know, the pier hasn't been cleared yet. And even if it was declared safe, *The Barbara* is still out in the middle of the bay. I'll admit it, rowing out there tonight is not on my top ten list."

Gabe stepped back into the living room just as Elton was pushing himself to his feet again. "It's been a day, and this old man is going to bed. There's the spare room. You can share the bed in there, or one of you can take the couch. Bicker quietly, please. I, for one, would like a decent night's sleep."

He shuffled off and disappeared down the hallway. First Gabe, then Casey glanced at the couch. The piece of furniture was hardly big enough to earn the name. It wasn't long enough for Elton to lie on, much less either of them.

"I'll take the recliner, you can take the bed," Gabe said, his expression as grim as if he'd offered to throw himself into a pit of hungry lions. "The recliner is—no offense—Elton-shaped and lumpy. I think you might end up in more pain."

Casey already regretted the time he'd just spent on it; it felt like a violation of Elton's personal space, and it'd done his aches and pains no favors. However—

"It's not a big deal. I'll take the recliner." Casey was resigned to not getting much, if any, sleep anyway. He could always drop to the floor once Gabe left the room.

"Seriously, it's fine. I'll take it."

"I said quietly," Elton called out, his voice muffled by walls and a shut door. "Just share the damn bed, it won't kill you. Spare blankets are in the hall closet if you need more than what's there."

"I don't know, it might kill one of us," Gabe muttered darkly.

Common sense fled.

Now Casey wanted to prove to Gabriel and Elton that it really was no big deal if they shared a bed. They were adults. Sharing a bed didn't mean they'd jump each other's bones. He shook his head—which, again, hurt—because that was not what he wanted to be thinking about.

Even if that's exactly what had crossed his mind.

Considering just how long it had been since he'd been remotely intrigued by someone, that someone being Charming Fucker was a head-shaker in and of itself. It wasn't being gay in a fucked-up lumberjack-man's world—although that did play a small part—it was merely the way Casey was built. It was easier and less difficult to be alone. Trust did not come easily to him, and attraction was complicated.

Gabriel Karne it was not the one to make it easier.

Another thought intruded; Greta could never know this happened. If she did, he would never be able to convince her that there was nothing going on between them.

Did he want nothing?

Casey threw out, "Elton's right, it's no big deal," and decided not to examine why too closely he went with that.

"Fine," Gabriel said, throwing his hands up. "Fine, we'll share. It will be fine, everything will be fine."

If nothing else, agreeing to share the guest bed was worth Charming's dramatic response. Casey suppressed a smirk. He wasn't clueless, he knew that Gabriel Karne was attracted to him.

But was it possible that Charming was also flustered by the push-pull between them?

Huh.

TWENTY

Gabriel

Sometime after midnight, not too far into Thursday

GABRIEL BLINKED up at the bedroom ceiling, uncomfortably aware of absolutely everything. His breathing. Casey's breathing. The coarse sheets brushing against his skin. The fucking ticking of a clock somewhere in the house. Where the fuck was the damn thing? Bowie's breathing. The patter of rainfall and the creak of siding. Keith making herself comfortable under the bed.

Everything was not fine. Half of his body was on fire, and the other half was freezing. Casey Lundin was a blanket hog. Casey Lundin was hot. He shifted for the twentieth time and reconsidered the recliner but dismissed it—again—because, as he'd pointed out, it was Elton-shaped. Gabe was a natural-born cuddler, which, considering who was next to him in the bed, was also an issue. He felt like every single cell in his body was literally reaching for Ranger Man.

When they'd first retreated to the spare room, he'd managed to drift off fairly quickly after the day they'd all experienced. But eventually, the insanity of the past few days had interrupted his slumber, repeating an endless loop of Casey's still form on the ground, and soon enough he'd fully woken. Now he was on his back and wide fucking awake. Intensely and uncomfortably aware of Casey's massive slumbering form mere inches from him.

His sexy, complicated, slumbering form.

Now Gabe's brain was demanding a cuddle. It would be so easy for him to roll over and tuck up against Casey's strong back. Then the replay loop would end, Gabe was certain.

There was a spark between them, Gabe was pretty much almost one hundred percent certain of it. It was that tiny *almost* part which kept him from doing anything massively stupid. Carefully, he repositioned himself again, putting a few more inches between their bodies, and reminded himself that he hadn't fled to Heartstone just to fall into bed with the first available human. Or unavailable one.

Especially not one who'd chased him out of the park his first night and cited him for trespassing—which, fine, was a ticket he'd earned and still needed to pay. And accused him of being a con man—which, okay, was the truth, even if that was his past. And didn't trust Gabe on general principle—Gabe was always drawn to smart men. Casey Lundin was smarter than most.

The mattress shifted and a grumbly voice came out of the dark, "Jesus Christ, what do I need to do to get some sleep over here? Injured, remember? What the hell has you all wound up?"

Shit. Gabe scrambled to come up with something before his mouth opened and he word-vomited.

"It's just—"

"You are gay, right? Or at least bi? A man occupying the same bed as you isn't out of the ordinary?"

"Ah—no?"

A chuckle escaped Casey. His laugh? Also, sexy. *Dammit.*

"You mean you don't know?"

Casey flipped over so he was on his side and facing Gabe's profile, and Gabe abruptly was even more aware of him than he had been seconds earlier.

"I mean, *yes.* Fuck you, yes, I am a happily bisexual man. And therefore, *no*, a man in my bed is not unusual. As you well know, considering my ex was the last body we found. But I never imagined a scenario where the man would be you. Not that I don't find you attractive. I do." Oh, fuck, his mouth had gotten away from him after all. "I just, never mind, this conversation is ridiculous—I'm going to sleep now."

He moved to flop over onto his side and face away from Casey, even though he knew that sleep would now prove to be impossible. Fine. He could sleep when he was dead.

The mattress jiggled, and Gabe twisted to look over his shoulder.

"The hell?" he whispered.

Casey was right there, looming over him. Gabe opened his mouth again, to say something smart like *Menacing is not conducive to sleep.* But before he could utter a single word, Casey leaned in and pressed his lips against Gabe's.

Oh. *Oh.*

The kiss was all tongue, sloppy, and over too fast. Who cared if it was sloppy? Not Gabe, he was greedy, he wanted all the messy kisses Casey would give him and turned toward the man to chase all that messiness. But Casey pulled away, and in the dark, Gabe couldn't read Casey's expression. Reaching out a hand, Gabe found his chest and felt the jackhammer of Casey's heart against his splayed fingers.

"Do it again," he demanded.

For once, Casey didn't argue with Gabe. He leaned in, and they were kissing again. Thank fuck. Gabe could've kissed Casey for the rest of the night, either more of that first sloppy-messy or this slow-intense, but reason reminded him that they needed to sleep and that Casey was injured. This time it was Gabe who stopped.

"We keep going and no one is getting any sleep. And, as much as I adore Elton, I don't want him in the audience."

Casey snorted. Laying back on the bed, he scooted them both around so Gabe was the little spoon. Which didn't take that much effort; the bed didn't offer a lot of extra square footage.

A large warm hand landed on Gabe's hip and stayed there.

"That was okay? And this?" Casey wiggled his fingers.

"God, yes," he hissed. "That was incredible. I want to do more of that, with you."

Somehow, even with Casey's hand burning a hole through his skin, Gabe managed to fall asleep and stay that way.

Up until all hell broke loose a few hours later.

LOUD BANGING against Elton's front door was immediately followed by Bowie barking and growling like the knocks had personally offended him.

"Motherfucker," complained Gabe when he fully resurfaced. "Why? What the fuck time is it?"

A man's voice called out, "Sheriff, open up!"

"Just a dang minute," Elton yelled.

Daylight had not yet made its presence known to Heartstone, so it couldn't have been later than seven or so. Gabe rolled to standing and spent ten seconds digging out his absolute last pair of jeans and tugging them on over his long underwear, then pulling his grubby Mariners sweatshirt over his head. Yet another piece of clothing he'd left behind at Elton's that he was thankful for.

For his part, Casey settled for the clothes he'd worn the day before. Keith had been perched on a windowsill but shot under the bed at the racket, from where she hissed at them all.

"I kind of want to join her," Gabe said morosely.

"Yeah, well. Let's see what fuckery is going on now."

Gabe followed Casey out into the living room. Elton had the door open a crack but was blocking it with his body. A uniformed officer stood on the stoop, and another was standing out in the rain. The top-step officer Gabe recognized as the one and only Sheriff Rizzi, and the one getting soaked was Deputy Eagan.

Rizzi spotted Gabe and Casey over Elton's shoulder and pointed at them. "Gabriel Karne, you're under arrest for the murder of Peter Vale, also known as Peter Stevens."

Gabe blinked. Being arrested for murder had not been on his to-do list for the day. "I'm sorry, what?"

"You have the right to remain silent. Anything you say can and will be used against you in a court of law."

"Eli," Elton began, "what is this? You know Gabe didn't have anything to do with Peter Vale's death."

Rizzi shoved some paperwork into Elton's face, presumably a warrant, but he whipped it away too quickly for any of them to read.

"The fuck you're arresting Gabe," growled Casey, grabbing Gabe's biceps.

"We can do this the easy way or the hard way, Ranger Lundin, but Karne is coming with us. Eagan, this is your time to shine, cuff him."

Dropping his hand from Gabe's arm, Casey stepped between Gabe and the door, either to block Rizzi from coming in or to keep Gabe from leaving, Gabe wasn't sure. It didn't matter which because either one would end up with both of them arrested.

"Casey, don't do anything stupid. Let me be in charge of that."

Casey turned on him, his expression something close to devastated. "How can you crack jokes right now?"

Gabe stared back at him, trying his best to telegraph that all would be okay. At least Eagan was there, right? Suddenly, he wondered if this was how Mickie Lundin had been arrested, ripped from his home in front of Casey and his family.

"I got you and Elton in my corner, right, Ranger Man?"

Casey nodded.

"Then everything will be fine," Gabe said with a great deal more confidence than he felt.

Rizzi, apparently satisfied that Gabe was coming without a struggle, moved down the cement steps to wait next to Deputy Eagan.

"Let's get this over with." Gabe slipped his feet into his work boots, grabbed the jacket Casey had lent him, and stepped outside to place himself in the custody of the one person on Heartstone Island he trusted the least. He didn't trust Spurring either but there was no sign of the chief deputy. At least Deputy Eagan was present; Gabe sensed the younger deputy was a good person. He turned back to the door. "We'll get this sorted out. You two got this. I'll be back by lunchtime, and you'll regret it. Maybe make that call to a lawyer friend."

He tried to figure out a way to insert the word backpack but failed. But he knew Elton and Casey would keep it safe, for now anyway.

With that, Gabe stepped out into the rain and held his hands out in front of him.

Until recently, Gabe had never deeply considered the

phrase *all hell breaking loose*. It had just been one of those sayings that was tossed around. And now he'd thought it twice in less than thirty minutes.

"Sorry about this, sir," Deputy Eagan whispered as she snapped the handcuffs around Gabe's wrists. "It's protocol."

"Ah yes, protocol. One of my favorite words."

The back door of the cruiser was open already, and he could see the security screen that protected cops from bad guys. Eagan led him toward the car, placing her hand on the top of his head when he bent to slide inside.

"You know, I've never actually ridden in the back of one of these before," he said cheerfully, looking up at the young deputy. "First time for everything."

"You'd be shocked to learn how many people tell me that."

The cruiser had been parked at an angle, effectively blocking in Elton and Casey. As if they would try and stage some kind of getaway. Gabe briefly amused himself by imagining a car chase that circumnavigated Heartstone with Elton taking the lead in his twenty-five-year-old, six-ton beast while Casey, hunched over the Wagoneer's steering wheel, took the back.

Without further conversation, Deputy Eagan walked around the back of the vehicle and slid into the driver's seat. Gabe kept his attention on Rizzi. Something was off, something Gabe couldn't put his finger on. The sheriff shot a scowl toward Elton's house, shook his head, and started toward the cruiser. Was he limping? Gabe wasn't sure if he'd had a limp a few days ago. Assuming not, how had he acquired it? Maybe by attacking Ranger Man in the dark? Gabe wouldn't be shocked to learn Rizzi had been behind the assault. Did he know about the backpack, that it had been found? Was he or one of his "friends" responsible for putting it there?

Casey and Elton remained in the doorway. Gabe was disappointed he couldn't give them a little finger wave, but the hand-cuffs made it impossible. Instead, he blinked his eyes several times and pretended to blow kisses. Elton squinted at him. Ranger Man's reaction, a mix of horror and disgust, was exactly what Gabe had been aiming for.

Lemons and lemonade, right?

The cruiser's engine rumbled to life and Deputy Eagan began to steer them off Elton's property and onto the main road. Gabe thought about trying to make small talk but decided Rizzi didn't deserve it and what he had to say might just piss him off anyway.

Instead, Gabe sat back, albeit uncomfortably, and watched the island's scenery pass by.

A MERE FIFTEEN MINUTES LATER, they were turning into the TCSO parking lot. The pit in Gabe's stomach that he had been trying to ignore the entire ride was morphing into a pothole.

How had Rizzi gotten the arrest warrant signed so quickly? Again, the thought that those papers hadn't really been a warrant crossed his mind. Gabe knew *he* hadn't murdered Peter, so maybe Rizzi had a judge in his pocket too? He would not be surprised. However, he hoped Elton and Casey were on the phone to a lawyer they trusted because he wasn't opening his mouth again until he had legal counsel.

Rizzi took the lead, while Deputy Eagan escorted Gabe into the foyer. Elton's crush was sitting behind the desk, her bespec-tacled eyes widening comically when she saw Gabriel come through the door. The arrest warrant must have arrived before she had. Which seemed—odd.

She gaped at them for a second and shook her head as if trying to make sense of it all.

Join the club.

Her gaze flicked to the left and down the hall that led to the various offices and the interview room Gabe had had the pleasure of visiting twice already that week. Gabe absently wondered if they'd aired it out yet.

"Um," she said, half rising from her chair. "Sir?"

"I don't have time for anything right now," Rizzi said dismissively, moving—still with a slight limp—in the direction of Althea's gaze.

"Althea," Eagan said, getting the older woman's attention, "we need to get Mr. Karne checked in properly. I'm going to take those cuffs off, sir. I don't believe you're a threat."

"Thank you, I promise to behave."

Eagan rolled her eyes and smirked a bit. "Why do I think that is not always the case?"

"It's like you know me. But I will today."

As soon as his hands were free of the cuffs, Gabe shook them out. He never wanted to feel that helpless again. No BDSM for him.

"Oh, right. Yes, let's get started." Althea blinked and reached for her mouse, clicking the desktop computer awake. "It's just that the sheriff has a visitor. Mr. Stevens asked to wait in his office." She glanced up at Deputy Eagan. "He said it was important."

Gabe's ears perked up at the mention of the name Stevens. This was a development he never would've predicted. No way would he have put money on Stevens showing up here, not after how he'd been yesterday.

"I'm sure it is," Eagan replied. "Mr. Karne, as soon as Althea has the paperwork printed and we've filled it out, I'll take you back to get fingerprints. Once that's taken care of, the interview room is the next stop."

"Oh, yeah, I missed that place. Home away from home.

Before all that, however, I'd like to make a call to my lawyer," he said mildly.

"Yes, absolutely." She smiled and nodded at his mention of his phone call. "Do you need privacy? We have a phone in the back, and I can step around the corner."

Gabe shook his head. He was just gonna call Elton anyway, make sure they'd started the ball rolling. "Here is fine."

There was a comfortable-looking plastic chair positioned at the corner of Althea's desk, and Gabe settled in.

"Let me get you an outside line." Althea fiddled with the complex-looking equipment. "I swear I could pilot the space shuttle from this damn thing—"

Althea's musing was interrupted by raised voices, one of which Gabe knew was Rizzi's. The shouting was followed by the explosive crack of a gunshot. Even Gabe, who hadn't grown up around guns, recognized that sound.

"The hell?" Eagan said, her eyes wide.

The three of them stared at each other for a millisecond, then Gabe jumped to his feet. Eagan darted down the hallway. Althea stayed still.

A second shot shattered the silence.

"Maybe that will get your attention! Maybe now you'll start listening!"

The speaker's voice was unrecognizable, filled with both fear and resolve, but Gabe's educated guess said it was Stevens.

"Get over here, under the desk!" Althea whispered. "Those are gunshots!"

She grabbed for Gabe's arm and tried to drag him around to her side of the desk, but he resisted, instead listening for more shots or other sounds that indicated they needed to get the hell out of Dodge. There were none. The only voices coming from the other room were indistinguishable murmurings. Was that Eagan or another officer?

And how the hell would the two of them fit under that desk?

The desk phone jangled to life. Althea dropped his arm as her attention darted to the caller ID screen.

"Should I answer that? What should I do?" Althea's whisper oozed panic, her voice starting to rise.

"Please, Althea, take a few deep slow breaths before you hyperventilate. Ignore the call," Gabe encouraged. What would she tell someone calling now? *Sorry, we have a possible hostage situation?* "Deputy Eagan has things under control. You just stay right here safe and sound and I'll check it out."

"I don't think you should interfere. I think you should stay here—"

"Just gonna take a look-see. I'll report back."

Dammit, Gabe was out of his element around all these law-and-order types. Where was Ranger Man when he needed him?

Going against his personal sense of survival, Gabe started down the familiar hallway.

You never have had a decent sense of survival, Chance.

Clearly, the only way to find out what the hell was going on was to insert himself into the situation. Or, at the very least, linger on the outskirts of the drama and collect information.

Behind him, he heard Althea's deep intake of breath and a rushed expulsion. That was a shock; when was the last time someone had done what he said?

At the end of the hallway, a young deputy he hadn't had the pleasure of meeting until that moment tried to stop him. "Sir, you can't—"

Gabe shook his hand off and kept moving into the large space where the deputies had desks. Along one side were a couple of empty offices—one looked like it was used for storage —but the action was taking place across the bullpen where, Gabe suspected, Rizzi's office was located.

It was early in the day still, so the office wasn't fully staffed yet. Probably a good thing if Stevens was threatening people with a gun. Those present were gathered around a door that opened into the larger corner office. It even had a glass wall that allowed spectators to watch what was going on inside. As Gabe approached, one of the officers, a young man Gabe hadn't had the pleasure of meeting, turned and raced past him, heading for parts unknown.

Deputy Eagan was present, of course. One hand rested on the service weapon at her hip, but she hadn't drawn it—yet. She was using her body to block the office door. That was of no consequence because one of the officers still there stepped to the side and those huge interior windows gave Gabe an excellent view of what was going down.

John Stevens sat casually in a guest chair, one ankle balanced across his knee like he was just hanging out with his old friend Sheriff Rizzi whom he often visited at work, which was probably the truth. Which was also probably why no one had questioned Stevens's arrival early that morning.

"—I had plenty of time before you returned to rig this office, you know. Your officers trust me, don't they? They're used to me coming in and out. There was no reason for them to be concerned by my presence."

Rizzi was seated as well and was very much directly in the sight line of the Glock that Stevens held in his hand. He wasn't in a chair but perched on the edge of his desk directly across from Stevens. Even if Stevens was shaky—which he did not appear to be—the man wasn't going to miss from four and a half feet. Gabe thought he spotted at least one bullet hole in the metal desk, and Rizzi's holster was empty.

"Sir. Mr. Stevens. Put the gun down. Surely there's another way to solve this."

Gabe had to hand it to Deputy Eagan. Her poise was

calming and kept the rest of the deputies and staff from panicking.

"I've thought long and hard about this, Bree, and no, there isn't another solution. But before that eventuality, everyone needs to hear what Rizzi is going to say. Come on, Eli." He waggled the gun. "It's time to share your story with everyone. Let's talk about what's been going on in Twana County for years. Decades."

"John, it doesn't need to end like this." Rizzi spread his arms out from his body slightly, his palms tipped toward the ceiling. "Let's talk about this man to man. We can work it out."

Gabe figured they were past the work-it-out stage. Stevens was a man on a mission. From his body language, Rizzi must have recognized it too. He shifted a bit on the desk, as if trying to get out of Stevens's range.

The ex-prosecutor waggled his gun, staring back at the sheriff, his gaze flat, emotionless. Dead. Rizzi stopped moving. When Stevens opened his mouth again, he was speaking clearly enough that everyone present could hear and understand him.

"The time for working things out has passed, Eli. I've got the documents, evidence saved. But really, I think what has to happen right now is that these fine gathered witnesses hear the sordid tale in your own words. How you used your office for personal gain. How—with my help, I admit that—you put people who were in your way, or relatives of people in your way, behind bars. Sometimes merely because they were an inconvenience to your narrative. Between us, we fabricated evidence, altered paperwork, coerced confessions. I'd bet good money that almost every case you've touched during your tenure is tainted."

The sheriff shifted again ever so slightly, which had Gabe wondering if he had another weapon hidden somewhere, close enough to try and grab.

"But you finally went too far, didn't you? You killed my son or had him killed. I cannot abide that. One way or another, we all pay for our sins."

"Now, John—"

There was a blast from the gun and another ragged hole appeared in the desk, this one about two inches from Rizzi's thigh. Gabe had to give it to Rizzi for staying put.

"The time to start talking is now, my friend."

TWENTY-ONE

Casey

Thursday morning

"I'M GONNA TAKE A DAMN SHOWER," Elton announced. "And then we'll deal with this, as Gabe would say, fuckery."

Casey responded with a grunt. It was the best he could manage after watching Gabriel leave. His heart hurt. It was impossible not to recall Mickie's arrest, how Rizzi had dragged him off. Mickie had never come home.

He and Elton had watched the sheriff drive off with Gabe handcuffed in the backseat and under arrest for the murder of his ex-boyfriend. The asshole had had the temerity to wink at them and blow kisses through the glass, as if the situation wasn't dead fucking serious. When they got him back, Casey would happily strangle him. And kiss him again. The jury was out as to what would happen first.

Kissing Gabriel last night had almost been an act of desperation on Casey's part. He hadn't been able to sleep with the man squirming beside him. But once he had felt Gabe's lips against his, Casey'd known he needed to do it again. For whatever reason, the dissolute con man was who Casey wanted, and Gabe seemed to want him back.

While Elton cleaned up, Casey worried as he gulped his first cup of coffee. Relived the kiss. When Elton was done with his morning routine, they'd put their heads together and decide next steps for getting Charming back ASAP.

Who would've predicted that Casey would want the infuriating man back?

Dammit, who would have predicted he'd want the guy back here and not on his merry way elsewhere.

He was just about to refill his cup when yet again someone knocked on the fucking door, startling him and interrupting his brooding.

"Who the fuck now? Bowie, quiet." Casey'd had about enough of unexpected visitors for the rest of his life.

Bowie huffed and darted his trademark Look toward Casey, but quieted and headed back to his spot in front of the couch.

Setting his mug on the kitchen counter with a decidedly grouchy smack, Casey went to find out who wanted something now. Hopefully, the cops weren't back and ready to arrest him or worse, Elton. He did not have the patience for Rizzi's bullshit but also couldn't come up with a legitimate reason why the sheriff would be back so soon.

Through the window, he saw a recognizable brown van idling at the end of the drive. The delivery guy hopped back in behind the wheel just as Casey opened the door.

"Your package is right there," the perky driver called out. "Have a great day!"

At least someone was having a good day.

Glancing down, Casey saw a cardboard One-Day Delivery envelope leaning against the siding. Picking it up, he went back inside.

"Elton, there's a package for you."

"Who's it from? I haven't gotten my shower yet." Elton emerged from the hallway, a worn, red-checkered robe wrapped around himself.

Casey read the return address. "John Stevens."

"Huh. What would he send me?" He held his hand out. "Pour an old man another cup of coffee, the shower can wait."

Casey stood his ground. "Open that first." He had a weird feeling, almost as if the envelope was demanding to be opened.

Elton squinted at him like he was planning to argue that coffee was more important. Instead, he perched on the edge of his recliner and ripped the envelope open. Inside was a slim sheaf of papers. Pulling them out, Elton started to set the envelope aside but, out of habit or because he felt something, he peered into it first. Then for good measure, he turned the packet upside down and shook it.

"Nope, nothing else."

Casey sat on the arm of the couch so he could read over Elton's shoulder.

ELTON: BY THE TIME YOU READ THIS, I WILL BE DEAD. CONSIDER THIS DOCUMENT A CONFESSION AND ADMISSION OF MY GUILT, WHICH STRETCHES BACK ALMOST THIRTY YEARS AND AFFECTS MANY PEOPLE WHO THOUGHT I WAS A GOOD AND DECENT PERSON.

I WAS NOT. I USED PROTECTED INFORMATION FOR PERSONAL GAIN. I ENTERED INTO AN ILLEGAL CONTRACT

WITH ELI RIZZI. WE BEGAN WORKING TOGETHER WHEN HE WAS JUST A DEPUTY AND I WAS A RELATIVELY NEW PROSECUTOR. OVER THE YEARS I RECEIVED MONIES AND GIFTS FROM ELI RIZZI AND OTHERS TO INFLUENCE CRIMINAL AND CIVIL CASES TO THEIR, AND MY OWN, BENEFIT.

BY THE TIME YOU READ THIS, ELI RIZZI WILL BE DEAD TOO.

"This is not good," said Casey, rising to his feet. His heart was thundering, trying to pound out of his chest. "Very not good. We need to get to the station."

Quickly, he punched in the number for the Sheriff's Office, but the phone rang several times with no answer before going to voicemail. He could think of only one reason why and that was because John Stevens was already there, and he had a weapon. Like many folks in Twana County, Stevens was comfortable with guns.

And Gabe was there. In custody. In fucking handcuffs. And Althea Mortine. Bree Eagan.

Casey thought he might throw up. He was ready to race out the door, but Elton was mumbling through the last few sentences of the confession aloud.

"BLAH, blah: *The sordid details of our working relationship are saved on my home office computer. I've included my password among the documents here. I trust you will get the evidence and this letter to the correct authorities so a proper investigation can be instigated. This confession does not absolve me of my crimes, but maybe in the end I will have done some good by ridding the world of Eli Rizzi, at whose feet I lay the blame for the murder of my only son.*"

"Goddammit all to hell," Elton said as he set the papers

down on his puzzle-slash-dining table. "I need to get my damn clothes back on. You're not going down there without me, I forbid it. I only hope we're not too late." Elton glanced at his wall clock on the way to his bedroom. "And I'm driving."

Casey didn't immediately respond, he was too focused on trying to drag oxygen into his lungs. There was an unstable man at the station. With a gun. Where Gabe was. And Gabe was not known for keeping his trap shut when he should. He snatched up his keys and parka, ready to bolt.

Some days—the ones that ended in Y—there was just no arguing with Elton Cox, so he waited while Elton got ready to go.

CASEY WASN'T sure what he'd expected when they arrived at the Sheriff's Office. Maybe sirens wailing and a SWAT team dressed in black, toting massive weapons?

Things were quiet. No one was rushing out of the building. There was no screaming or shouting. And best of all, no gunshots. He reminded himself that they weren't one hundred percent certain Stevens was there. Maybe the ex-prosecutor had somewhere else in mind, a different convenient venue to ambush Eli Rizzi and erase him from the planet. However, when he spotted Stevens's Mercedes parked in the lot sans driver, his stomach twisted into a more painful knot.

"Dammit, he's here. Or at least his car is."

Elton grunted and didn't bother messing with the lot, he just double-parked directly in front of the entrance. "What are they going to do, give me a ticket?"

One of Rizzi's wet-behind-the-ears uniformed deputies appeared as they approached the entrance. He tried to stop them from entering, but Elton just shook his head and Casey glared. The deputy stepped aside.

"Sirs, we have a situation," the kid called after them.

"We know and that's why we're here." Elton flapped Stevens's confession in the officer's face and kept moving. The old man could be surprisingly fast.

At first glance, they didn't see anyone else in the small lobby.

Shit.

"Althea?" Elton called out.

A whimper was followed by a soft rustling, then a pale and frightened-looking Althea slowly rose from underneath her desk.

"Oh, Elton," she whispered.

Tucking the papers under one arm, Elton stepped around to gently grasp Althea's outstretched hands. If they hadn't been an item before, they were now.

A gunshot exploded in the quiet. Althea whimpered and shook. "Oh no, another one."

"Go," said Elton, nodding toward the bullpen with his chin.

Stomach clenching, Casey went.

A weight lifted from his shoulders when he spotted Gabriel lingering between several law enforcement officers, one of whom was Bree Eagan. They were huddled near the front of Rizzi's corner office, presumably trying to figure out what was going on inside.

Casey had a height advantage. He stopped behind the group and peered above their heads through the glass wall.

Rizzi was perched on the edge of his desk and focused on the man sitting in front of him. John Stevens, who had a weapon pointed at Rizzi's crotch. Casey winced. At four or so feet, there was no chance he'd miss, and a shot to the groin was not how anyone wanted to go.

"It's time for you to start talking, Eli, telling some truths. Maybe some highlights? Share with these good people what you've been up to all these years. How you coerced confessions and framed the innocent. More recently, why you had my son murdered and killed Deter Nolan yourself. And maybe why you needed Gordon MacDonald behind bars for a little while earlier this year, safely out of the way."

Rizzi didn't speak, and Stevens waggled the gun.

"If you want to do this the hard way, that's fine with me." He squeezed the trigger and then there was a ragged hole in the leg of Rizzi's slacks. Stevens was good—the bullet missed Rizzi's calf—but Casey would bet Rizzi had felt the heat of it.

Rizzi jerked backward. "Jesus Christ!"

"Stay fucking put. You have one more chance."

Why hadn't Eagan or one of the other officers taken Stevens out yet? Casey glanced around. And where was Emmett Spurring? As the sheriff's right-hand toady, it seemed like he would be in attendance. He also wondered what had been said before he and Elton arrived.

"No one is going to believe a coerced confession, John," Rizzi countered with remarkable calm.

Stevens barked out a dry, dead-sounding laugh. "That's rich, coming from you. But don't you worry, I have measures in place to make sure the information I tucked away over the years gets to the right people. I just want to hear you say it out loud. Confess, tell these people just how lawless you are." Stevens side-eyed the group watching and caught Casey's eye, then turned back to Rizzi. "Let's start with Maya Crane—although there are more names, of course there are. I know most, not all, but most of them."

The mention of the girl whose murder his brother was currently serving time in prison for had Casey pushing closer so that he was standing directly behind Gabe. He wanted to hear every word, he *needed* to.

Rizzi spotted him then, his flat dark gaze meeting Casey's

through the glass. For the first time in his life, Casey saw a flicker of worry, just a tease of it, cross Rizzi's face. It wasn't much, but fear looked damn good on the asshole.

"Come on now, don't be shy, Eli. I've said one name for you. All that's left is for you to fill in a few of the details. Just one or two things no one else would know or do you need me to add another? I've always wondered about Suzie Warner too. The jig, as they say, is up, my friend." He leaned a few inches closer to his hostage. "I won't miss the family jewels from here."

"I—" Rizzi swallowed and glanced around again, no longer calm, clocking the gathered officers who were now waiting for him to speak. Not one of those present was actively looking to disarm Stevens; they too wanted to know what Rizzi was hiding. At the mention of a murdered girl and a missing girl, the atmosphere in the bullpen became almost electric.

Bree Eagan shifted her stance, seemingly impatient to hear what was coming next but also ready to intervene as needed. Casey wondered how Rizzi had managed to hire someone so competent.

"Eli ..." Stevens waggled his Glock again, his hand steady.

"Maya Crane's death was ... unfortunate," Rizzi protested, his eyes were wide with panic. "She was in the wrong place at the wrong time! If she hadn't—" He cut himself off. "You helped, you made sure evidence went away, was swept under the rug."

Casey's jaw clenched, his molars grinding against each other at Rizzi's use of the word unfortunate. It bothered Stevens too,

"When you kill someone to silence them, it's murder, Eli. And yes, I did help pesky evidence go away. An innocent young man, Mickie Lundin, went to jail in your place." Stevens nodded. Had he glanced in Casey's direction again?

"That girl's death was an accident! She wasn't supposed to

die. The situation got out of control, you know how young men are."

Stevens shook his head, disappointed, and waved the gun again. "More."

Rizzi's gaze darted toward the crowd of watching law enforcement officers, then he licked his lips and swallowed. "All the Crane girl needed to do was stay quiet, but she wasn't going to do that, was she? She had to be dealt with."

There was a collective gasp from those watching, including Casey. What had happened to Maya was her being *dealt with*?

"And the guilt for what happened afterward is mine. Thank you, Eli, that's what I needed you to say out loud, with witnesses."

Rizzi appeared to be speechless. That or he was trying to figure out what to say that would get Stevens to point his gun a different direction.

Stevens spoke again, "And my son, Peter? Why did you have him killed?"

Rizzi shook his head. Casey didn't know if that meant it hadn't been on his orders, he didn't know, or he flat-out refused to answer.

"See, Eli, his murder was the last straw for me, which is saying a lot when you consider all we've *collaborated* on for years."

Somehow, Casey knew—everyone witnessing had to know—what was coming next, but it still seemed to happen in slow motion as well as too fast for anyone to stop. The weapon in Stevens's hand was no longer pointed at the sheriff; instead, the old lawyer directed the business end at himself. Casey thought he saw him mouth *I'm sorry* before pulling the trigger without hesitation.

There was a fleeting, weighty silence and then the station erupted into chaos. A few deputies slapped hands over their mouths and turned away from the gruesome sight. Casey also had to look away and noted that Gabe was slightly green and turned his back on the scene at the same time.

Casey had been so fixated on what was happening that he hadn't realized Elton had joined them. He'd been early Special Forces—a Frogman in the fifties—and now merely shook his head and muttered, "What a waste."

Before the gun thumped to the carpet, Deputy Eagan took charge.

"Eli Rizzi, I am taking you into custody for the murder of Maya Crane."

Casey expected Rizzi to fight her off, to try and escape, but perhaps he realized the jig was up. Or Stevens's self-inflicted death had shocked him into silence. He stood up and turned around. Deputy Eagan cuffed Rizzi and read him his rights, then she and the deputy who'd initially tried to keep them out of the building led their now ex-boss away, presumably to a holding cell.

"No one, and I do mean absolutely no one, is to leave this building without my express permission," Eagan called out, then disappeared with the former Twana County sheriff.

Deputy Eagan wasn't gone for more than a few minutes, which made Casey wonder if she didn't trust everyone to obey her directive. Looking around at the still pale faces, he didn't blame her.

Surveying the bullpen, her eyes landed on Casey, Gabe, and Elton. Pointing at them and then to the interview room, she said, "You three, get in there and keep your butts in chairs until I come and get you. Do not think about leaving the premises until someone has questioned you."

Elton held out the signed confession almost as a peace offering, the papers crumpled from being stuffed under his arm. "I received this today. I'm going to hang on to it for now, to see it gets to the right people. But you can read it if you like."

Eagan quickly scanned Stevens's confession and handed it back to him. "We'll need to make a copy of this. Please, into the room now."

"Well," said Gabe with what had to be feigned brightness, "that was a bit more excitement than I expected from my morning. How about you two?"

TWENTY-TWO

Gabriel

Thursday

THEY WERE STUCK in the poorly ventilated TCSO interview rooms for several hours since each responding agency wanted to interview them. Eventually, they were separated and taken to different rooms, various offices appropriated for the task, then brought back together to wait it out in the original room—which unfortunately still smelled like fear-sweat and Spurring's dirty socks.

The state investigator was a guy around Gabe's age who introduced himself as Lane Boyd. Sizing him up, Gabe immediately decided that Boyd was not one to fuck around with.

"I'd like to talk to all three of you at once," Boyd said in a way that wasn't a question or a polite request. "As we've already established, my name is Lane Boyd."

Gabe waited for him to share the rest of his title. He did not, which again gave Gabe more reason to think that Boyd was not someone to fuck around with. The agent was quietly perceptive, one of those who didn't miss much and probably heard more than suspects wanted him to. Not that they were suspects.

Boyd set his cell phone on the table, poked at the screen, and then looked up at them.

"This interview is being recorded. Please state your full names and dates of birth."

Once that was over with, and Gabe had tucked away the knowledge that Casey's middle name was Hank, the next round of questioning began.

"Tell me about this backpack you discovered and consequently removed from a possible crime scene." He directed this quasi-request at Casey.

Casey leaned back in his seat, crossed his arms over his chest, and shot the investigator his signature Look. The chair squeaked slightly, protesting his bulk.

Lane Boyd did not blink, he didn't even breathe funny, which Gabe found impressive. He met Casey's stare with his own equally unreadable one.

"I am exceedingly unimpressed that you, Ranger Lundin, along with your associates Gabriel Karne and Elton Cox, removed what potentially could be vital evidence in a missing persons case."

"It was a decision made in the moment," Casey responded dryly, equally unimpressed and unintimidated.

Gabe reminded himself that Casey was law enforcement in his own right. Which, as a former con artist, he shouldn't find as hot as he did.

"I didn't know, and still don't, if it was Rizzi or someone else who attacked me. I made the snap decision not to leave the bag up there. Suzie Warner's family deserves to know what's been found after all these years. They deserve closure—especially after what happened in there."

Boyd grunted noncommittally. "What else can you tell me about the encounter last evening." Again, not a question.

Casey repeated what he'd told Gabe and Elton, with both of them filling in bits and pieces as he did so. Boyd winced when Casey described the out-of-the-blue attack.

"It's a damn good thing your friends showed up."

They were all silent for a heartbeat. Gabe couldn't say what everyone else was thinking, but Casey could easily have been killed and maybe his body hidden away like the missing girl's. They might never have known what had happened to him.

"I don't know what it is about that site," Casey said, breaking the silence, "or Gordon MacDonald's property that has Rizzi and other unknowns buzzing like disturbed hornets. Maybe it was because Rizzi knew Suzie Warner's bag was hidden up there—because he was the one who hid it?"

"But you aren't convinced," said Boyd.

"I'm not convinced that's the only reason." He shrugged. "But it could be. I could be wrong."

"I'm going to need to take that bag into custody."

Did he want to cuff it too?

Casey must have sensed Gabe was about to lose control of his snark; he drew his eyebrows together and turned his megawatt glare Gabe's direction. Sexy. For his part, Gabe released a deep sigh and rolled his eyes. It was Elton who rose to his feet and dug around in his pants pocket. Pulling out his keyring, he handed it to Boyd and rattled off his address and where they'd left the bag. "The dog's name is Bowie, and he probably won't bite."

"The cat's name is Keith, and she probably will," Gabe added.

"Bowie and Keith, got it." But it was said with a smile, so Gabe decided Lane Boyd was at least okay.

Boyd called in yet another G-man and gave him the lowdown on the backpack and Elton's address. "Right, boss, I'm on it. Be back shortly."

The door hadn't yet clicked shut again when Casey spoke again. "My brother, Mickie Lundin, is behind bars for the murder of Maya Crane because of the lying asshole sheriff. How long before he's freed?"

Boyd glanced up from the papers he'd been flipping through to look across the table at Casey. He had piercing blue eyes, and Gabe was tempted to make a Paul Newman joke but managed to keep his mouth shut.

"It's a process. Release could happen as early as next week. But don't get your hopes up because we do need to go through the files and interview Rizzi, and don't forget, it's the holidays. However," he added quickly at the impending thunderstorm looming in Casey's expression, "it won't be months. There's just a lot of paperwork."

Through the room's window, Gabe watched Chief Deputy Spurring walk in. By his expression, he was as stunned as everyone else in the building. How deeply involved was Spurring? Had he been a part of Rizzi's web of lies? Gabe supposed that Lane Boyd and others would be tasked to ferret out that information.

There was another movement in the bullpen, and over Casey's shoulder, Gabe saw Rizzi emerge from wherever they'd been keeping him. The still handcuffed ex-sheriff was being led out of the station by one of Boyd's unnamed G-men, probably to be taken to a higher security location. Spurring backed up far enough that his back hit the wall behind him.

Was he afraid or just getting out of the way?

"Hey, don't miss this," Gabe said, nodding out the room's one window and toward the bullpen.

Casey twisted to see, his eyes narrowing as he watched Eli Rizzi being led away in disgrace. "Couldn't have happened to a better man," he said. "I'd say that prison is too good for him, but I imagine it's going to be pure hell." He returned his focus to those at the table.

"You'll bring in forensic investigators to check out the site?" Casey asked Boyd. "Sooner rather than later?"

"Weather depending, yes."

"You'll need an expert, someone who knows the area."

"Are you offering your services?"

"No one is more familiar with The Valley than me or my work partner, Greta Harris."

Boyd cocked his head. "It's against protocol, but one of us will call you when we have a team together. We'll likely contract with WCF, they're top-notch when it comes to cold cases, and they'll at least need a guide."

Gabe was a bit surprised that Boyd shared that much information but maybe he realized it was the only way to keep Casey from interfering. And even then, it probably wasn't going to be enough.

"WCF?" Elton repeated, his eyebrows a fuzzy white line across his forehead.

"West Coast Forensics," Boyd clarified. "This is exactly the kind of case they excel at. And Kimball Frye, the owner-slash-COO, owes me a favor right now."

THEY WERE ALLOWED to leave the Sheriff's Office in the late afternoon, after being unnecessarily reminded once or five times not to talk to *anyone* about what they'd witnessed. On their way back to Elton's, they detoured for a much-needed meal at the Geoduck Inn.

"Oh my god," exclaimed Gabe when they walked in the door, immediately feeling his shoulders start to relax as he drew in a deep breath. "Carb and saturated fat heaven. I'm not going to regret a single bite."

Elton chose the same table next to the windows as the last time Gabe had been there with him, and the same waitress— possibly owner—came over with menus for them.

"We'll take three cheeseburger specials and three waters," Elton said before she could leave.

"Alright," she laughed. "You guys are hungry."

"It's been a day," Elton confirmed.

She walked away and they were all quiet for a second, just looking at each other. Then Gabe snorted and Elton chuckled.

Casey stared at them both for a few seconds more before letting a smirk curve his lips. "*A day* is one way of pitching it."

CASEY'S CELL phone buzzed while they were stuffing their faces with fries and burgers.

"It's Greta," he said before answering. "Hey, Greta. Yeah, I'll brief you tomorrow. Oh, nice. That's great news. One sec." To Elton and Gabe, he said, "The person we rescued the other night regained consciousness." The phone conversation continued for another minute, consisting mostly of grunts and yesses on Casey's part. Gabe finished his meal and proceeded to steal one of Casey's fries, and Casey glared.

Gabe shrugged and grinned back. "A toll for cell phone at the table."

"You're lucky he doesn't take your hand off," Elton said.

"I'll risk it." Gabe reached out for a second fry. "They must make these from scratch, slice up the potatoes and everything.

Best fries I've ever had." He felt confident making the statement since french fries had been one of Heidi's few weaknesses. They'd sampled them up and down the coast and inland as well.

Casey narrowed his eyes and swatted Gabe's hand away with one hand as he clicked off and put the phone down with the other. "Normally, rescuers send people off to trauma centers and we never know what happens to them, whether they live or die. But when Carlos woke up, he asked his medical team to personally thank us for him," Casey told them. "And if you take one more of my fries, it will be you at the trauma center."

"Tough talk, tough talk," teased Gabe, taking another fry regardless of the impending danger. Maybe because of it. "That's cool that the guy wanted you to know he'd made it. Folks like you and Greta make a real difference out there," Gabe said around another of Casey's fries. He had the fleeting thought that he might regret the greasy meal later, but likely not. He would probably need ice cream. "I'd like to meet her."

"Greta and her wife, Abby, are good people," Elton said. "They usually have a shindig over the holidays. I'll make sure you get an invite."

Gabe had kind of put the holiday season out of his mind. In the best of times, the holidays meant little to Gabe; they'd moved too often to collect any decorations. Now that he thought about it, he realized he'd already seen houses with colorful lights hanging off the eaves and blow-up Santas and other creatures gracing their lawns all over the island.

Who wants to cart around that crap, Chance?

"But Calvin Perkins is still in the wind," Casey said, bringing Gabe back to the present. "In the wind and, frankly, not looking so great. He has a den, a hideout somewhere up there, but even in the dark, I could tell he's been living rough. I'm planning on heading up The Valley early tomorrow morning regardless of Agent Boyd. I can lend a hand, at least provide another set of eyes. I'm sure Greta will go with me."

"I've been thinking, could Rizzi and Stevens have done all this underhanded shit on their own for years?" Gabe mused. "No way. I'd bet my third cell phone in a month that Stevens was just one wing of what Rizzi had been involved in. Possibly not, but I have a gut feeling."

People like us always listen to our instincts, Chance.

TWENTY-THREE

Gabriel

Late Thursday

GABE SHIVERED and hunched into his Casey-jacket to avoid the wind's chilly fingers. There was a decidedly icy nip to the air, but at least it wasn't actively raining, a welcome change from the weather of the past few days. Inserting the key he'd borrowed from Elton into the padlock, Gabe twisted it and let himself onto the dock. Closing the gate behind him, he slowly made his way toward *The Barbara*. His footsteps echoed hollowly over the dark water of Riddle Bay while he mulled over what he wanted to say to Casey. That in and of itself was out of the ordinary—Gabe wasn't exactly known for planning conversations. And he just didn't *do* relationship conversations.

Christ, he was exhausted. Bone fucking tired. After stuffing themselves to the point of pain at the Geoduck, they had been quiet on the drive back to the old man's place. There was too much to think about, especially for Casey and Elton. Gabe's involvement had been pure chance—which was remarkable.

"I'm heading out," Casey had announced in a tone that said he wasn't going to listen to arguments against his decision. "There's a lot of thinking for me to do."

Almost before he or Elton could respond, Casey had gathered up Bowie and was gone.

"I don't think Casey should be alone with his thoughts for long. That boy has a tendency to brood," Elton had told him after watching Casey drive off. "Keith and I will be fine here, I'm gonna put my feet up and pretend to work on the crossword puzzle. Take the truck."

He'd been dismissed. Practically ordered to check up on Casey. So here Gabe was, and there was *The Barbara* at the end of the pier, bobbing in Riddle Bay, back in the spot she belonged. But did Gabe belong here? He didn't know. Belonging was foreign to him.

Now is not the time to reflect on your upbringing, Chance.

Fine.

Gabe didn't like that Casey was alone either, it didn't sit well with him. But why? What was his purpose in coming out here? Was it for Casey or himself? When did Gabe become the cheer-up committee for moody park rangers?

In a flash of brilliance, he'd stopped at Norskland General Store and picked up ice cream, a quart of The Duc and the Earl. A nice touch, he thought. The Earl Grey tea flavor with French madeleines mixed in was incredible, and Casey seemed to have a sweet tooth. And he'd also picked up something else—no one could say Gabe didn't pay attention.

He couldn't stop remembering Casey asking Agent Boyd when his brother would be freed. And about how long Casey had been alone, not just tonight. He'd been abandoned by his parents. They'd left him to fight for Mickie on his own—for reasons even Gabe couldn't imagine justifying. Heidi had had her faults, but Gabe knew in his heart that she never would've left him behind like that.

People on the island were going to be talking about this day for years. Gabe couldn't begin to imagine the sheer number of cases investigators were going to have to go through. The innocent—and even not-so-innocent—who'd been caught up in the Rizzi-Stevens machine were going to maybe get a chance again.

People like Mickie Lundin, whose twenties and thirties had been stolen from him. The whole thing made Gabe feel sick to his stomach. He realized he'd stopped walking and forced his feet to start moving again. His target was Casey Lundin. What he had to do was get there, he'd ad-lib the rest.

That morning while Gabe, Elton, and Casey had been witnessing history and then answering a million questions, the fire marshal had left a voicemail for Casey saying that, while the *Ticket* and *Shangri-La* were losses, the pier itself was declared safe. Thank fuck because Gabe knew he wouldn't have been up to rowing himself out to *The Barbara* tonight. Forty might be the new twenty—maybe it was the new thirty—but at forty-four and counting, he was still closer to fifty, and the past few days had been stressful.

What was he even thinking coming out here? Other than the fact that a bossy old man had told him to.

Put a pin in it.

Christ.

He loathed the phrase "We need to talk," or anything remotely related to those words, but Casey had been the one to kiss him last night. Casey did not seem like the type of person to casually kiss—Gabe totally was, but never Ranger Man. Therefore, the kiss was important and meant something, and Gabe wanted that. He wanted to be important to Casey. Thus, they needed to talk.

Gabe reasoned that he also wanted to distract his brain from what had gone down at the Twana County Sheriff's Office today, and Ranger Man would do.

The man is more than a distraction, Chance.

Stevens's confession and accusations had already set a great deal in motion, including, Gabe hoped, the imminent release of Casey's brother. But sorting out the fuckery wasn't going to happen tonight. Another reason Gabe had decided to interrupt Ranger Man's evening. Surely the man wasn't asleep.

Before Gabe drew close enough to knock on *The Barbara's* hull, Casey emerged from the cabin onto the deck.

"Don't take up a new career that requires sneakiness."

"Wasn't trying to be sneaky. You wouldn't know I was coming if I was trying to be quiet. Permission to board?"

"You're asking permission? Again, that doesn't seem very Charming Fucker of you."

"Ha, ha, ha. I brought an offering. Ice cream."

"What flavor?"

"The Duc and the Earl, from Jewel Creamery." Gabe held the bag up for Casey to see. "I got to taste-test it, surprisingly delicious."

"Well, in that case, come aboard."

Casey led the way into *The Barbara's* cabin, where Bowie greeted Gabe with a tail thump.

"Have a seat and let me grab a couple bowls and spoons," he said, toeing off his moccasin-style slippers.

Gabe hung up his jacket and set his boots next to Casey's before claiming a spot on the curved bench seat. "Still jealous of your table." Unlike the one on the *Ticket*, Casey's table was big enough to spread out at without bumping elbows.

Opening a cabinet, Casey got out bowls, one blue and one gray.

"Sorry, I don't really care if my dishware matches," he said, then added two spoons and sat across from Gabe.

"No worries." Gabe opened the bag with a flourish. "Ice cream also does not care." He pulled out the quart-size container and set it on the table before reaching back in. "I brought these too. They were not easy to find." Next to the bowls, he set the flat wooden spoons Barry had found for him in the stockroom of the grocery store. "But I draw the line at the 'frozen dessert' these things normally accompany."

A genuine smile curved Casey's lips, and he reached out and slid one of the wood spoons toward himself. "You remembered."

"Of course I remembered. I'm not in my dotage yet."

A smiling Casey Lundin was—a lot. Gabe had already known he was in trouble when his main objective was to get more of that. To have Casey smile at him like he was a weird flat wooden spoon. Go figure.

"Not too far into it anyway," Casey snarked, peeling the lid off the ice cream.

"Hey," Gabe protested, "I've got a few good miles left in me. No guarantees about the rest though."

Casey used one of the metal spoons to scoop their dessert into the bowls. "I bet you have plenty of mileage on you. But maybe I should kick the tires a few times before committing. Do you come with a thirty-day warranty?"

Gabe laughed, he couldn't help himself. This flirtation, or whatever this was, was unlike anything he'd experienced in the past. He'd never taken things this slowly. But considering this was Casey Lundin, slow was probably a good thing.

"About last night—" Gabe started.

"A terrible movie, by the way."

He wasn't wrong, but Gabe refused to be sidetracked. He was a man on a mission.

"Nice try, Ranger Man. Look, I'm just gonna say it. I know we got off on the wrong foot, what with the trespassing thing and your general 'follow the rules' stance." Gabe laughed at Casey's raised eyebrow. "Okay, maybe it was the sexy devil-may-care attitude I bring to the yard. But—"

"Yes."

Gabe felt his eyebrows shoot upward. "Yes, what?"

"Yes, let's see where this goes." Casey waved a hand back and forth between them. "Warning, it's been a long time since I've dated. But for reasons I cannot fathom, Bowie likes you and Greta is sure she will."

"She hasn't met me yet, but that problem is easily solved. Of course she'll love me."

"I think it's your modesty that intrigues me," Casey said, but his smile stayed in place. "You did bring the funky spoons."

"See? I *can* think of others."

Gabe relaxed against the back of the bench, pleased with himself.

"What's yours?" Casey asked.

"What's my what?"

"What's your wooden spoon?" Casey held up the spoon-shaped plywood.

Gabe opened his mouth to say something probably something stupid, but the thing was—

"I don't have one."

Casey frowned. "You don't have a sentimental memory? Something that you've saved for a rainy day? A recollection you set aside to bring out when you feel nostalgic?" He held the spoon up. "When I see these ridiculous spoons, I think of when my family used to visit Long Beach—the world's longest beach, supposedly. Anyway, we'd always go to Marsh's Free Museum, and Mom would let us get the little cups of ice cream."

"Uh, yeah, no." Gabe shook his head. "Nope. Heidi, my

mother, did not take vacations. She was maybe the least sentimental person I've ever known. I can't think of a single nostalgic memory."

Sentiment doesn't pay the rent, Chance.

"Well," Casey said, shooting him an unexpectedly gentle look, "maybe we can create one."

Gabe blinked moisture out of his eyes.

"There's a lot of dust in here." There was no dust. *The Barbara* was the very definition of shipshape.

AFTER ONE LAST drag around the insides his bowl, Casey set it and plywood splinter down. "That was incredible. Excellent choice. Now, um, uh, do you want to see my etchings?"

"What? Etchings?" Gabe asked, looking up from his also empty bowl, confused by the abrupt change of subject. Ice cream to etchings, what the hell.

"I keep them near my bunk." He snorted a laugh and shook his head. "I'm so not good at this, I don't do this"—he waved a hand between them—"very often."

"Ohhh." Gabe nodded and allowed a wise-ass smile to curve his lips. "Yes, please, I'd love to see your etchings. Did people really fall for that back in the day?"

Casey stood up and set the empty crockery in the sink.

"No idea, you're the elder in this scenario."

TWENTY-FOUR

Casey

Thursday

"SO, where are these etchings of yours?" Gabe asked as he paused on the other side of the threshold and looked around Casey's bunk in one sweeping glance.

Because *The Barbara* was a modest-size sailboat, there wasn't a lot of open wall space. Casey had an Ansel Adams calendar pinned up and a framed snapshot of Mickie and him from Casey's tenth birthday.

"I keep them under the bed. That way, they're easier to find when I lure sexy, gullible, older men to my lair."

"Gullible, me? Pffft."

Casey leaned one shoulder against the doorframe and watched as Gabe sat on the edge of the mattress and bounced up and down.

The hell? "What are you doing?"

"Testing the springs, of course. I mean, if you're kicking the tires, this old man needs to make sure there's no chance of injury. You could easily break me, you know. I'm delicate."

"You are not delicate."

"Not going to let me have my harmless fantasy, are you?"

Casey's gaze caught Gabe's amused one. The man seemed to have a bottomless well of affability. He supposed that it was a helpful character trait for a con man. Or a boyfriend. He shifted his stance, recognizing that he was slightly anxious.

"I, ah, don't have any condoms and haven't been tested in a while. It's not as if I do this sort of thing often."

"*This sort of thing.*" Gabe repeated Casey's words with an added saucy-eyebrow waggle. He patted the open space next to him. "We've had a fucking long-ass day. Let's just get to know each other a little better. Sit here next to me, I won't bite. Actually, that's not true, I might, but I do believe in consent. Come on." He tapped the blanket again when Casey didn't move. "I'll make it worth your while."

"Is that the best line you have?" Casey asked as he moved to occupy the spot next to Gabe.

"Just one of many, don't you worry. Before the kissing and whatnot, before we go any further, I feel like I should warn you about something else."

"Oh? What's that?" Casey was fascinated by Gabe's lips, how his tongue snuck out to wet them as if he too was antici-pating what was about to happen.

Gabe leaned closer, his mouth just inches from Casey's now. He had to hold himself back from grabbing his chin and pushing Gabe down against the mattress.

"I'll ruin your reputation. It's a given," Gabe said, licking his lips again.

At that, Casey cocked his head and frowned. "What, my reputation for being a hard-nosed bastard?"

"Yep," Gabe responded with a serious nod.

"Are you really going to kiss me or just talk about it?"

A smile slowly curved Gabe's lips, making the crow's feet at the corners of his eyes appear. He slid his hand around the back of Casey's neck and pulled him all the way in until their lips met. Casey was lost, but Gabe's hold anchored him.

With a grunt, Casey twisted around so he could push Gabe backward onto the bed.

"Is this okay?" he asked, nuzzling Gabe's neck, ending with a buss below his ear.

"Don't stop," Gabe panted, sounding slightly out of breath and slurry. "So good, everything's good."

"Yes," Casey whispered against Gabe's cheek, pleased that it was him driving Charming to the edge. "So good."

Casey allowed his instincts to take the wheel, delving further into Gabe's mouth, exploring him with his tongue, reveling in the soft cries and whispers of pleasure he elicited. The intense feel of Gabe's body underneath Casey's—hard but yielding, needing while also giving. So much sensation at once was threatening to overload his system, but in the best of ways.

After what seemed like both hours but also only seconds, a deep, teeth-clenching groan tore from Casey's throat. Almost of their own accord, his hips thrust against Gabe's—into Gabe. They were fully dressed, but their erections skimmed together and apart again, offering a tantalizing tease of release.

"Jesus." Casey started to move away, forward, he wasn't sure.

"Casey," Gabe hissed.

With a strangled groan, Gabe arched up into Casey's body. Somehow, he also managed to get a hand down the front of Casey's worn jeans and into his boxers, wrapping his fingers around Casey's rigid cock.

"Ah, just... hold on." He was going to come, but he needed to feel Gabe's orgasm too.

"I am," Gabe responded with a wrecked laugh.

Casey muscled them onto their sides, all but ripping open the front of Gabe's jeans so he would have access to him. Gabe did the same for him, and seconds later his fingers were wrapped around them both, at least as much of them as he could hold.

Watching Gabe's hand while experiencing the slick, silky hardness of them rubbing against each other had Casey's brain fuzzing out so that he was seeing white. It had been so long for him, so long since he'd felt this way.

"I'm—I'm not—I can't—" His balls were painfully hard. The visual of Gabriel's long fingers, the heads of their cocks appearing and disappearing within their hold, had him gasping. He wanted it to last but he also needed to come.

"Do it, come for me," Gabe rasped. "You're so hot to the touch, so hard."

Casey's cock pulsed and he came so hard he saw stars and maybe even an asteroid, and then the sight of his come spilling over Gabe's hand made him pulse a second time. He came back to himself just in time to catch the last of Gabe's long groan of ecstasy as he too spilled over his fist.

For several minutes they lay there staring at each other, mouths panting and chests heaving as—at least for Casey—the world came back into focus. Gabriel was probably trying to come up with a witty remark.

"Holy cow," Gabe whispered. "Can we do that again?"

Okay, not so witty.

"But not right this minute," he clarified. "I want to clean up and then cuddle."

"Cuddle?"

"Yes, cuddle. I like a good cuddle, and after the day we've had, I deserve it."

"I think I had the same day you did."

"That's my point."

With a snort, Casey heaved himself to his feet. "Stay here, I'll be right back."

"As if I was going anywhere."

He wiped himself down at the bathroom sink and then carried a clean warm cloth back to Gabriel. In the bedroom, Casey discovered that Gabe had divested himself of his clothing and turned the bedcovers back but hadn't flipped them over himself.

"Seems a little late, the horse already left the barn," Casey remarked.

Casey took a moment to appreciate Gabe's body. His chest hair was shot through with silver streaks much like the hair on his head, and a faint scar bisected several ribs on his left side. Casey wondered what had happened. Instead of asking— because who knew what conversational detour they'd end up on —he quickly tidied Gabe up, tossed the washcloth into his hamper, and stripped down.

"Scoot over, I get the outside of the bed."

With a grin, Gabe scooted, pulling the blanket over himself and holding it for Casey to crawl under.

"Cuddle, huh?"

"Definitely cuddling, it's almost my favorite part. A close second anyway." The last was followed up by a massive yawn.

Casey was on his back, although that wouldn't last long. He was usually a side sleeper. Lifting his arm, he invited Gabe to fucking snuggle into his side, which Gabe did with a contented sigh.

"'Night," Gabe murmured, snaking an arm out across Casey's stomach.

Casey looked down and Gabe's eyes were already closed.

What was this sorcery? Two weeks ago, he'd never wanted

to see the man's face again. And now? Now Gabe's face would be the first thing he saw tomorrow morning.

And Casey had to admit he was looking forward to it.

EPILOGUE

Gabriel

Midwinter

"QUIT TWITCHING, you're driving me and Bowie bananas."

Gabe spun around to narrow his eyes at Casey instead of continuing to glare out the enormous plate glass window that framed an incredible view the Strait of Juan de Fuca and the San Juan Islands.

"Quit twitching? That's rich of you. You aren't heading into the lioness's den."

Casey's eyebrows drew together. "I'm here, aren't I? Kind of am."

"Fine. You are, you both are," Gabe acknowledged, including Elton with his words, "and I appreciate the sacrifice. You didn't have to join me on this—" He threw his hands up, unable to come up with the descriptors that would summarize it properly.

"Meet the relatives event?" Casey said with a stupid smirk.

"Yes, that. I don't know how I was maneuvered into attending."

"Because Claribel Delacombe invited you."

"Thank you, Elton, for reminding me. I don't know what to do with *relatives*! I've never had any extended family before. This is so far out of my comfort zone I can't see the shore!"

"Just so you know now, you don't say no to Claribel Delacombe, not ever," Elton continued, ignoring Gabe's panic. "But especially not when it's her birthday."

"Apparently not," Gabe muttered. He shoved his hands into his pockets and continued to watch the ferry dock loom out of the mist.

Seconds later, the ferry bumped against the pilings. They had arrived at Piedras Island, and Gabe was seriously considering not getting off the boat.

"Come on." Rising to his feet, Casey held out his hand. "Let's get back to the car."

He and Casey had been dating—for lack of a better word—since the day Eli Rizzi had been arrested on a variety of charges and John Stevens had ended his life. And Gabe was still having trouble getting used to Casey being there *for him*.

Just as he'd never had relatives, he'd never had a partner who looked out for him. The relationship was still new, and Gabe had plenty of time to screw it up, but he knew he didn't want to, which made everything infinitely more difficult.

Christ. Gabe would never have predicted it would be he who struggled with acceptance. Not acceptance, he corrected himself, with *believing*. Different from acceptance.

Every adult relationship he'd been in before, Gabe had known prior to them even beginning that they would come to an end. They always did, didn't they? And yet, Casey Lundin didn't seem to be going anywhere. What was he supposed to do with that?

Taking a breath that Gabe hoped Casey would understand was not reluctance but something different, an emotion he couldn't name, he accepted Casey's outstretched hand.

"Okay, but if it's too much, I get to call Uncle."

"Gabriel." Gabe sighed. He did like it when Casey called him Gabriel. "We've got your back."

CLARIBEL DELACOMBE'S birthday party was being held at some resort on Piedras Island. Apparently, the limited number of living blood relatives Gabe could claim all resided on the island, along with the dead and buried ones. With the exception of his mother. A quick search had revealed that The Brooch had begun its life as part of a lime mine operation and when that market failed early on, the owners had converted it into a resort for the well-off. The guest rooms were named after famous and not-so-famous Northwest artists, and the management seemed to lean hard into the vibe. They also had an award-winning chef on staff. That was a glimmer of hope anyway. He might at least eat well while being interrogated.

Still, Gabe was pleasantly surprised when they rounded the last curve in the road and he got his first glimpse of the resort basking in the rare January sunshine. There was a large three-story building as well as several other structures, all of which looked well-maintained with fresh paint and planters, just waiting for the weather to improve in a few months.

Something else also caught his eye.

"Is that what I think it is?" Gabe pointed toward the water where, between a few massive evergreen trees, he thought he spotted a lighthouse, but it was difficult to tell from the back seat.

"It is, indeed, a lighthouse. I've heard it's supposed to be haunted," said Casey.

Was that a skosh of wonder lacing his tone? Gabe peered over the seat at Casey. Did his Ranger Man have a romantic soft spot for lighthouses? It made sense to Gabe, seeing as Ranger Man was his own sort of human lighthouse, a beacon of sorts.

"Back in the old days, rumrunners used this area as a drop. Canada is literally a few miles that way," Elton told them. "Supposedly, someone was left behind once, and it didn't turn out well. But I can't imagine that the smuggling stopped when the Coast Guard came in. I'd bet that the runners just became sneakier."

"Okay, that is seriously cool. Can we go up into it? I hope we can."

"I should've known that the less law-abiding aspects of your heritage would appeal the most."

"Hey," Gabe protested while Elton snickered. "I'm calling shotgun next time, old man."

"Are you ready for this?" Elton asked once they were parked.

Gabe sighed, staring around at the beautiful grounds and various buildings. It didn't look like it was going to kill him. "As ready as I'm ever gonna be."

After a great deal of discussion back on Heartstone, Gabe had insisted they time their arrival with the beginning of the party. His reasoning was that he'd be able to blend in with the other attendees and be generally ignored. Surely there would be a lot of other guests. After all, Claribel was some sort of island matriarch if Elton was to be believed.

"You're not being taken to the executioner, Gabriel," Casey said with a chuckle.

"Fine." Taking a final deep breath, Gabe stepped through

the door Casey'd opened for them. Once inside, he blinked for a second, trying to get his bearings.

Alas, the older woman he'd met a few months ago was lying in wait. There was no other explanation for her being *Right There*. Gabe wondered if Elton had texted her from his new cell phone. If so, Gabe might have to lose it for him. Would she have a cell phone, though?

Focus, Chance.

"Ah, Gabriel!" Claribel said with fiendish delight as she moved toward him, an intricately carved walking stick clutched in one hand to support her and her free one reaching for Gabe.

Two men attended Claribel, one on each side. The one on the right was Shay Delacombe, whom Gabe had met previously, and the other could only be Niall Hamarsson. Except for the scowl, there was no denying the two shared similarities. And Gabe too. He may have wished he could deny them, but all he had to do was look in the mirror. He was, of course, the best looking of the three.

Gabe took Claribel's hand and bussed a kiss across the top of it.

"Such a gentleman," she crowed before swatting Shay on the shoulder. "You hulks could learn a thing or two."

"Gabe," Shay said with a friendly smile, "this is Niall Hamarsson."

"Yes, the other half brother." Gabe turned to Casey. "This is Casey Lundin, my—"

"Boyfriend," Casey supplied, shaking Shay's and then Niall's hand.

Gabe could not fathom why Casey, who insisted on "going slow," was the one announcing their boyfriend-ship to the entire world. He decided that his confusion revealed more about him than about Casey and that it was something he'd deal with later.

"Ha! I knew it," Claribel practically chortled. "Come now,

don't keep an old lady standing around. The party's in the ballroom."

"Er, what year are we celebrating for Claribel?" Gabe murmured as Niall stepped over to walk beside him.

"Whatever year I damn well want to," Claribel said, changing her course to head toward a hallway that likely led to the ballroom.

Elton snorted and Shay coughed into his fist. Niall grunted. Gabe wasn't sure if the sound was supposed to be a laugh or not.

"We don't think it's actually Claribel's birthday," Niall murmured back. "She just wants an excuse for all of us to wait hand and foot on her."

"If I did want to be waited on, it's not working, is it? Cody and I were forced to plan the whole thing ourselves."

Niall scoffed. "And she has selective hearing."

"As if either of those two would give up Party Control long enough for the rest of us to voice an opinion," said Shay. "Don't worry, Gabe, we'll protect you," he added with an irritating and slightly oily chuckle.

"Who's this Cody person?" Gabe did not need to meet yet another new-to-him relative today.

"Cody's the owner-manager of The Brooch," Shay said. "I'm sure you'll meet him later."

"We're not related, are we?"

Niall snorted. "Thank fuck, we are not. You'll meet Mat and Ryder later, they both had to work."

Mat Dempsey, Gabe knew was Niall's husband while Ryder Mann was married to Shay. He was fine with waiting to meet them. Sometimes the extrovert in him needed a rest.

Niall and Shay steered Gabriel and Casey to a table in one corner, and Gabe noticed Elton take Claribel's elbow as they continued toward the table of honor.

"Is that a bingo wheel?" Gabe asked, nodding in the direction of a silver basket filled with numbered balls. It sat at a place of honor near the table Elton settled Claribel at.

Shay replied, "Yes, and she cheats, so don't take her bets."

"Noted." Why wasn't he surprised to learn that Claribel didn't play fair?

"Dinner and an ungodly number of pastries are coming soon. Can I get you something to drink?" Shay indicated the open bar.

"Nothing alcoholic for me, but I love a good berry fizz." Gabe always felt a bit weird about not drinking. Alcohol was such A Thing in society, but he might as well tell them right out of the gate.

"Me neither these days," Niall said, pulling a chair out. "Ben's been making some great spritzes lately. They're pretty popular."

"What do you want, Casey?" Shay asked.

Casey looked over at the bar. "I'll tag along and see what else they have. Hang on to Bowie for me."

Gabe took Bowie's leash, glad to have something else to focus on. Bowie sat on his haunches, his eyes on his favorite person, a glitter-bow collar adding to his aplomb.

"We'll be right back," said Shay. "Play nice."

The last bit was hopefully aimed at Niall. Gabe had no plan on bringing attention to himself in any way. The strategy was a quick meet and greet, birthday wishes, eat fast, and then escape the island maybe with a detour to Jewel Creamery on the way. Gabe hadn't even made hotel reservations. They would be on the last ferry or the three of them would be sleeping in the car. Four, if he counted Bowie.

He and Niall watched the other two slowly walk toward the bar. Shay was a hand talker so Gabe could tell that he was saying something to Casey. He low-key wished he'd gone along with them. Shay Delacombe was imposing in the same way that Casey was, but he had a more polished and civilized air to him, probably from his career as a lawyer.

Niall, on the other hand—the other brother, whom he hadn't met before today, and that had been perfectly fine, thankyouverymuch—had an edge of menace to him. Gabe tried to think of something they had in common that wasn't Niall being on one side of the law and Gabe the other.

He got nothing.

"So, your neck of the woods is keeping WCF busy these days," Niall began.

Gabe grasped the conversational life preserver. "I guess we are."

He'd heard from Casey that a forensics crew had begun to set up around Snowcap Estates about a week ago. While it was midwinter, the weather this year had been mild, especially compared to how fall had ended. At least, that had been Casey's reasoning as to why they hadn't waited until spring.

"We haven't heard much about how things are going."

Gabe knew that Casey hated not being a part of the operation, but he understood why he wasn't. Didn't stop him from grumbling about it though. They were both looking forward to the spring, when Casey would have less time on his hands. Out of prison after almost twenty years, Mickie Lundin probably was too. Casey was overprotective of his older brother, to the point of being slightly suffocating. Gabe could understand Casey's reactions, but he also understood that Mickie wanted his freedom, his space to discover who he was now.

"Early days yet, but Ethan's one of the best and he has a great team."

"They're looking specifically for Suzie Warner's remains, right?"

"Between you and me, yes. Not that it's a secret, I suppose. But yes, since her backpack was found there, the assumption is that she was buried or dumped somewhere close by. From what Ethan has said, though, it's a large area and some rough terrain. And it's been a while, so we have to hope that animals have done minimal damage. Or at least not carried everything off."

Gabe hadn't thought about that. It was going to be awful if nothing was found after all this time.

"I wouldn't be surprised if they find more than Suzie."

"Are you two talking shop?" Shay asked, setting Gabe's drink down in front of him.

"Busted," said Niall.

"Did you tell him the Colavitos have been taken care of?" asked Shay.

Gabe felt his eyes widen as he stared at his two half brothers.

"No," said Niall with a shake of his head. "I thought I'd let you do the honors."

"What did you do?" Gabe asked, feeling a bit breathless.

"We have friends—legal friends, I assure you—in high places who, as it turns out, were already investigating Colavito and his dealings. They just pushed their case to the top of the list. He and several others were taken into custody last week on various racketeering charges. Thousands of counterfeit handbags were discovered at a known warehouse, as well. So," Shay finished, twitching his eyebrows up and back down, "they won't be bothering you again."

"Wow, that's—that's incredible," Gabe said. "Thank you."

"Pfft, don't thank him, he just made a phone call. Someone else did all the work. Typical lawyer."

Casey took the seat next to Gabe. "Who's a typical lawyer?" he asked. "And can you pull some strings so we can visit the lighthouse?"

. . .

THEY STAYED, of course.

Later that night, after the festivities were over, Gabe and Casey somehow ended up occupying a suite on the second floor. It was beautifully appointed, and Gabe was particularly fascinated by the artwork fixed to the walls.

"I think these are originals," he said, leaning so close to the sketches that his nose almost touched the glass.

"They are. I read on their website that most of the artwork was produced by artists who stayed here during the Great Depression and after."

Gabe turned toward him, intending to say something, but whatever he'd had in mind was lost. Casey lay back on the bed, the covers flipped to the side. He was wearing only a pair of bright red cotton boxers and a smile. A wicked smile.

"Cody's done a great job with the place, hasn't he?" He shifted and lifted his arms to slide his hands behind his head.

Gabe allowed himself a few seconds to absorb the magnificence that was a naked Ranger Man. Casey Lundin was better for Gabe than any drink. And he, for reasons Gabe couldn't comprehend, was his.

For now.

"Are you trying to kill me?" he teased, brushing his insecurity aside. Casey was old enough and mature enough to know what he wanted. "I'm an old man!"

"Old man," Casey scoffed. "I don't know how you do it, but in reality, you're younger than I am. Probably, like Claribel, you have a deal with a demon."

Claribel was a force one could only admire, not aspire to. She seemed to have Casey's number, so to speak. That evening, she'd teased him mercilessly about knowing that he and Gabe were together back when she'd first met them a few months ago.

The deeper Casey dug his heels in about not being together yet at that time, the harder she'd grinned and poked until Niall told her to knock it off.

While Casey was discussing demons, Gabe hastily stripped down to his briefs, scattering his clothes across the carpeted floor. Bowie pointedly huffed his disgust at human shenanigans and curled up in a corner with his back to them.

"You know," Gabe said, easing onto the bed so he could lay next to Ranger Man, who also doubled as a furnace when it was cold. "You should be worried. I could get used to this same bed thing."

"You're supposed to get used to it, Gabriel." Casey sounded slightly exasperated. "The point of being together is the *together* part."

"I'm damaged goods. Together is a concept."

"We can be damaged goods *together*."

"I suppose that works," Gabe said, mimicking Casey's position, hands behind his head and eyes on the ceiling. "I just don't feel worthy of you."

The sheets rustled, and the next thing Gabe knew, Casey was lying on top of him, pressing him into the mattress. His warm, strong hands cupped Gabe's face.

"You are worthy, Gabriel Karne," Casey, said staring into his eyes.

Without giving Gabe a chance to respond, probably knowing it would be something along the lines of "I think you need a cognitive assessment," Casey covered Gabe's mouth with his, effectively cutting off his rejoinder.

The thing was, Gabe was uncomfortably aware that, against his best judgment—all judgment had fled him when it came to Casey Lundin—he'd fallen in love with Ranger Man. But Casey was not ready for declarations, not yet. So instead of revealing his heart, Gabe wrapped his legs around Casey's calves and held him tight, arching against the hard panes of his muscled body, returning the kiss.

Telling Casey that he loved him without saying the words.

END FOR NOW...

BOOK THREE:

Skin Game

Life is settling down, right?

It's a new year, the former con artist has a permanent-for-now address, and even Keith-the-cat seems to like it there. No more rickety sailboats and living out of go-bags for Gabriel Karne.

Romance-wise, he and Ranger Man are easing into things. A lifetime of habits are hard to break—for both of them. Gabe even has a job, sort of.

Will Gabe regret agreeing to it? Probability is high.

In the midst of the side hustle, he receives a letter from a stranger who says they have some of his late mother's belongings.

Then a young woman shows up on his new doorstep claiming to be his long-lost daughter, and she appears to have the documentation to prove it. It's not impossible, and yet...

Gabe wasn't born yesterday, and Heidi Karne was his mother, after all.

The next time Gabe sees the young woman, she's dead.

It will be fine. Everything will be fine.

.   .   .

SKIN *Game*

DO you NEED to learn a bit more about Casey's elusive brother?

Stolen Hearts — free in exchange for joining my newsletter!

AFTERWORD

This is a work of fiction, created without use of AI technology. Any names, characters, places or incidents are products of the author's imagination and used in a fictitious manner. Any resemblance to actual people, places, or events is purely coincidental or fictional.

Elle Keaton's creative body of work cannot be used in any manner for the purpose of training AI.

The author, Elle Keaton, supports the right of humans to control their artistic works. No part of this book has been created using AI-generated images or narrative, as known by the author. The primary style sources used in the writing of this book are the online versions of the Merriam-Webster Dictionary and The Chicago Manual of Style. Due to their inherent limitations for fiction-writing and the author's personal style choices, there are instances where other style guide rules have been consistently applied. Region-based idioms, age- or era-appropriate slang, UK spelling and style rules, and other deviations based on specific dialects may inform some of these choices. Should you have questions, please contact the author at: dirtydogpress@gmail.com

www.ingramcontent.com/pod-product-compliance
Lightning Source LLC
Chambersburg PA
CBHW030903060726
47591CB00005B/1397